A SEAT AT THE table

P. ROSE

I dedicate this book to those seeking love while chasing their dreams because two things can be true.

A SEAT AT THE *table*

THE PLAYLIST

Apple Music

Spotify

PART ONE | March 2023

One

If she didn't know any better, Maya Thompson would have believed that she was having a heart attack. Her heart was pounding through her chest and when she rubbed her hands together to calm herself, they were clammy. Her anxiety always got the best of her when she needed to shine and that evening, she needed to do more than shine.

She needed to glow.

"Lord." she breathed. Her black pumps paced a small space of wood laminate while she played back the speech she had written, edited *and* memorized in two weeks.

"The arts have been the heart of Cascade City for many years. And today, they have become a cornerstone in our community, allowing not only for the youth but adults alike too…" She paused.

The words vanished from her memory like a dry eraser

to a whiteboard.

"Shit." Maya hissed.

"Ooh, is that part of the speech?" Maya's co-worker, Nina Walker asked. She stepped behind the red, crushed velvet curtain holding two drinks. Maya immediately recognized the Rum and Coke with lime as hers and she salivated at the thought of the ice cold liquor coursing through her system. A dose of liquid courage didn't hurt anyone. Nina beamed and handed Maya the drink.

After two short chugs from the highball glass, Maya could feel the nerves fading as the alcohol melded with the roasted shrimp cocktail and mini beef patties she devoured earlier when they walked into the 3C Community Art Center. A smile curved her full, red lips and she felt the weight in her shoulders and neck shift.

"Thank you." She said then finished off the drink.

Nina raised her tall cylinder glass topped with two chemically bright red cherries, a contrast to the frothy white concoction of her drink.

It was definitely a Pina Colada.

"Are you okay?" Nina asked.

Maya smiled nervously but nodded with confidence.

"I'm good. Just a little nervous. I didn't expect Robert and Tim to elect me to give this speech tonight."

"And why not? You're well spoken, beautiful and—"

"The darkest woman at the firm." Maya finished.

"I was going to say better connected to the community and besides, Zetta in Accounting is darker than you." Nina remarked. "Isn't she from Ghana?"

Maya gave Nina a sharp side eye but smiled. "She said that's what her ancestry report said."

Nina said, "Do you believe her?"

"Nina!"

Her colleague sipped her drink and shrugged her bare shoulders. Maya noted Nina's slim frame in the black lace cocktail dress. It was more of a wedding reception look than black tie event with its sweetheart neckline and black platform pumps that she wore to finish the look, but Maya knew that Nina didn't care. She was a paralegal; a tiered right hand to Maya who served as one of two Special Counsels at the law firm. Nina was glad to be outside instead of at the confinement of *Sterling, Turner & Associates* on a Thursday night.

Maya on the other hand, wasn't. She would have preferred to be in her office in one of her favorite power suits, thumbing through Public Defender cases for the next week, finding the ones that she really connected with; instead, she was dressed in a black satin, twist front dress and looking all the part of a beautiful socialite with a cause. It wasn't the speech that bothered her— hell, it wasn't even the dress, but Maya wanted to be working the crowd, introducing herself and talking about *her* mission.

Hi, I'm Maya Thompson, I work for Sterling, Turner and Associates and I am ready to help my community learn and understand the court system that will allow them the same opportunities as the...

She never knew how to describe "them;" using words like "fortunate" or "affluent" felt wrong but they were the truest terms. At home, she often practiced her elevator pitch with a hard smile, showing all her teeth accompanied with the stiffest posture possible.

"When you stand tall, people know you mean business." That's what her father told her when she was a little girl and it's been instilled in her ever since.

Hi, I'm Maya Thompson, I work for Sterling, Turner and Associates and I am dedicated to helping my community learn and understand the judicial system in order to increase their odds of success in an already tumultuous environment.

It was the best way to pitch herself and the most dangerous one too. Selling herself as a public defendant "for the people" was frowned upon by the higher ups at *Sterling and Turner*, especially Timothy Sterling, Esquire, but Maya didn't care. She had a mission; she had a purpose, and nothing would come between her and her dream.

It was Nina's lip smacking that brought Maya back to reality. She was looking down into the tall, empty glass like she found a prize at the bottom and said, "I think I'm gonna get another one of these." Nina pointed to Maya's empty glass. "Another one? To take the edge off?" She asked.

Maya shook her head. "No. I gotta stay focused." She said.

Nina shrugged. "Okay. I'll be back then." She slipped past the long curtain, leaving Maya with her anxiety and the fragments of her speech.

Maya drew in a deep breath, exhaled then returned to her speech. "Thank you all for coming out tonight to support not just the arts but also our wonderful community."

Marcus Johnson stood hunched over the west end of the bar; his iPhone in hand and one earbud stuck in his left ear. It was his signature look, as he spent a great portion of every day attached to his phone. If he wasn't making calls or sitting in on virtual meetings, he was sitting behind his computer, creating codes, building applications, and bringing his business one step closer into the hands of the community that raised him. That night, Marcus was multitasking: Supporting his sister *and* preparing to close a business deal.

The bartender passed him a *Stella Artois* beer, its emerald, green bottle glistening with condensation. Stellas were for celebrations. It was a tad bit early to celebrate; however, Marcus could feel success in the air. Not to mention it was only beer that he recognized in a sea of local IPAs. He nodded to the lanky bartender then placed a ten dollar bill on the table.

"Open bar, sir." The bartender said. He was prepping a tall glass for what looked like a Pina Colada.

Marcus nodded. "All the same. Saluté." He raised the bottle, took a drink then returned his attention to his phone.

It was a three-way call in progress between Marcus, Darnell Epps, his business partner and a man named Wayne Carlson.

Carlson was a man with so much money that he didn't have anything else better to do with it besides spend it and invest it. He was known as a "big tech guy," who lived in California and vacationed in the likes of Italy, France and Brazil just because he could. It was a mystery about what Carlson did for a living, but it was never that big of a mystery for people to dig deep into the man's life. No one cared because, well, money was money.

Marcus and Darnell were introduced to him in early January after Marcus reacted to a post Carlson made on Instagram.

It was a motivational quote from Colin Powell about success. Seeing the words of wisdom was just what Marcus needed at the time, a reminder that there isn't a secret sauce or special potion to success, it's all about hard work, learning from failure and perseverance.

Marcus knew failure. He knew hard work too, but he definitely knew failure. He knew the struggles of being a Black owned business, not to mention, the only Black owned tech business in a sea of hundreds of white owned ones. He knew the struggles of being denied business loans and opportunities that were supposed to be afforded to everyone.

"You don't have enough collateral."

"I'm sorry but we cannot back you at this time."

The excuses were endless but no match for Marcus' dedication to his business and sitting on his fourth call with a multimillionaire was confirmation for him. Marcus was on the right path. If Carlson agreed to invest, it would be a major win for his company and he would be another step closer to growing, expanding and giving back to the community that helped strengthen him.

Darnell spoke up on the call; his rough voice had an edge to it that his childhood friend and business partner was often nervous about, yet when he spoke about the numbers, that rugged voice captivated listeners and seemed to dissolve any assumptions people may have had about his burly friend. Darnell had an ability to code switch from DMX to Steve Jobs at the drop of a dime.

"Mr. Carlson, last year, InnovateCore's profit almost doubled. We were shy of the six-figure mark by less than sixty-thousand dollars." Darnell said. "You won't find numbers like this from other small tech businesses."

Wayne Carlson whistled into the phone.

He was impressed. After the first two calls, Marcus picked up their potential investor's quirks; it was a game for him.

Guess the quirk and land a deal.

Carlson responded in whistles and grunts. Whistles were good. Grunts were bad and it was the grunts that Marcus loathed. When he grunted like a Pitbull sensing danger, Marcus knew a negative remark or rebuttal would follow. And Wayne Carlson whistling on their call was indeed a good sign.

Darnell dove deeper into the finances while Marcus drank his beer, taking in the scenery of the art gala. He paused every few seconds to listen for his name or a good spot to chime in on the call; however, his partner was on a roll and wasn't coming up for air anytime soon.

Marcus scanned the packed space with guests dressed in their best evening wear. The invitation suggested black tie attire, so he selected a dark green suit with a golden dress shirt. To keep the color scheme going, he wore a green tie, matching suede shoes and a gold pocket square.

A string quartet played some unknown classical tune as guests walked around surveying the art on display. Servers walked the length and width of the space, dressed in black slacks, white button shirts and slim black ties. There were at least a dozen of them weaving through the space, carrying silver trays with champagne or random hors d'oeuvres. A server headed toward him; she was short with auburn locs secured in a tight bun atop her head. On her tray, she had some small finger foods that looked like pies and smelled like heaven.

"Excuse me, what are those?" Marcus asked then glanced at his phone to make sure he was still muted.

The short girl stared up at him then raised the tray a little higher for him to see. "Crab Empanadas and Chickpea Fritters with Coconut Chutney." She said.

Marcus would have preferred a burger with fries, but he settled on two of the empanadas. He thanked the server who gave him a twice over, smiled then sauntered away.

She stopped at a couple nearby, offering up her platter to them while taking another side glance at him.

"Well, aren't we the popular one?" A familiar voice came from the left of him. Marcus turned and smiled as his sister, Olivia approached him with open arms.

"Lil sis." He said with a bright smile and strong embrace. When they pulled away he raised an eyebrow.

Olivia eyed the ruffle in his brow. "What?"

"You look great." His voice was sincere and softer than normal.

Olivia bowed her head, hiding her smile but he could see the apples of her cheeks swelling. "Thank you. It's been a minute since I've had to get this dressed up." She motioned to the cream colored satin jumpsuit she wore. The neckline fell off her shoulders with belled sleeves; watercolor flowers were painted across the chest and down one of the pant legs and her gold, strappy sandals twinkled under the overhead lights.

Despite Marcus having Olivia by almost three years, it was his little sister who went gray first and instead of freaking out, the artist within her accepted it. By the time she graduated art school, Olivia had dyed her entire mane a silver gray and shaved the sides. That night, her loose, gray coils were pinned into a chic mohawk with gold barrettes.

"Are you enjoying yourself?" Olivia asked.

Marcus said, "I am. This is very nice." He glanced around the room again then heard his sister groan.

"Seriously?" She said.

"What?" Marcus asked.

"Really?" Olivia's voice seeped with irritation.

"What?" He asked again.

Olivia stepped closer to him and through gritted teeth she spoke. "Are you on a call right now?"

"I umm..." Marcus stopped; her eyes burned into his chest, and he felt a tinge of guilt when he tapped his ear-bud. "Look, I had to get on this call. It's a big deal and—"

"Every call is a 'big deal'" for you, Marcus. Every single one." Olivia said.

Marcus protested, "Oh, come on now. I'm here. I'm supporting you and your art."

His sister folded her arms. "Oh yeah?" She asked.

"Absolutely." He smiled.

Olivia sucked her teeth. "Which one is mine then?"

Marcus' stomach dropped then his eyes darted from the left, to the right and returned to his sister. "I think it's—"

"You don't know, do you?" Olivia asked.

He raised a hand then his shoulders. "To be fair you never tell me what you're working on." He said.

His sister sighed. "I have been trying to tell you about this show, but you can't seem to return a call or text message from your own sister lately."

Marcus said, "I'm sorry, O. I know this is an important event for you and—"

"And *you* promised to be here." She said, her dark brown eyes glazed with disappointment.

Marcus pulled his sister in for another hug; Olivia resisted before her body relaxed into his bear hug. He kissed the side of her shaven head then looked at her.

"I am here to support you. I promise, but can you give me ten minutes to wrap up this call then you and this event will have my undivided attention?" He asked.

Olivia stared at him.

"Please?" He poked out his bottom lip and made it quiver.

Olivia laughed then rolled her eyes. "Fine." She said, "Hurry up, the keynote speaker will be up soon, and I really want to connect the two of you."

Marcus' lip returned to normal, but his face twisted. "Why?"

"Because you two have similar interests and I have something that I want to pitch to you and her."

"*Her*." Marcus said. "Her?"

"Yes. What? Oh, you think I'm tryna hook you up? Boy please." Olivia laughed. "Never that."

"Haha my ass. You better not be." He said.

"Whatever. Go on and wrap up your call, okay?"

Olivia walked into the crowd of guests and Marcus returned to the bar. His beer was still cold, and Darnell was on a tangent about revenue. He nodded to himself then took another swig from the bottle. Marcus glanced at the end of the bar to a woman dressed in a black lace dress. She didn't seem as formal as the other guests, in fact, she appeared out of place as she sipped what looked like a Pina Colada.

The bartender set an identical drink in front of her, she smiled, and Marcus saw her mouth "Thank You" before her eyes locked on him. The woman gave him a flirtatious grin and waved before she picked up her refill then floated away from the bar and into the crowd.

Just then Marcus heard Darnell tag him in. "Marcus projects that 2024 will be a big year for the business."

Marcus cleared his throat, prepped himself to code switch then unmuted his phone. "Correct. InnovateCore is ready to launch a brand new element of technology that will help not just our local community but other communities in a major way."

Two

♥

M arcus had his beer bottle in a death grip; Wayne Carlson had spent over an hour on the phone with him and Darnell and he was ready to decide. The silence among the airwaves was thick; he wished he had a joke to tell to cut through the tension then Carlson broke the stillness.

"Gentlemen, first off let me say that you two are doing a great job with InnovateCore. I can tell that this means a lot to the both of you."

Marcus' throat was dry but his beer bottle was empty. Wayne wasn't saying anything that neither he nor Darnell had heard before, in fact most rejections started off like that.

"First off let me tell you…. blah, blah, blah, we cannot move forward with funding."

Marcus refused to believe that Wayne would do the

same thing, yet all the signs were there.

Wayne continued. "You both have an ear to the street and to your community and that is what business is all about. Learning and knowing your audience better than you know yourself."

"Absolutely." Darnell replied.

Wayne chuckled. "You two have found the problems in your community and in technology and you want to solve them. And I love that."

He loved it. Wayne Carlson, bajillionaire of the world said that he "loves" what they are doing.

Marcus' grip on the empty beer bottle eased.

"Fellas, I would like to invest two hundred and fifty thousand dollars into InnovateCore."

The room went still, and Marcus' heart leaped into his throat. "Wha-what?" He asked. "Did you just say that..." He trailed off as a shock surged through him.

"I did, Marcus. I want to invest in InnovateCore today!"

Darnell let out a booming hoot while Marcus struggled to contain his excitement; he did a small celebratory 2-step then glanced around to make sure no one noticed.

"Mr. Carlson." Marcus said.

"Please call me 'Wayne.' We are doing business together now." He said.

"Yes." Marcus chuckled nervously. "Yes, yes. Wayne,

thank you for this!"

"No, thank you! I will have my assistant reach out to you and Darnell to set up the money transfer then we can talk about further growth, okay?"

Marcus and Darnell agreed.

"Go be great, fellas." Wayne said then ended the call.

Marcus finally exhaled while Darnell continued to rejoice. "Man, this is great! Can you believe it? We just got Wayne Carlson to invest a quarter mil in our business."

Marcus said, "I- I can't believe this." He rubbed the back of his head; the base of his neck had started to hurt from all of his smiling, yet the soft throb was nothing compared to the realization that they had secured a top level investment from one of the richest men in the United States.

"So, what's next?" Darnell asked, eager to keep the momentum going.

"We wait for Wayne's assistant to reach out to us." Marcus said. "Until then, I'm going to enjoy my sister's art show."

"Oh man, I forgot about that." Darnell replied.

"Well, there's still time to come through and check out the art. We can grab a drink after to celebrate this impressive win."

"Nah. I have Quentin tonight." Darnell said. "And I have been promising him that we would watch Spider-Man for the last week."

"It's cool. I understand." Marcus said. He looked ahead; Olivia was waving him toward the small stage set up at the far end of the event space. She pointed to the watch on her wrist and mouthed the words, "Come on."

Marcus raised a finger then returned to Darnell. "You just gonna leave me here to celebrate this amazing win on my own?"

Darnell chuckled, "Man, I'm sure there are plenty of women in that room who wouldn't mind having a glass of champagne with you."

"Here you go with that." Marcus rolled his eyes then motioned to the bartender for another beer. The bartender nodded, grabbed another green bottle from a small refrigerator then placed it in front of him.

A wave of applause came over the crowd. "Somebody sell something?" Darnell asked.

"I don't think so." Marcus glanced at the stage again and saw a woman standing under the spotlight. She took her place at the podium, scanned the audience as her full red lips curved into a smile that lit up her dark eyes. "Damn." Marcus sighed.

"What?" Darnell asked. "Did Olivia sell something?"

"No." Marcus said, "Let me call you back, man." He didn't wait for Darnell to respond; Marcus ended the call, slipped his phone into the pocket of his dress pants before gravitating toward the stage.

"And in closing, we must remember that our community is sacred. Every one of us has an opportunity to make it greater every single day. Thank you." Maya smiled and the audience erupted with applause.

Olivia joined Maya on stage, hugged her tight then whispered to her. "That was one hell of a speech."

"Thank you." Maya said. She stepped away from the podium, Olivia took her place, grabbing the microphone and beaming into the large crowd.

She said, "Thank you to Maya Thompson for that wonderful speech. Please know that Maya is available for legal aid through *Sterling, Turner and Associates*. They are located at the Fremont Building on the fourth floor, right?" Olivia looked to Maya to confirm.

She nodded.

"That's Sterling, Turner and Associates at the Fremont Building, fourth floor. Maya is a phenomenal lawyer who has been a guiding light in this community for some time now. Thank you again, Maya."

The audience continued to applaud as Maya made her way off the stage; Nina was a few feet away, practically jogging in place with outstretched arms. She hugged Maya joyfully. "That was amazing!" She said, "You sounded like a real politician up there. That speech was perfect. You really do have a lot of love for this city don't you?"

"I do." Maya said.

"I saw Robert and Elena in the crowd too. Robert looked like a proud father as always."

"Really?" Maya asked. She wished that she would have seen him in the crowd but she was too busy trying to make sure that she remembered every word she wrote and found herself fixated on a few clusters of people as she spoke.

It was a technique she picked up in speech class from high school. She hated the class, at least she did initially. Despite having dreams of being a Supreme Court judge, Maya detested public speaking, so it was her guidance counselor who recommended that she take the class her senior year.

Her Speech teacher, Mr. Powers picked up on her nervousness instantly. After Maya gave an ironic speech on the importance of confidence, Mr. Powers pointed out that she in fact lacked it.

"All your points were great, Maya." He told her afterward. "You know your stuff but tell me," he pushed his thick, horn rimmed glasses up the bridge of his nose then asked her, "How can I take you seriously on the subject matter when you stand here before me lacking the very confidence needed to deliver your speech?"

His critique made her feel small. How could she lack confidence when she knew the material? Needless to say, that semester at City Bluff High School was one of the roughest for Maya, but it was Mr. Powers who taught her how to present confidence even when you don't feel it.

"You gotta find your colors." He said.

"Find my... colors?" She repeated the phrase like she was learning a new language.

Mr. Powers said, "Yes. To help you stay calm and focused and look confident, find colors to your left, right and center that you connect with. Don't think about the faces, think about the colors. Focus on the colors and talk to those colors. It will help you. Trust me."

During her last three speeches in the class, Maya found her colors: from the chilling blue of a classmate's cardigan to the warm auburn glow of another's hair. Maya connected with the colors and when she did, her voice traveled across the room and her confidence radiated from her like pure electricity.

That night, in the 3C Community Art Center, Maya found her colors before she started her speech. First it was a jewel toned magenta to her right, as she spoke that magenta shimmered and glowed like a neon sign. In the center, she connected with a pale shade of blue, it reminded her of a pool reflecting the warm summer rays. When she connected with that blue, she felt a calmness wash over her until the nerves slithered away. Then, to her left, she noticed the richest shade of green she had ever seen. It reminded her of a forest. Lush. Sacred and warm. Her eyes and her entire being were drawn to the green and with every chance she had, Maya turned in the direction of that green and spoke with absolute confidence.

When she stepped down from the podium, she scanned the crowd quickly for another glimpse of that green, but it was gone.

She wanted to see it again and meet the owner.

"Maya!" Olivia's voice cut through her concentration. Maya blinked then turned her smile on as Olivia approached her and Nina.

The two women celebrated her with another round of hugs then Olivia clasped her hands together and spoke. "Thank you again for doing the keynote tonight."

"No problem. Anything to help support." Maya said.

Olivia's face glowed. Her smile seemed to spread further across her glossed lips as she pulled something from the abyss of the crowd. "Oh, Maya, I want to introduce you to my brother."

"Brother?" Maya said. "You have a brother?"

"Yes." Olivia finally snagged a hand from the ensnared audience and Maya's eyes widened.

That lush shade of green.

Her green.

"Maya, this is my brother, Marcus, Marcus Johnson and Marcus this is my best girl, Maya Thompson."

Three

♥

Marcus stood before the mystery woman who had taken the stage just moments ago; he stitched her name and face into his memory.

Maya.

She extended a hand; her long, slender fingers were adorned with gold rings made to resemble leaves. He noted her left ring finger bare.

A plus.

Her skin was a decadent shade of sable, a subtle contrast to the black dress that she wore. Her shiny, black hair was streaked with caramel blonde highlights and pulled back with soft, short tendrils framing her oval face. Her lips were painted a luxurious red hue that held a gentle smile.

"It's a pleasure to meet you, Marcus." Her voice was as soft as velvet with a hint of allure.

Marcus took her hand in his, careful not to squeeze as he

savored the contact. He wanted to close his eyes and revel in the moment but refrained. When he released her hand, it felt like he was still holding it.

"Liv, you never told us you had a brother." A shorter woman next to Maya spoke. Marcus remembered her from the bar. The Pina Colada woman. She gave him a once over and grinned.

"It's not something I feel the need to bring up all the time." Olivia said.

Maya's brown eyes surveyed Marcus, then Olivia then her smile widened, revealing two neat rows of teeth. Marcus smiled back at her.

"I see the resemblance for sure but Liv, your last name is Martinez." Maya said.

Olivia shrugged. "Hey, I had to get something in the divorce, right?" She laughed then nudged the shorter woman who joined in on the joke.

"Got it." Maya said. "Are you an artist too, Marcus?" Maya asked.

"God no" He chuckled. "You don't wanna see me paint. I can barely draw a pie graph."

Maya laughed. It was a genuine laugh too and it was cute. Soft for the public yet loud enough for those around her to hear that she was entertained.

"Marcus is an entrepre-negro." Olivia joked. "He's got

his own tech company with his best friend."

The shorter woman perked up and behind her hazel contacts, Marcus saw a glimmer of intrigue. She stepped closer. "Oh yeah? What's it called?"

"InnovateCore." He said with pleasure. "We started it from the ground up." Marcus looked to Maya to see if he had lost her interest, but he hadn't. She was still staring at him with her attentive, dark eyes.

"InnovateCore." Maya repeated the name. "I've seen that name around town before. You recently did some data analytics for the new computer systems at the police precincts, right?"

Marcus stood a little taller and his face started to hurt from the smile that felt fixed to it. "Yeah, we did." He said.

"Impressive." Maya said.

Olivia chimed in. "See! This is why I thought it would be great for you two to meet."

Marcus glanced at his sister; Maya was staring at her too.

"Why is that?" Maya asked.

"Well, I have two projects that I am working on with the help of Cascade City Community Arts and I would love it if you two could join me and my team."

"Really, Liv?" Marcus said. "We just closed this deal with this investor and—"

Olivia cut him off. "Seriously? We need to celebrate that

too! I'm gonna go and grab some champagne for all of us and then I can tell you about the projects, okay?"

"Liv. Wait a minute." Marcus tried to reach for his sister's arm, but she slipped into the sea of guests, leaving him alone with Maya and her friend.

Maya couldn't tear her eyes off Marcus but when Nina nudged her then cleared her throat, she adjusted her focus and smiled nervously. "Goodness, my manners." Maya said. "Marcus, this is my co-worker, Nina." Maya gestured at her friend like a new car. "Marcus Johnson. Nina Walker, one of the top paralegals at Sterling, Turner and Associates."

Nina stepped closer, separating Maya and Marcus. Her hand shot out so fast, Maya thought she struck Marcus in the face. "It's a pleasure to meet you, Marcus." Nina said.

He took Nina's hand, shook it slowly and Maya noted a flush of disappointment that flooded Nina's face when he didn't take her hint. "Nice to meet you too." He said, releasing her hand.

Nina pushed a strand of black hair behind her ear and cleared her throat.

Strike one. Maya smirked and knew that Nina wasn't done.

"How long have you been running InnovateCore?" Nina asked.

Marcus shoved a hand in his green dress pants and Maya caught a glimpse of the gold watch on his wrist. Its finish gleamed but it did not sparkle. Vintage. Possible family heirloom? When his eyes lowered then rose again to Maya, they smoldered without effort. When he smiled, Maya wondered if he was flirting with her or just being polite, she returned his smile with a soft smirk.

Maya studied Marcus; he was struggling to explain his job in simple detail. She could see his brain searching for general words to replace jargon and when he couldn't find the right words, he would laugh nervously while rubbing the back of his neck. He used his large hands to animate his words, and his deep voice vibrated when he referenced some of the highlights of his business. Even in her heels, Marcus stood two inches taller than Maya, with a build that screamed former high school and possibly college football player.

Defensive line for sure.

He had a classic Caesar fade with a few sprinkles of gray at his temples and in his perfectly groomed beard. Aside from the flecks of gray, Maya couldn't guess his age and thought it would be rude if she tried, so she let her eyes return to his green blazer. The cut fit him well, highlighting his large shoulders and sculpted arms.

When their eyes locked again, Maya blinked to end her mental cross examination only to realize that she missed Marcus' response to something. His eyes told her that was waiting for an answer. His question was directed at her.

Maya's face flushed as she giggled softly then said, "Goodness. I'm sorry. I totally missed that question."

"Damn, did I bore you already?" Marcus smiled and Maya saw deep dimples piercing his cheeks.

"No. No. My brain was still processing my speech." Maya said.

Nina chuckled then chimed in, "She always does that. She's a perfectionist. Always striving for the best."

"Aren't we all?" Marcus asked.

Maya's face burned as her eyes darted from the floor then back to Marcus. He was still looking at her.

"We are." She breathed.

Olivia sang "Excuse me" while shuffling her way back into the small huddle. She managed to juggle a bottle of champagne and four glass flutes with her small hands. "The champagne has arrived." She said, "And I brought more people to come and celebrate with us."

From the outer crowd, two more guests joined their

group. Maya grinned at the sight of them.

"Robert, Elena." Maya said and hugged the both of them before they greeted Nina.

Robert Turner was the second partner in the law firm's namesake. He was an older black man with a clean, bald head. He wore red circle framed glasses that Maya knew were fake. He always wore them for informal events. He believed that they gave him "some edge" he told her. Robert was known for his tailored suits, decorative pocket squares and monogrammed cuff links, but that night, he wore a pale blue Oxford shirt with his sleeves rolled up and navy blue dress slacks. He wore a red tie that was embellished with an African pattern, along with brown leather shoes that matched his slim, leather belt.

On his arm was his beautiful wife, Elena. Robert's wife matched his short stature, but that evening the strappy, silver heels she wore gave her an inch over her husband. Elena wore a curve hugging, black sequin jumpsuit and a black sequin headwrap. Salt and pepper tendrils peeped from beneath the fabric.

"We made it by the skin of our teeth." Elena said with a radiant smile that highlighted her high cheekbones and flawless bone structure.

"Why? What happened?" Nina asked.

Elena's thin brow caved in, giving Nina and Maya the

"You already know" look.

Maya did know. "You two on grandparent duty again?" she asked.

"*Again*?" Elena laughed, "It feels like it hasn't stopped. Ever since RJ moved back in town with little EJ, we barely see RJ, but we always see EJ."

Maya shook her head. "Is he working?" She asked.

Robert spoke up. "Yeah, our last damn nerves but we didn't come here tonight to talk about that boy, we came to enjoy the evening."

"Well, you're just in time, Mr. Turner, because we are celebrating my brother, Marcus and Maya joining me on two big projects for the community."

Robert and Elena looked at Maya then Marcus. Robert pointed at Marcus; his face shifted into an inquisitive grimace. He was trying to place a home with Marcus's handsome face. "You're Marcus Jones, right?"

"Johnson." He corrected him with such professionalism Maya couldn't help but smile.

"Yes. Yes. I'm sorry. Marcus Johnson. You have a tech company, right?" Robert asked.

Marcus nodded. "InnovateCore." He said.

Robert raised a highball glass that was a less than a quarter full. Maya knew it was whiskey.

"InnovateCore. What do you guys do again?" Robert

asked.

Maya saw Marcus take a deep breath, prepping to answer the same question again and without hesitation, she offered an assist. "Marcus was just telling us how his company created the new software at the courthouse for their online system."

Marcus tilted his head. "You *were* listening then." He beamed, blessing Maya with another glimpse of his dimples.

"I'm a lawyer." Maya said. "No detail escapes me."

Robert said, "This is very true. Maya is a our secret weapon at the firm." He wrapped an arm around her shoulder and grinned proudly. "Olivia, what do you want with my lead attorney anyway?"

Olivia had already helped herself to a round of champagne; directly from the bottle. She blushed, wiped her mouth with the back of her hand then spoke. "Oh! Well, the owner of the Fremont building reached out to 3C and asked if we could create a mural on the side of the building. He wants something that represents the city and all of the various elements throughout it. I wanted Maya and Marcus to help with the concept and maybe help us paint it too." She batted her eyes at Maya and her brother.

"You want *me* to paint?" Marcus said. "You know I have zero creative talents, right?"

Olivia said, "It doesn't take much to hold a paintbrush. Plus, I have a team of artists who have already agreed to help. I know that you and Maya have done a lot for the community professionally and personally. It was only right that I invite you two in on this." Olivia said, "I really want this mural to showcase what Cascade City is all about."

"Which is?" Nina asked.

"The people." Maya answered. "I have lived in this city for most of my life. It's home to me and always will be. After law school, I knew that I wanted to come back here because I really do love this city. It just sucks that there are parts of this city that are so broken and run down that the police hate to go there. It's like the wild, wild west in certain areas. They struggle to get medical attention and I have heard too many times about how the police often refuse calls. And let's not forget the lack of adequate legal assistance."

Robert scoffed and Maya shot her attention his way. "Those parts of the city should be condemned." He said. "They're drug infested and brimming with criminals."

Elena nudged her husband in the rib. "Robert, don't start." She warned. "I think you forget that *you* grew up in the very parts that you ridicule now."

"Cascade City is for everyone." Olivia said. "And I want

this mural to display that. Which brings me to the second project." Olivia's grin widened. "In addition to the mural, 3C has approved for me to host the first ever Cascade City Summit. It will be a celebration of our city and kick off with the mural reveal. I wanted to see if InnovateCore could help us create a website for information and sign ups and if Sterling, Turner and Associates would be willing to let us utilize Ms. Thompson and her legal expertise to speak to the community."

Maya caught Robert perk up. Anytime he could plug the firm, he would do it and anytime he needed someone to "connect" with the people, Robert nominated Maya.

Robert said, "I think that is a wonderful idea. And Maya would love to help."

"Robert, don't you think Maya should make that decision?" Elena asked.

He laughed. It was loud and obnoxious but who would correct him? Not Elena and certainly not Maya. "This is Maya's thing." Robert said. He raised his glass to Maya and winked. "She loves coming out to events like this and showing the community that Sterling, Turner and Associates is committed to being here for the people." He said.

Maya looked at Marcus. His lips were pulled in a straight line. He didn't like Robert. She could tell.

Yes, her boss was a handful but she was used to it.

When Olivia looked at Maya, she noted her best friend's eyes were identical to Marcus'. Deep pools of life and joy. Olivia's eyes shimmered at her. "What do you think, Maya?" She asked.

"Of course, Liv." Maya sealed the agreement with a hug before Olivia turned to her brother.

"Marcus?" Olivia sang. "What about you?"

Marcus exhaled. "When have I ever said 'no' to you?" He asked.

Olivia laughed. "Never and I don't expect you to start now."

He nodded.

"Can I help too?" Nina's voice was higher than it needed to be.

"The more the merrier." Olivia said.

Nina rejoiced with her eyes fixed on Marcus. The cunning look in Nina's eyes was like a viper ready to strike. Maya knew she was locked in on Marcus.

"This is gonna be great." Olivia gushed, finally handed flutes to Marcus, Maya and Nina; Maya and Marcus watched her as she poured. "I don't have cooties, y'all." She said.

Robert and Elena tightened the circle, raising their drinks in the air alongside Maya, Olivia, Nina and Marcus.

Olivia cleared her throat. "A toast to greater things on

the horizon. To an overabundance of success and making sure there are plenty of seats at the table so we can all eat."

The group cheered, tapped glasses then downed their drinks. As the bubbles settled in her stomach, Maya questioned if it was alcohol or butterflies because when she glanced around the circle, her eyes always found Marcus staring right back at her.

And she liked it.

PART TWO | April 2023

Four

♥

Marcus pulled into the south facing parking lot of the 3C Community Arts Center. The art center was the heart for Cascade City and the commonplace for most events. From black tie galas in the winter and spring to themed rooftop nights in summer. The 3C building had it all; however, during the day, the historic three story building served as an open gallery, a local gift shop and a communal workspace for artists. His sister Olivia was one of the first artists to stake claim in the building as a residential artist and became a community art teacher. Her popularity and skills made her one of six art instructors in the building with an exclusive space of her own to teach and create.

Marcus cut the engine of his 2014 Land Rover and heard the roar of another engine down the street. In his rearview, he saw a pearl white 2022 Corvette hit the corner, pull into the lot then slipped into the space alongside him.

He shook his head as his partner and best friend, Darnell rolled down the window and hit the gas. The car screamed from the stressed acceleration and his best friend's eyes lit up.

"Listen to that lion roar." Darnell howled out the window.

Marcus climbed from his truck and watched Darnell wiggle and shimmy like a fish on a hook until he was free from the confines of the flashy sports car. "Man, why do you do that to yourself?" Marcus asked.

"Do what?" Darnell asked. He pulled a black backpack from the passenger seat then closed the driver's side door.

"You're damn near three times the size of that car. You need an SUV or a truck." Marcus said.

Darnell was stocky and was an inch shy of six feet tall. When he wasn't in the office or spending time with his son, Darnell was in the gym and buying shirts two sizes too small. He tapped the hood of his gleaming car and laughed. "Man, are you crazy? This was the best gift I ever gave myself and I'm gonna ride this thing 'til the wheels fall off."

"That won't take long." Marcus muttered.

Darnell asked, "What was that?"

"Nothing. Come on. I bet Liv's already looking for us."

Marcus grabbed his worn leather messenger bag, closed the rear passenger door and led the way toward the art center's entrance.

"When was the last time you treated yourself?" Darnell asked.

"What?" Marcus jotted their names into the security logbook; the scrawny guard behind the desk gave them a sheepish smile paired with a limp salute before the two men moved toward the elevators.

"When was the last time you treated yourself? I mean really spent something on *you* and not ICore?"

The elevator doors opened and they walked in. As the doors closed, Darnell nudged Marcus' shoulder with his. "Better yet. When was the last time you went out on a date?"

Marcus gave him a side eye. "When was the last time *you* went on a date?" He asked.

"This isn't about me, besides, I have my hands full with Quentin. I'm talking about you. It's been how many years since Kiana rejected you for the hundredth time?"

Marcus said, "Is there a reason why you're bringing this up right now?" He couldn't control the anger that crept into his voice.

Darnell raised a hand. "My bad. I just think that you should take care of yourself a little more. You know, buy yourself something nice. Take a trip. Go on a—."

Marcus' sharp gaze made him freeze.

"You know what I mean." Darnell said.

Marcus nodded. "I don't have time to date right now. We have too much going on." He said. "We just closed this investment deal with Carlson, we have a laundry list of new projects to coordinate and now we're helping Olivia."

Darnell interrupted, "Correction, *you're* helping, Liv. I'm here for moral support and to see if your sister has some fine ass artist friends."

"Really?" Marcus chuckled.

Darnell shrugged. Marcus shook his head, and the elevator doors opened to the third floor.

Just weeks ago, the very space was overflowing with artists, art supporters and the *Who's Who of Cascade City*, but when Marcus and Darnell stepped onto the third floor, the space echoed with voices and was void of the freestanding bar, servers and patrons. The white wall installations that were planted throughout the space were gone, along with most of the art. The white walls of the open floor held a few pieces of art and the sunlight that passed through large floor to ceiling windows filled the room with natural light and warmth.

Marcus and Darnell followed the echo of voices until they found a long folding table with a crowd of people huddled together. Olivia was the first to look up; her gray hair was pulled up in a messy bun with a paintbrush sticking out of it like a dirty hairpin.

"You're late." She said when she approached him and Darnell, hugging them both before looking at Marcus again.

"Sorry. We made it though." Marcus said. He offered another hug but Olivia playfully shrugged him off.

"You did and thank you. Come on, let me introduce you and D to everyone." Olivia said.

From a distance, Marcus scanned the group until he saw her jet black hair and those soft, brown highlights and that brilliant, wide smile. Marcus felt his chest tighten and his stomach flipped.

Olivia caught the group's attention, "Alright everybody, I want to introduce to you the final members of this project. Please welcome my brother, Marcus Johnson and his best friend slash business partner, Darnell Epps. They are the founders of InnovateCore."

The group was a collective mumble of greeting, except Maya. She waved at them, her eyes on Marcus. He smiled and waved back, letting his eyes linger on Maya a few seconds longer than he should have.

"Take a seat anywhere, you guys. We just started brainstorming ideas for the mural." Olivia said.

Darnell made a beeline for Maya and her paralegal Nina; Marcus chewed his bottom lip as he watched Darnell beamed from ear to ear while staring at both women. He didn't think Darnell would be Maya's type, yet the feeling that simmered in his chest and sent his heart into overdrive felt a lot like worry.

Darnell shook hands with Nina then Maya. He held her hand until Maya let it slip from his hold in the most elegant way then she glanced at Marcus.

"Good to see you made it." She said.

"Thanks." Marcus replied. The simmer in his chest died but his heart quickened and his face heated.

Maya said, "I thought you were gonna chicken out on this deal with me." Her smile was just as warm as he remembered.

She was dressed in slim, black pants, held up by a set of suspenders. She wore a white turtleneck that clung to her upper body beautifully, giving Marcus an opportunity to take in the full shape he had the pleasure of viewing at the gala. Maya had a long torso, thick thighs, wide hips with a perfect curve in her back. She was a few inches shorter than the last time they met, and Marcus noticed that she had on a pair of black, jeweled flats. Her black tie glam makeup was gone, instead, her look was simple: glossy, nude lips and a high ponytail that complimented her natural curls.

She was stunning.

"Hey Marcus." Nina smiled broadly. She was in a black two piece pants suit and white heels. Marcus realized that they must have left the office and came straight to the meeting.

"Hey Nina." Marcus said with a polite smile.

Olivia clapped her hands, the vibration echoed in the large room. "Alright everyone, let's just start brainstorming ideas for the mural. I want to get a good collection of ideas then we can start building a sketch from there."

With Darnell seated between Maya and Nina, Marcus sat down to Maya's left. When she stepped away to grab a bottle of water, Darnell punched his arm. "Ow. Man, what the hell?" He asked.

Darnell put a finger to his lips then leaned close to his ear. "So, you weren't gonna tell me, huh?" He said.

"Tell you what?" Marcus asked.

Darnell's lips twisted and one of his bushy eyebrows rose up into his forehead. "Really, man? You know good and damn well what I'm talking about? You didn't mention Maya."

Marcus stifled a laugh while his computer powered up. "I met her at the art gala." He said.

His friend was looking past him, at Maya; she was locked in a conversation with two other volunteers who were also grabbing water. Darnell's eyes narrowed, he bit his lip and shook his head. Marcus imagined Maya feeling Darnell's eyes burning a hole into the back of her head while she spoke. Marcus leaned forward to obstruct his view.

"Hey." Darnell said.

"Stop it." Marcus warned.

Darnell shrugged. "What?"

"This is not the time nor the place." Marcus said.

Darnell tilted his head again and said, "You're right. I'll catch her when we take a break."

"Can you please act like you're interested in this?" Marcus replied.

"If it means I get to spend time with *her* then color me interested." Darnell grinned as he retrieved a small notebook from his ICore logoed backpack, along with a pen.

Maya returned to her seat with a bottle of water then leaned over to peek at Marcus' laptop.

She leaned a little closer to him. "Is that organized to you?" She asked, nodding to the screen saturated with multiple folders.

"Of course." Marcus said. He looked at a yellow legal pad in front of her, overflowing with notes, sketched boxes and small post-it notes. "To each his own, right?"

Maya's arched brow lifted, and her full lips curved into a smile that Marcus knew would weaken him for as long as he experienced it. He wasn't sure if he would be strong enough to keep his daydreams at bay, let alone his desire for her.

After an hour of brainstorming, Maya watched Olivia write down every idea that was said or blurted out on a mobile whiteboard. When she threw the thick, black dry erase marker on the table, she exhaled hard before she looked out at everyone seated around her. "Alright. Let's take a break then come back and narrow all of this down." She said, motioning to the chaotic whiteboard.

A chorus of sighs and rejoice came over the table; Maya watched as people stood up to stretch their legs and check their phones. A small group headed to the elevator to take advantage of suggested vending machines on the second floor. Nina was digging in her bright pink, Kate Spade bag and pulled out a matching wallet.

"Does that vending machine take debit?" Nina asked.

"I think so. If not, here." Maya said and pulled a folded five dollar bill from her pants pocket. "Could you grab me a Dr. Pepper too?"

Nina grabbed the bill and clutched it to her chest. "God

bless you, woman. I'll be right back."

Nina hurried to the elevator and Maya returned to her legal pad. She offered some ideas for the mural during the brainstorming, but her head had been elsewhere. She stared down at her collection of notes, ideas for slides and bullet points that she had been organizing and rearranging for months.

The full picture was coming into view. Her vision was a step closer to reality.

And she was ready.

"Analog. I like it." Marcus' deep voice filled her ears.

Maya looked up and he was standing beside her, phone in hand and that charming smile on his face. When she saw his dimples appear and couldn't help but smile back. He reclaimed his seat beside her then tapped on her legal pad. "Don't you think you should have that on a computer?" He asked.

"Why?" Maya replied.

"Auto save, of course." Marcus said.

Maya shook her head. "No. I prefer it this way."

Marcus looked at the legal pad again; his head tilted from one side to the other as if he was trying to decipher a secret code. "What is all of that?" He asked.

Maya sat up taller in her seat. "I'm preparing to pitch a new legal initiative to Sterling and Turner. If I can get them to get on board this could help so many people who are still tangled in our legal system, including some who are currently serving time."

Marcus eyes' met hers again. He said, "What's the initiative about?"

It was all her ideas, concepts and procedures, written down in great detail. Maya had kept her vision under wraps and wasn't ready to tell anyone but her day with Robert and Timothy was coming and she had yet to practice her pitch. Marcus shifted his chair closer, awaiting her response. Maybe he was being nice, either way, Maya could share it then gauge his reaction. She needed to know that her idea could work.

He smiled with his eyes; they were the warmest shade of brown Maya had ever seen. They enclosed her like a blanket and for a moment, Maya felt safe. She swallowed. Nervous to go deeper into her ideas and because.

It was Marcus.

Maya cleared the dry mass that had formed in her throat and explained to Marcus in short detail her vision for a legal program within Cascade City that not only supported the community, but helped aspiring lawyers and legal advocates opportunities they often never had. As she spoke, Marcus nodded, asked questions, he even smiled at certain highlights that Maya loved herself.

"Cascade City was founded by a diverse group of people and over time, our legal system here has seemed to lose sense of that. I believe that we can get it back and this." she tapped her notepad. "This is how I believe we can do it." She said.

Marcus clapped loudly, a few people at the table looked over at them but said nothing. Maya's face flushed and she looked away. "Stop it." She said.

"Nope." Marcus clapped louder. "This is great. How long have you been working on this?" He asked.

"Too long." Maya sighed. "I have been outlining this for three years now, but it's been living in my head for over a decade. I just recently proposed a meeting to discuss it with the firm."

"How do you think they'll take it?" Marcus asked.

Maya shrugged. Her moment of hope slipped when she thought of the odds. "I'm not sure. Sterling, Turner and Associates isn't very diverse." She said.

"But they have you though." Marcus said.

"Yeah, thanks to my father." She laughed nervously then said, "I feel like I have to prove myself every single day there. Despite my track record. Despite my wins. Every day is a new battle. You know what I mean?" Maya glanced at him; his eyes were already on her, but his smile slipped and his lips created a line across his face. "I'm sure it's not easy for you either." She added.

"Of course not." Marcus said. "Being a black entrepreneur is already hard enough and then I turn around and decide to start a black owned tech business. When I tell you, I have received more 'Thanks, but no thanks' than 'Yes, we're ins' in my life to last me a lifetime, but I don't give up. And neither should you. This idea, this initiative was given to you for a reason. I believe that you can change their minds."

Maya smiled. Her eyes burned with tears but she fought them off. She couldn't remember the last time she felt like someone understood her. "Thank you." She said. "Thanks for letting me ramble on like that."

"It wasn't rambling. It was a pleasure. It really was." Marcus said.

They heard the elevator chime, the doors opened, and Nina's boisterous laugh exploded onto the floor. Darnell exited alongside her with a few others in tow. When Nina saw Marcus close to Maya, she trotted ahead of Darnell with a can of Dr. Pepper held out in front of her.

"Here ya go, Boss Lady." She said with her eyes on Marcus.

"Thank you." Maya said.

Nina's attention went back to Marcus "Marcus, Darnell was telling me about this big investment deal. That's the one you mentioned at the art gala, right?" She asked.

Marcus nodded.

"Sounds like you guys are really making moves out here. I hope you're keeping the right support systems in your life." Nina popped a chip into her mouth and chewed it slowly.

Maya shielded her face to hide the laughter that begged to escape.

"You know, I was just talking to Marcus about the importance of taking care of yourself." Darnell said. "We've been working like crazy with no days off and I think we need to let off some steam."

Maya looked at Marcus; he mouthed the word "No" while shaking his head.

"Let off some steam, huh?" Maya said before she looked atDarnell. "And what did you have in mind, Darnell?" She asked.

Marcus' hefty friend grinned; the man was practically vibrating when he spoke.

"We should take a drive into Chicago. Go to a nice spot for dinner, have a few drinks and maybe hit up the pier."

Maya and Marcus exchanged looks again but Nina's excited squeal broke their gaze. "A night in the city would be great." She said then nudged Maya. "Maya, you could use a break too."

"I'm pretty busy." Maya said. "And we promised Olivia to help with this mural and the summit."

Nina's youthful smile fell until she was pouting like a child who had just been punished. Nina groaned. "You know I love you, but you can be a real buzzkill."

"Sue me then." Maya smirked.

Five

♥

The Cascade City Summit committee dissolved in a week's time. There were arguments of prior engagements and packed schedules that justified their departures. Nina told Maya that she was finally off the waiting list for a spin class that she had been raving about and couldn't miss the opportunity. Maya told her that she understood without pointing out that her days were hectic too, overflowing with court cases, briefings, along with her preparation for her presentation, yet she kept her commitment with Olivia.

A guilt trip didn't change Nina's mind.

The final team was Maya, Olivia, a half a dozen artists and Marcus. As a team, they were finalizing the mural along with drafting the structure of the summit. Olivia pitched a creative aspect for the summit including a community art show with grand prizes for various categories and Marcus suggested a shopping tent where local vendors could set up shop.

He said, "We have to remind people of all the small businesses that thrive within our community. We could even do a few food trucks. I know few that D and I have worked with."

Olivia shrieked, "Yes." She attacked her whiteboard with vigor, noting the need to recruit food trucks and to designate space for the vendor's tent.

Maya listened intently as Marcus shared more ideas to make the summit about the community and not about making money. He spoke passionately about Cascade City; his hands were elevated and his deep voice echoed throughout the room. Maya loved how he captivated the small group. All eyes were on him as they listened intently. Clearly, he wasn't the type who struggled with public speaking. Olivia wrote down every idea Marcus threw out and Maya did too. He was glowing, beaming from ear to ear, and Maya admired it.

"Bro." Olivia said. "These are great. I think this is exactly what we need for this summit. We want to show the community what's available to them and the impact that we all have on this city."

Marcus nodded while typing away on his laptop.

Olivia capped her dry erase marker then flipped the

whiteboard to reveal the working ideas they had for the mural. The whiteboard was covered with words and rough sketches in red dry erase marker. "Okay, with community being our common theme here, let's revisit this mural." She said.

Maya studied the rough sketches and words; she had written down the mural concept to study at home and the office. On her legal pad, she jotted down her thoughts and questions related to the concept ideas. Maya tapped her pen on her legal pad rhythmically. Olivia's head tilted.

She said, "Maya. I know what that drumming means. What are you thinking?" Olivia asked.

Maya looked at the whiteboard again. She said, "I still have my reserves about including the American flag."

Olivia's brows caved in. "Yeah?"

Maya said. "I think it could be a little cliché. Don't you think so?"

"It represents cohesiveness." Olivia replied.

"Does it though?" Maya leaned forward on the table; her eyes scanned the concept art again. "Almost every mural I have looked at online seemingly has a nod to the American flag in it. Why?"

Marcus said, "Because it represents freedom." He leaned forward and glanced at Maya from two seats down. "Cascade City is a place of freedom."

"It is?" Maya asked.

Marcus perked up and his smile challenged her. "You don't think so?" He asked.

Maya said, "Cascade City is more than a place of freedom. We have one of the most artistic cities in the state of Illinois. Why don't we celebrate that? Why don't we celebrate the creative freedom over the colonized freedom."

Marcus hit the *Wakanda Forever* salute and howled like the Black Panther's adversary M'Baku. The committee and Maya laughed.

"Haha. I'm serious though. Why don't we create our own take on the American flag? Switch it up and celebrate the creative diversity that our city has to offer."Maya said.

"I see where you're going with that." Marcus said. "But do you think that the community as a whole will understand it? I just fear that some people will try and say that we are defacing the American flag or trying to erase it. Call me crazy but I know we have some MAGAs dwelling among us."

Maya giggled and Marcus responded with a soft smile. "You could be right." She said.

Olivia clapped gleefully, snatched up her black dry erase marker and started to sketch something onto the whiteboard. She said, "I think I got it."

She stepped away from the whiteboard to reveal another concept. She had sketched a paintbrush dripping with paint that bleed into the creation of the American flag. "Creative unity. We are the creators of unity and freedom." Olivia said.

Maya beamed, "I love it." She glanced at Marcus. "Any qualms with that?" She asked.

The smirk that spread over his face felt more flirtatious than satisfied. "None at all. I think it really brings our ideas together." Marcus said.

"And I think we have our mural, guys." Olivia said. The group applauded and Maya caught a glimpse of Marcus. He gave her another Wakandan salute and she returned it gracefully.

Marcus offered to give Olivia a ride home and to kill time while she locked up, he helped Maya fold chairs and clean up their work area. Maya had her hair pulled up in a messy bun and she wore black rimmed glasses. He wanted to compliment her when she walked in earlier, to tell her that she looked beautiful in glasses but refrained. He knew that the second it came out, he would get tongue tied and end up saying something else or freezing up completely.

He had spent the afternoon staring at her side profile and feeling a flush of excitement whenever she looked toward him. When she smiled at him, her plump lips curved in a delicate smile. He could only imagine what they felt like if he kissed her.

Marcus was pulled from his daydream by Maya's laughter. He shook his head then looked around; she had removed all of the chairs except the one he had gripped in his hand.

"Damn. My bad. I must have zoned out." He said.

Maya laughed, "It's cool. I do it all the time."

"Forget to fold chairs?' Marcus asked sheepishly.

Maya giggled again. "Zone out." Her laugh warmed his soul.

"Gotcha." Marcus added his contribution to the set of chairs that relaxed against a wall. "Feels good to finalize that mural and the premise of the summit." He said.

"Absolutely. It's a shame so many people dropped out though." Maya said. "We're gonna need all the help we can get."

"Yeah. I'll get Darnell to use some of that muscle for more than running his mouth." They both laughed. Maya pulled a black garbage bag from its bin and Marcus ran to her side. "Whoa. Let me do that." He said.

He slipped between her and the bag, gathered the ends

of the plastic bag then tied it off.

"You think I'm fragile or something?" Maya asked. Her tone was playful and sexy. "I could have done that."

Marcus said, "I know but I would never hear the end of it if Liv found out that I let you or any woman for that matter handle the trash while in my presence."

"Touché." Maya said.

Marcus set the bag next to the elevator then grabbed his phone from his pocket to study it.

"Running late for something?" She asked.

Marcus said, "No. No, I was just checking to see if Darnell hit me back. There's a convention this Saturday and he wanted to make sure that we were going. I told him I was still down so we have been trying to confirm what time he wants to meet so we can ride together."

Maya's eyes flickered before she exclaimed, "You're talking about the Tech and Business Convention in Chicago."

Marcus' brow elevated. "*You* know about the TBC?"

"Yes. I attend every year. I actually love technology." She said.

"Are you going this Saturday?" The question came so quickly that Marcus's heart shot into his throat. He said, "We have some extra passes. Maybe you and Nina would like to join us?"

Maya laughed. "She's not a techie but she does seem to

be smitten with *you*. I'm sure she would love to tag along."

Marcus looked away and he heard Maya's laugh again. "Are you blushing?" She teased.

"No. I'm not." He said.

"Mmm hmm. Well if you have extra passes then yes, I would love to attend."

Marcus wanted to reach for her and hug her then kiss her but he suppressed the idea. Instead, he said, "Could you text me your email address? I can send you the pass that way."

"Why don't we just meet here, Saturday morning and we can all go together. Or is that too much?" Maya asked.

"That's." Marcus cleared his throat. He felt like a little boy talking to his crush. "Yeah, that works. We can meet here Saturday at nine."

"Nine a.m. it is." Maya replied.

"Nine a.m. for what?" Olivia skipped into the room with her art bag in hand and a large grin on her face. "What's going on?" She asked.

"Maya and Nina are coming with Darnell and me to the Tech and Business Convention in Chicago on Saturday."

Olivia rolled her eyes. "Eww. Nothing good ever happens before one p.m. anyway. You ready to go, big bro?"

"Yep. Come on, let's get you home." Marcus said.

Maya stepped to the elevator, pressed the button then

gathered the garbage bag with her free hand. Marcus opened his mouth to protest but when the elevator doors opened, she stepped in and winked at him. "See ya, Liv. Goodnight Marcus."

"Goodnight, Maya," he said.

Marcus kept his eyes on her until the doors closed then a surge of pain vibrated up his arm. "Ow. What the hell?" He said. He rubbed his arm and looked at his sister.

Olivia hit him again. "Why did *she* take the trash out?"

"What? She picked up the bag and stepped into the elevator. What was I supposed to do?" He asked.

The elevator opened again and Olivia ranted at him. "You are no good, I tell ya. Wait 'til I tell Mom about this."

Marcus groaned. "Why the hell would you tell Mom about this?"

"Because she raised you better than that." His sister said.

Marcus shook his head, pushed the button for the first floor and silently prayed for no traffic on the way to Olivia's house.

After a stop at the grocery store for essentials: wine, fruit and half off sushi, Maya stepped into her condo breathing a sigh of relief that her day was done. Her double duty day was finally complete.

Almost complete.

Maya remembered she had a case to review before she could end her day, and she needed to finalize her presentation for Timothy and Robert. After swapping out her dress pants for biker shorts and a hoodie. Maya poured herself a glass of Riesling, grabbed some chopsticks for her sushi then headed to her living room.

She opened her balcony door and let the early evening breeze fill the room. Maya plopped down on the chaise portion of her large, cream sectional couch then grabbed her briefcase. She had her laptop and legal pads organized in front of her when her phone rang.

The opening to *She Got Her Own* by Jamie Foxx- selected by Nina of course, started to play and Maya answered slightly annoyed.

"Hey Nina." She said.

"So how was the meeting?" Nina asked.

Maya removed her glasses to massage the bridge of her nose. "It was great. We finalized the concept for the mural, and we started planning for the summit." She said.

"Was Marcus there?" The way Nina sang his name made Maya roll her eyes.

After the gala, Nina wasted no time looking up *the*

Marcus Johnson.

Maya tried to express no interest in what Nina found but she had to admit that she was curious about him and his business; however, she preferred to get to know him rather than stalk him. In less than twenty-four hours, Nina had a complete background check on Marcus, down to his mother's maiden name then found a short biography on him in Cascade City's local mailer magazine, *Cascade Highlights*:

Marcus Langston Johnson born January 23rd, 1983 in Harvey, Illinois, came to Cascade City by the way of his father and mother, Charles and Eleanor (Shannon) Johnson. The late Charles Johnson retired as a professor at Northwestern where he taught Computer Science. Charles passed away in 2020 while his wife Eleanor, a retired registered nurse and community activist still calls Cascade City home. Marcus, a tech entrepreneur, is the oldest of two, his sister, Olivia Johnson-Martinez is a renowned artist and art teacher. Today, Marcus and Olivia continue the efforts of their parents and give back to their community as often as they can. Olivia supports the youth through the arts and Marcus launched his first tech initiative after the death in father in 2020 called

TechBytes in which he teaches the youth about technology innovation outside of social media.

"This is one hell of a background." Nina said and went on to read the rest out loud to anyone at the office willing to listen. When latched on to a man, Nina was as forward as they came and she studied men like college courses.

"Your dream man was there." Maya told her.

"Yeah? Was he looking fine? What was he wearing?" Nina asked.

Maya paused to ponder her question to recall what he wore to the meeting. He stepped off the elevator wearing black joggers with a cream colored hoodie that was large yet not too bulky. Maya made out that large frame of his behind the plush sweater and had fantasized about sneaking her hands under his hoodie to feel his chest and those massive arms a few times during the meeting. He had finished the look with a pair of black Air Jordans— his signature shoe and had his leather bag slumped over his shoulder.

Maya cleared her throat and laughed at Nina's inquiry. "Maybe *you* should have been there so you could have seen it for yourself."

Nina sucked her teeth. "You're no fun. You know that,

right?"

"Oh yeah? Well, if I'm no fun, how did I manage to secure us passes for the Tech and Business Convention in Chicago this weekend?"

"Ugh. You wanna go to that, Maya?" Nina groaned.

"Yes. I go every year, and *you* bailed on me last year." Maya said.

Nina's voice was dry as burnt toast on the other end. "Oh yeah. I know."

Maya said, "Marcus and Darnell will be joining us."

Silence passed through the phone and Maya thought Nina had hung up before she heard her squeal.

"Are you serious?" Nina shrieked.

"We're driving together Saturday morning." Maya said.

"I'm riding up front with Marcus then." Nina said.

Maya rolled her eyes again. "Who said that he was driving?" She asked.

"If he does then I am." She replied.

"Alright, Nina." Before she could continue interrogating her about Marcus, Maya excused herself from the call, reminding Nina that she still had to prepare for her presentation.

"You know that shit like the back of your hand, Maya. You're ready, I know you are." Nina said.

"Thanks." She said, then ended the call. Maya was getting ready to activate the *Do Not Disturb* feature on her phone when she noticed she had two text messages waiting. She opened her inbox and saw an unknown number; when she clicked on the message, her lips curled in a wide smile.

It was gif of Chadwick Boseman as the infamous *Black Panther*, repeating the iconic salute.

Underneath the short video was an additional message:

> Liv gave me your number. I hope that was okay.

Maya beamed against her will and sent her response:

> It's alright. I guess that means we need to keep in touch.

She saw three dots appear then disappear. He responded:

> I hope so.

As she stared down at her phone, Maya felt bubbly.

Was this what it felt like to have a crush on someone? It had been so long since she found someone attractive let alone actually liked someone. A rush of excitement, accompanied with dizzying blindness made Maya's stomach queasy. Then the emotional high crashed as quickly as it arrived with a thrust back into reality.

The thought of dating again made her anxiety flare up. Who even said that Marcus wanted to date *her*? Maybe he was just being polite. A gentleman looking out for his sister's close friend. None of what he was doing really screamed "I like you."

Maya looked down at her phone again. He sent another text. Maya decided it was safe to add him as a contact then read his message:

How do you take your coffee?

Six

A medium coffee with three creams and four sugars steamed in the cardboard carrier Marcus held along with a small box filled with assorted, fresh pastries from his favorite, local spot, *Java Peak*. Darnell sat in the passenger seat sipping his coffee and wolfing down a chocolate almond bear claw. He had his phone propped up on the dash of Marcus' truck to watch Instagram stories while he munched.

"Man, this bear claw is fresh as hell. I need to get my ass up earlier to grab more of these." Darnell said.

Marcus glanced over his shoulder and said, "You waking up before ten a.m. would probably give you a heart attack."

Both men chuckled. Darnell and Marcus had a strong bond; they were often mistaken for brothers simply because they were tall, burly and black. Aside from sharing love for football and technology, they were complete opposites, which was the magic that made them a great team. Darnell was one of the first people Marcus met when he and his parents moved to Cascade City. They bonded over their love for Chicago teams: the Bears and the Bulls and agreed that baseball was not their "thing."

In school, they were stars on their wrestling and varsity football teams as well as stellar students. Darnell excelled in math and helped Marcus whose strong suits were science and English. It was an even trade, so by the time they graduated, it was a no-brainer when Marcus decided that he wanted to start his own tech business and wanted Darnell on board. His best friend signed on immediately.

Together, they turned a business formerly operating out of a closet in their sweltering two bedroom apartment, into a two-room office space in their hometown and successfully servicing Illinois, Wisconsin, and Ohio.

It was a few minutes past nine a.m. and a small seed of panic planted itself in Marcus' stomach. He looked at his phone to check for a new message from Maya. No notifications, just the last message she sent about fifteen minutes prior:

> On the way to pick up Nina then heading to the 3C building.

He didn't want to be anxious, but he was. Marcus moved the drink carrier from hand to hand as he counted the seconds. The steady count started in his head before he started counting out loud. "Thirty-one, thirty-two, thirty-three."

Darnell poked his head out of the truck. "Hey. You okay out here?" He asked.

"Yeah. Just worried about Maya." Marcus said.

"You think she and her friend stood us up?" Darnell shoved the last of the bear claw into his mouth.

Marcus watched as powdered sugar settled onto best friend's logoed black Henley shirt. He motioned to Darnell to look down.

"Damnit." Darnell scoffed while brushing the white dust off his shirt then his face.

"Why would they stand us up?" Marcus asked.

Darnell sipped his coffee then looked at Marcus. "Why in the hell would two women, especially ones that look like them want to go to a tech and business convention?"

Marcus opened his mouth to protest but he pursed his lips together then smiled peacefully. He knew Maya was on her way. She didn't seem like the type of woman who would stand a guy up. But then again... Before Marcus's mind took a ride down memory lane, a smoke gray Volvo sedan pulled into the parking lot.

The car came to a stop next to Marcus's truck then the engine was silenced. The windows had a black tint, projecting a distorted reflection of himself; the driver's side door opened, and Marcus felt the panic dissipate yet his heart accelerated.

"I'm so sorry we're late." Maya said as climbed from her car. "*Someone* made us late." She added, darting her eyes to the passenger side.

"I stand corrected." Darnell said.

Nina emerged from the passenger side; her attention immediately shifted to Marcus. She smiled at him; her hazel eyes pleading for forgiveness. "Sorry. I overslept. I'm not up this early on a Saturday unless brunch is involved."

"It's cool." Marcus said.

Maya and Nina collect their purses from her car then walk toward his truck.

Nina pointed at the Land Rover. "Is this you, Marcus?" She asked.

"Yep! This is my baby." He said then slapped the hood lightly. Darnell stepped out of the truck; he towered over Nina, who was looking at him in a combination of wonder and fear.

"I told him to get a Corvette. He comes back with this." Darnell said.

Maya eyed the truck, looked at Marcus and smiled. "I think it suits you very well." She said.

"Thank you." He said before handing Maya her coffee. "Three creams and four sugars, right?"

Her lips were glossed again and when she smiled, the early sun glistened off the fullest part of her bottom lip. She took a sip and beamed. "It's perfect. I love the coffee at Java Peak."

"Really?" Marcus said, "I practically lived there when I first started. I mooched off their Wi-Fi for at least a year."

Maya laughed. "They have some of the best coffee and pastries." She said.

"Isn't that the place where Robert gets the muffins on Fridays?" Nina asked.

"Yep. Three dozen assorted, every Friday." Maya said.

Nina squealed, "Their muffins are so damn good."

"So are the bear claws." Darnell said.

"I'm partial to their cherry cheese danishes." Marcus said.

Maya shook a finger at him respectfully. "You know, I have yet to try one of those. Every time I go there, they're sold out."

Marcus grinned as he handed her the bag. "You're in luck then because I have one right here." He said.

Maya opened the bag; her eyes swelled when she peeked

inside. "Oh my God." She beamed.

"You want it?" He asked.

Maya reached into the bag for the pastry then withdrew her hand. "I couldn't." She said. "You just said it's your favorite."

"I eat them three times a week." Marcus replied.

"It's true, he does." Darnell said.

Marcus looked at Maya then winked. "Come on, you know you want it. See what the craze is all about. Trust me, you're gonna like it." He said.

Maya pulled the Danish from the bag, then took a bite. Marcus watched her while she chewed slowly then her eyes fluttered. Maya was having an outer body experience and Marcus added another thing that attracted him to Maya Thompson to his list. Her love for good food.

"Oh, sweet Jesus. That's delicious." Maya said.

Marcus lifted his hands in praise. "Told ya. The best Danish ever, right?"

Maya nodded and indulged in another bite. She said, "I could eat a dozen of these."

Marcus laughed. "I told you. You wanna finish that in the car?"

Maya nodded again.

"Alright, let's get on the road." He said.

"I'll ride up front with you, Marcus." Nina was already

in position to hop into the passenger seat; Marcus looked at Darnell, he shrugged then cocked his head toward the pastry loving Maya and grinned.

The McCormick Place was a scenic thirty-five minute drive for them and just minutes away from downtown Chicago. The popular convention center was constructed of four buildings with three of the four buildings linked together by what was known as the Skybridge. The space could hold a variety of events all at once with nearly two hundred meeting rooms and hundreds of thousands square feet of space. The Tech and Business Convention was located in the South Building which Maya and the group accessed via the center's Grand Concourse.

As they walked through the crowded lobby toward the South Building, Maya took time to study Marcus. During the drive, Nina monopolized the conversation with random questions. And thanks to her extensive deep dive, Nina had an advantage yet humored herself with the attention. Maya and Darnell chimed in, but Nina barely paid them any mind, because she had Marcus' full attention. So Maya and Darnell started a discussion of their own.

She learned that Darnell had a son and like Marcus, he was a real technology enthusiast. He went into detail describing his home office set up and Maya felt a ping of jealousy when he bragged about his record player set up.

"Surround sound speakers connected to the record player?" She asked him.

Darnell nodded with pride then said. "Yep. Cost me about two grand to get it just right but it was worth it."

He went on about the sound system before he inquired about *Sterling and Turner*, in which Maya felt inclined to give the general overview of the company to him. When she was done, Darnell said, "I had no idea we had black lawyers in Cascade City."

"Well now you do." Maya said with a soft grin and when she peeked into the rearview, she saw Marcus' eyes meeting hers.

Maya noted that Marcus and Darnell wore the same outfits– uniforms. They wore relaxed fit, long sleeve shirts bearing an embroidered logo on the left side of their chests. The logo was a capitalized I and C with a globe hovering in the space between the C. Both men chose dark denim jeans; Darnell wore a pair of Jordans but Marcus finished his look with a pair of casual oxford.

Aside from the Henley shirts, they carried something

embossed with their *InnovateCore* logo. A subtle strategy, yet bold enough to spark the typical networking question "What does that mean?" And thus, an opportunity would be born.

Marcus had a black, leather sling bag strapped across his chest and Maya caught a glint of silver beneath Marcus' Henley that was a thin, silver snake link chain. She scanned the rest of him for jewelry only to find he wore an expected *Apple* watch with a silver mesh band.

And no wedding ring.

Maya never thought to check for a ring before, she was relieved to find his left ring finger naked and free of a tan line too.

After checking in, the group gathered at the massive archway of the South Building , each of them scanning the program. Nina flipped through the glossy pages only to stop at the advertisements for merchandise. Darnell appeared to be more interested in the page of sponsors displayed on the back of the program. Maya glanced at Marcus; he was physically circling items in the program with a pen.

"So, you *do* own a pen." Maya said. His hand was mid-circle when his head turned toward her. "I thought you only used Apple Pencils."

Marcus made a mocking face to match the tone, repeating Maya jab. "Got jokes huh?" He said.

Maya shrugged and flipped through the programs. She made mental notes for a few seminars and noted the time for the mixer that was set to immediately follow the close of the convention. It would be held in the Grand Ballroom on the lowest level of the building and the dress code was noted as "Casual."

Maya had opted for light wash skinny jeans, a white, pearlesque, sleeveless tunic that she paired with burgundy cardigan. She chose a pair of wine colored flats at the last minute, remembering that they would be covering lots of ground on foot and learned her lesson from her first time at the convention, three years ago. An hour into walking the convention and she cursed herself for wearing four inch heels.

Marcus peered over Maya's shoulder; his face was so close to hers. She could smell the Teakwood aroma on his skin. It was fresh and soothing; Maya fought the urge to close her eyes and savor it, instead she glanced at him out of the corner of her eye. "Yes?" She asked.

Marcus didn't move, he kept his face close to her as he spoke. "There's a seminar starting in about ten minutes in Hall A1 on tech trends in 2024. You wanna start there?" He said.

"That's the one I really wanna check out." Darnell said.

"It's sponsored by CNet too."

Nina nodded and Maya wondered if she knew what *CNet* was.

"That's our first stop then." Maya said. "We can then move onto the vendor floor afterward."

"That's *my* spot." Nina said. "The goodie bags are always top notch."

Marcus smiled again and Maya's heart did something.

Was that a flutter or heartburn?

Darnell and Nina led the way with Maya and Marcus in tow; he was matching her stride. "Am I walking too slow?" She asked.

"No. I just wanted to walk with you and spectate." He said.

Maya looked at him with a pinched brow. "Spectate?" She said.

Marcus pointed ahead to Darnell and Nina who were talking and laughing.

It clicked for Maya then. "They do look cute together." She gushed.

Marcus agreed. "They do." Maya could feel a question looming, but Marcus cleared his throat as if to reset himself. "So, you're a tech girl?"

Maya giggled. "Is that how you're going to break the ice with the women in here today?"

"What?" He asked. Marcus' face hardened then softened when he smiled; he was getting familiar with her sense of humor. "No. I was seriously asking you that."

"Yes." Maya laughed. "I would like to consider myself tech savvy."

Marcus said, "Aside from your love for pen and paper, I would say that you're pretty tech savvy."

"How could you tell?" Maya asked.

"You have the latest iPhone, iPad and MacBook, so you're big on having a solid tech ecosystem. I noticed your bag has a built-in charging station which tells me that you're almost always plugged in and hate it when your phone goes under," He paused, squinted and pretended to think. "Twenty percent. You seem like the type who has a camera alarm system, some type of virtual assistant device, I'm guessing Alexa and that Volvo of yours has all the bells and whistles that scream 'techie'."

"Damn." Maya laughed. "You're good."

"Was I right?" Marcus asked. Maya rolled her eyes playfully when Marcus chuckled. "Yep. I'm right."

"Whatever." She said.

"Your turn." He said.

Maya looked at him like he spoke a foreign language.

Marcus said, "Come on, I know you picked up some things about me, you being one of the best lawyers in

Cascade City and all."

"I never said that." Maya said.

"Everyone else said it for you." Marcus grinned.

Maya tried to leer him, but he was too handsome to upset her. She laughed then said. "I'm a lawyer, not a detective."

"And both can read a person from a mile away." He replied. Maya laughed again then Marcus said, "I feel like you can read a person really well."

He was right. Maya had studied Marcus. From the night at the gala to the meetings at the art center; she had picked up vibes about him and the more time she spent with him, a new element would emerge and tempt her.

Ask him out.

Get his number.

Ask him if he's single.

Of course he's not single. Look at him.

Maya felt Marcus' eyes on her and the sensation made her flush. There was a spring in his step that was eager and comical. "Alright. Let me think." She said, "You're a diligent worker." She said.

"That's obvious." He replied.

"Can I finish?" Her voice was playfully sharp. Marcus pressed his hands together and bowed apologetically. "Thank you. As I was saying, you're a diligent worker.

You're passionate about your business and how you can pay it forward. You're well rounded too. I feel like you can talk football stats on one hand then talk about coding on the other."

His anxious smile turned into a full grin that made Maya giggle nervously. "That sounds like me." Marcus said.

"Of course it does." Maya replied.

"Anything else?" He stopped and looked down into her eyes and Maya's heart thundered in her chest. "What else do you think you know?" His voice was low, almost intimate.

Maya's face burned but she couldn't take her eyes off of him. "You have excellent taste in pastry." She smiled. Marcus broke their gaze with a chuckle before they walked into Hall A1.

Throughout the convention, Marcus caught himself staring at Maya longer than he expected. During seminars when he should have been paying attention, he watched Maya as she took notes or recorded highlights on her phone. He wondered what her social media looked like. Was it neat and organized or eclectic? Because she was a beautiful collaboration of organized chaos that only those closest to her had access to.

Yes, she was a lawyer which meant that she had to know a thing or two about the law, but she also understood business and technology, art and apparently a little bit of basketball. Marcus heard a snippet of the excited conversation Maya and Darnell had about Steph Curry and his potential for the next three years; the way her oval face lit up when she made a point that shot down Darnell's prediction was a delight to witness.

At the close of the convention, they made their way to the *Grand Ballroom* for the mixer. Everyone took a name tag, writing their names on the minimal blank space; Maya wrote her name in clean caps and added a starburst after the last A in her name. She looked at Marcus as she stuck the name tag to her cardigan. "What? We all don't have embroidered logos." She said then winked.

Damn. Marcus said to himself.

"We should stick close to each other." Nina said, she snaked her arm around Marcus' arm. His body stiffened and he saw Maya's face shift. Her lips were a plump line on her face.

"There's definitely strength in numbers at things like this." Marcus said, "But it's also a good idea to move around and network." Marcus maneuvered out of Nina's grasp then exhaled softly.

As a group, they navigated the large crowds. Darnell led the way toward the bar, Nina followed him, but Maya and Marcus fell behind. "Drink?" Marcus asked her.

Maya shook her head. "I'll wait." She then added, "You never know who you're going to meet at these things."

Good idea. He thought.

Marcus guided Maya away from the crowd at the bar as someone tapped him on the shoulder. He turned to find an older, black man smiling at him so hard, Marcus thought the man may have had him confused with someone else.

"Marcus Johnson, right? Of InnovateCore?"

Marcus gave Maya a worried glance, but she just smiled and motioned for him to shake the man's extended hand that he had not seen. "Yeah. That's me." He said.

"Wow! I'm Lance Wilkes. Of Wilkes Security. Your company helped me upgrade my data analysis system just last year."

A rolodex of names and faces passed through Marcus' head until it stopped on something familiar. *Wilkes Security*, Rock Forest, Illinois. They had been losing clients by the dozens because of their outdated technology and resources. In the age of CCTV cameras, facial detection and wireless systems, *Wilkes Security* needed to find a way to level up and even the competitive playing field in home security.

Lance's son reached out to InnovateCore and they went to work, analyzing what worked for them and what didn't. After the extensive review, ICore created a data analysis system that helped the family owned business identify patterns and trends in the home security field. The system helped *Wilkes Security* recognize errors in home security systems then offer home security packages ideal for apartments and small homes. Following their work with Lance and *Wilkes Security,* he sent them three more customers.

Lance's recommendation had been gold for them that year.

Marcus shook Lance's hand with vigor; both men were smiling. Marcus noticed his bright smile. He ignored the idea of veneers yet struggled to take his eyes off his stark white, perfectly capped teeth, a contrast to his smooth, dark skin. "It's good to see you, Mr. Wilkes."

Lance gripped his hand. "Hey, none of that 'Mr. Wilkes' mess. You call me Lance."

"Gotcha. Lance. How are you?" Marcus asked.

"Doing well. Doing very well. My son and I had a panel earlier today talking about aging alongside technology." Lance said.

Marcus smiled. He loved to hear when his clients thrived

thanks to *ICore*. And Lance's new smile confirmed that business was doing good. "How's business?" He asked.

Lance stood up taller and grinned. "Fantastic. We are in the top five of security businesses in Winnebago County. A true first for us. Home security has been on a rise, and we work with more small businesses now too"

"Congrats." Maya said. She stepped closer to look Lance in the eyes. The man's aged smile traveled to his eyes, taking years off his age.

"Oh my. Hello, I'm Lance Wilkes." He grabbed Maya's hand and kissed it. "And what's your name, beautiful?"

Maya played the game; she smiled politely and offered her name. Lance kept her hand in his, but she gracefully pulled it away.

Marcus loved how cunning she was at dismissing unwarranted attention.

"It's a pleasure to meet you, Lance." Maya said.

"That pleasure is all mine." Lance looked from Maya to Marcus who realized what the man was hinting without words.

Is she with you?

Marcus said, "Maya is a lawyer, Lance. She's one of the top attorneys in the Chicagoland area."

"Is that right?" Lance asked.

"It is." She said with poise. No one would have known

that less than two minutes ago, the man had slightly repulsed her. "Tell me more about Wilkes Security, Lance."

And just like that, Maya rerouted the conversation and opened a floodgate.

Throughout the rest of the evening, Marcus watched Maya network. She exchanged business cards, talked shop with coders, designers, even the bartender, not once did she flaunt her own expertise. When she did mention that she was a lawyer, she would dismiss it casually and return the attention to whoever she was speaking with. It was something about the way Maya carried herself that evening that made Marcus realize that he wasn't lusting after Maya.

He was falling for her.

Maya had playfully called "shotgun" and joined Marcus up front for the ride home. His truck was lively with everyone gushing over their favorite parts of the convention and the mixer. Marcus played back his personal highlights of the day with Maya. From her smile and her laugh to the way that she studied people as they spoke to her. How her brown eyes would stay locked on them until they were done.

It was astounding to him. And sexy as hell.

He had never met a woman so grounded and compassionate. It wasn't an act either. Maya wasn't like the blood sucking lawyers depicted on TV or the lawyer who he and Darnell initially had to help them with their trademark details; she was genuine and beautiful.

When they returned to the parking lot of the *3C Arts Center*, Darnell climbed out first with Maya and Nina following. Marcus felt his chest tighten with anticipation; his heart rang in his ears and all he could tell himself was to go for it. He was going to make a move.

Marcus was going to ask Maya out.

Life slowed but his words came out fast. "Would you like to go to dinner sometime?" He asked. His voice shook but his smile was wide and eager.

"Seriously? Absolutely." It was the confirmation that he imagined in his head, but the voice didn't match. "What day were you thinking?" The voice asked.

Reality came back to Marcus like a fastball to the face; his eyes adjusted, and he saw Nina standing outside the front passenger door, where Maya had stood just seconds before. Maya had moved to the back of his truck, retrieving her sponsor gifts from the convention. Nina stood outside of the passenger side, holding the phone charger that she had plugged into the USB slot on his middle console that morning.

"What?" Marcus said.

His heart plunged into his stomach and behind Nina,

Marcus saw Darnell shaking his head dramatically.

Then he saw Maya.

That bright smile that made him weak faded and her dark eyes shifted away from his sight. Nina, on the other hand, was smiling at him, vibrating in her skin when she said, "I'll text you. Maya has your number, right?"

"Yeah." The word barely left his mouth, but Nina was beaming. She thanked him for the ride then danced toward Maya's Volvo.

Maya tapped the car door and smiled; it wasn't genuine, it was painful. "Thanks again for the ride, Marcus. I'll see you Monday at the Summit meeting."

He wanted to scream for Maya to wait but his throat was dry, and his hands felt glued to the steering wheel. Marcus watched Maya and Nina climb into her Volvo. He wished her window tint wasn't so dark; he wanted to see her face again.

Was she really as disappointed as she appeared?

Maya's Volvo engine started, the car backed out of the parking space, and in seconds, she was gone.

Marcus' head dropped to the steering wheel with a soft thud. He groaned.

"What the hell just happened?" Darnell asked.

A wave of sickness soured Marcus' stomach as another guttural moan escaped him.

Seven

♥

Maya paced the pale gray carpet floor of her office, reciting the key points of her presentation to herself for the fifth time. Timothy decided to put her on the spot and offered Maya an hour of his time to share her initiative with him, Robert and a few members of the firm. Maya wanted to make sure her points were clear, concise and easy to understand because she needed them to understand that her initiative was not only important to her but their community too.

This was a win-win for everyone.

"With this initiative, I envision a system that not only upholds the principles of justice but actively works to address and improve systemic inequalities and provides a voice to those who may otherwise be marginalized within it."

Her phone vibrated on her desk. She had silenced it since

Saturday and had no plans on taking it off. Maya ignored the initial alert. "With this initiative." She said.

Her phone buzzed.

"With *this* initiative."

Another buzz.

"*With this.*"

Then another.

"Shit." Maya hissed. She snatched the phone from her desk, looked at the screen and sighed.

Messages from Marcus. She rolled her eyes then opened her inbox despite herself.

His first message read:

> About last night...

His message was followed by a series of photos.

Maya sank down into her leather office chair and clicked on the first image. It was two dinner plates along with one of Marcus' large hands. She noticed Nina's gold bangles opposite him.

Nina adored those bracelets and bragged about them whenever someone complimented her. "They're Cartier knock offs but you gotta be a pro to notice that." Nina told her.

The second photo was Nina on her phone. She appeared to be scrolling while Marcus held up his glass of wine; Nina was oblivious to the camera *and* the moment. Maya giggled to herself then flip through three more photos featuring Nina and her cellphone, then Marcus sent another text:

> Such wonderful company.

It was the last photo that made Maya erupt in full, boisterous laughter.

It was a picture of Marcus at *Java Peak.* He sat posed with a cup of coffee and a cherry cheese Danish. Under his selfie he said:

> Wish you were here.

She smiled at her phone, then responded with a heart emoji.

The heart emoji was a good sign. Marcus smiled at his

phone's screen, but in the midst of his joy, his emotions took a nosedive as he stepped into his home office. The text he sent to Wayne Carlson was read but not responded to. He had sent the message twelve hours ago; to follow up on their scheduled meeting to discuss the investment and collecting payment.

Marcus' nerves were frying.

When his phone rang, Marcus ignored the caller ID and answered swiftly. "Marcus Johnson." He said.

"Damn man. Why you answering the phone like that?" Darnell's voice came through on the opposite end. "You good, bro?" He said.

Marcus sighed, rubbing his right temple. "Have you heard from Carlson?" He asked.

Darnell said, "Wayne Carlson? No. Why?"

"Have we received anything from his assistant?" Marcus asked. Darnell confirmed that he didn't receive anything in his inbox and confirmed that the business email inbox was clear too.

"You're nervous aren't you?" Darnell asked.

"Yes. It's been three weeks." Marcus said.

Darnell scoffed. "Actually, it's been four, but that man is busy."

"Doing what?" Marcus chuckled nervously. "He may be loaded but I doubt his schedule is jam packed."

"I'll shoot him an email." Darnell said.

Marcus said, "I sent him a text last night."

"Let me email his assistant and see if she can help us out." Darnell replied.

Marcus sighed again and said, "Thanks, man." He could hear Darnell typing and mumbling to himself before confirming that the message was sent.

"Did you hear back from Maya?" Darnell asked.

"I did." Marcus said as joy returned in a small, tingling dose. "She should be at the committee meeting tonight so I hope I can talk to her face to face."

"Good. I knew you two were feeling each other." Darnell said.

Marcus scoffed, "What?" He walked the length of his personal office.

"Don't lie, man. I saw the way you two were laughing and chit chatting at the convention. It's okay to like someone. " Darnell said, "Hell, I was impressed when you asked her out."

"I didn't ask her though." Marcus said. He studied the large dry erase calendar he had affixed to the burnt orange accent wall. Its white surface was covered with dates in black marker, important information in red and business payouts noted in green.

"I saw those pics you sent me. Looks like you and Nina

didn't hit it off too well." Darnell chuckled.

Marcus laughed dryly. "Did you think we would?" He said.

"Why did you even go forward with the date anyway?" Darnell asked.

Marcus said, "Because I didn't want to hurt her feelings. Rejection sucks and rejection in front of everyone hurts like hell."

Darnell whistled then said, "Man, you gotta let that Kiana mess go. And if I'm being honest you dodged a bullet when she rejected your proposal. She was too damn bougie."

Marcus nodded to himself and let the memory transport him back to the last New Years Eve party he ever attended.

The invite announced an all-white event and from head to toe, which Marcus and Kiana did not disappoint. He wore white dress slacks and a matching turtleneck and Kiana decided on a white turtleneck dress. It clung to her slim frame while accenting areas that he knew Kiana wasn't fond of, yet her pride told her to flaunt it. Marcus remembered laughing to himself as he watched her squeeze into the dress that she purposely ordered one size smaller than usual.

"It's too small." He told her, but Kiana didn't care. She

managed to get in the dress but struggled the entire night to sit down. She even refused to dance with him out of fear that she would bust out of the spandex, cotton blend dress like a can of biscuits.

It was at the stroke of midnight when all the guests were cheering and toasting to the next 365 days that Marcus pulled Kiana away from the crowd, took a knee and proposed.

Where there should have been a look of happiness, excitement or surprise, Marcus watched Kiana's eyes narrow at him, scrutinizing him and the ring he held out for her. His heart raced so fast he thought it would shoot from his body and take off.

Kiana glared at him. "Are you serious?" She said. Her voice was hard and rusty. Her thin brows were stitched tightly together. "*You* want to marry me?" She asked.

"Of course." Marcus told her and felt his confidence evaporating into the celebratory ether. His smile wavered and sweat accumulated on his forehead. "Come on, baby. What do you say?" He asked.

Darnell's heavy voice broke Marcus' trance. "Hey! We got a message from Wayne." He said. Darnell mumbled a few lines of the email under his breath. Marcus made out some words:

"I apologize for the delay... It's been hectic over here."

His partner rejoiced, "Got it! He wants to do a meeting next Monday. Please tell me that works for you."

"Monday afternoon." Marcus said.

"Cool." Darnell went to work on the reply. Marcus could feel him grinning through the phone. "Alright, that's done. Next item on the agenda, asking Maya out."

"I can't." Marcus said.

"Why the hell not?" Darnell asked. He imagined his best friend on the other end with large arms folded across his chest.

"Too soon. I just took Nina out. How would it look if I asked Maya out immediately after?" Marcus asked.

"Like you're *really* interested? You *do* like her." Darnell said.

Marcus replied. "I do."

"But..." Darnell sang.

"But I- we have a lot of work to handle around here and so does she."

Darnell interrupted him with a loud groan. "Come on, Marcus. This is *our* business, but it is not our lives. You need a life. Forget about Kiana, forget about your shitty date with Nina and ask Maya out." He said.

"But I can't take her where I took Nina though." Marcus said.

"Oh hell no." Darnell laughed. "You need a better date,

and I know where you should go. Check your IG." He said.

Marcus pulled his phone from his ear, tapped the Instagram icon and saw the red and white icon notifying him that he had a direct message. He opened his inbox and found the latest message from *d_epps17*.

Seventeen had been Darnell's jersey number throughout their football career; he had been willing to hurt and/or bribe players for that number at the start of every season. The latter always worked, Marcus only recalled two guys actually getting beaten up by Darnell for it.

He opened the message, and a brightly colored digital flyer appeared on his screen. Marcus switched from the internal speaker to the speakerphone. "What's this?" He asked.

"You know Celine's kicks off the annual opening of their beer garden with a jazz night. It would make a great 'Sorry I asked the wrong girl out' date for you and Maya. Don't you think so?" Darnell said.

Marcus studied the flyer again. The event was advertised as *"Jazz in the Cascade at Celine's"* with a live jazz band, drink specials and their popular food truck.

"You should call Maya right now and ask her." Darnell said.

Marcus replied, "I can't. She's at work but I'll be seeing

her tonight."

"Great. Ask her tonight while y'all paint or doing whatever y'all be doing over there." Darnell said.

"Shut up. You know I volunteered your muscle to help out at the summit too." Marcus added.

"Of course you did." Darnell laughed.

They laughed together then Darnell shifted into business mode. He started a conversation about a new client and once he started talking in numbers, Marcus zoned his business partner out and studied the flyer again. While he studied at the flyer, Marcus imagined him and Maya slow dancing together.

Joy consumed him again.

The committee meeting was in full swing; Maya was working with an artist and cohort of Olivia's named Jo and a barista from *Java Peak* named Brittany. The three of them were organizing all the businesses who had signed up for the summit and donated to host booths. Brittany tackled the business cards that were dropped off at the coffee shop while Jo handled the half sheet forms that she collected over the weekend. They took turns reading off contact names, email addresses, phone numbers and donation amounts to Maya as she typed them into a spreadsheet.

Maya paused then checked the count. "This is amazing." She said.

Jo and Brittany looked at her intently. "Forty businesses have donated and we have thirty-two vendors so far."

The barista, Brittany, was the first to respond. Maya had complimented her on her bright red hair when they first met and that day, she had her hair in two, short French braids. "I know we have more business cards at the shop too. I just grabbed this batch before the jar started over-flowing."

Maya said, "You know, I think we should create a booth chart for the vendors' tent. We can categorize each business based on their specified fields."

Jo, who had streaks of black paint on her hands and arms nodded eagerly. "Oh that is a great idea."

Maya opened a new workbook and went to work designing the chart. Olivia approached their chattering group with a glowing smile.

"How's it going, ladies?" She asked.

Jo and Brittany raved about the idea of the chart; Maya's eyes met Olivia's. They were wild with excitement.

"You love an organization chart don't you?" Olivia smirked.

"Sure do." Maya said.

Olivia clapped her hands together. "You think your bosses will be interested in getting a booth?" She asked.

"Well, they've already put down a substantial amount for a sponsorship." Maya replied. "I don't see why they wouldn't reserve a booth too."

"They really love throwing money around like that, huh?" Olivia asked Maya.

"Of course. It brings in business every time." Maya said before her eyes wandered to Marcus.

She had kept her distance from him the entire night, but she couldn't help sneaking quick glances at him from across the room. He had spent the first hour of the meeting clicking away at his laptop. When their eyes locked, Maya would hold his strong gaze until her face flared with heat, then she'd break the connection. She felt like she was in high school all over again and fawning over the finest guy in school. Her stomach knotted with excitement every time he looked in her direction.

"Let's call it a night, everyone." Olivia said, standing in the middle of the room, stretching her arms high above her head. "We will continue tomorrow and don't forget Saturday morning; we are meeting at the Fremont building to work on the mural."

There were sounds of confirmation followed by a chorus of chairs scraping across the wooden floor, rustling paper and laptops closing. Maya looked at Marcus; his eyes were on her again. She cleared her throat then looked at Olivia. "Hey, Liv, do you need a ride home?" She asked.

Olivia grinned as she tightened her high ponytail. "Nope. I have a ride *and* a date."

"Date?" Marcus repeated the word as he pushed away from his chair and he puffed out his chest. Maya and Olivia giggled at his brotherly theatrics. "Who are you going out with?" He asked.

"Nobody you would know." She joked then peered at Maya. "He's an artist from Chicago I met a few months back. We have been playing phone tag for weeks and we both finally have some free time."

"Congrats." Maya said. She slipped her legal pad in her leather briefcase then gave Marcus a final look before she started to walk toward the elevator. "Well, be safe and have fun. I will call you tomorrow regarding that Chicago bakery that wants to be a sponsor."

"Great and see you Saturday too, right? 9am?"

"9am." Maya repeated. She pushed the button for the elevator then looked over her shoulder. Marcus was shoving his laptop into his bag. She wondered if he could make it in time to take the elevator down with her, then she imagined him missing the elevator...just for a little dramatic effect. Like in the movies.

The elevator chimed, the doors opened and Maya stepped in.

"Hold up." Marcus called. Maya's hand grasped one of the doors and she watched him shuffle to the elevator. They both waved to Olivia until the doors closed on her, then the elevator made its descent.

Maya drew in a slow breath; suddenly she wished that the building was more than three stories high. She turned to Marcus and smiled. "I gave my presentation by the way." She said.

His eyes swelled. "Really? That's great. How did it go?" He asked.

Maya said, "They put me on the spot but I did pretty damn good, if I say so."

Marcus laughed softly. "That is wonderful." He said. "So what's next? Do they have to approve your project?"

A grin warmed Maya's lips and Marcus stared at her, trying to read her delight. She said, "They approved it almost instantly."

"Oh shit." Marcus rejoiced. "It was *that* easy?" He asked.

"Yes." Maya smirked. "Per the firm's request, I can get started right away," she said.

"Really? Just like that?" Marcus asked.

"Just like that." Maya repeated. "I submitted my budget

immediately."

Marcus raised a brow. "A budget huh?"

Maya mirrored his brow lift. "It pays to be special counsel." She said.

"I see. Congratulations." He smiled. His dimples pierced his face, triggering his youthful side.

"Thank you. I wanted to see if InnovateCore would handle the tech elements for me. I want to create a website and have some ideas for a few databases too. Would you be able to assist me?" Maya asked.

"Of-of course." Marcus stammered. "Thank you."

"And we will pay too." Maya said quickly.

Marcus chuckled. "Thank you. I appreciate you thinking of us." He said.

Maya's smile widened. She said, "You're welcome. I know that you believe in helping improve the community, especially *our* community. And I know that with an opportunity like this, I do not want to give it to some John Doe tech company." He nodded and his smile warmed Maya to her core.

"Thank you, Maya." Marcus said. They way he said her name made her grip the rail.

The elevator came to a halt then opened to the main floor. Outside, the last remnants of the sun had faded as dusk took over the city. "Can I walk you to your car?"

Marcus asked.

"Sure." She said.

They walked in silence; Maya wanted to mention the photos from his date with Nina but decided it was in bad taste or at least too soon. Instead, she said, "Nina said that she had a nice time."

Marcus scoffed playfully, "Then she and I have different versions of that date." He stopped abruptly and turned to her. "Maya, you know that I didn't mean to ask Nina out that night, right?"

She bowed her head. "I had a feeling, but I didn't want to assume. Plus, I knew Nina had a thing for you."

"I couldn't tell during our date." Marcus said.

"Yeah. That surprised me too." She said. Maya looked away for a moment then returned her gaze to Marcus. The tension between them was magnetic and Maya could feel something hanging in the evening air.

Marcus said. "I did want to ask you if you would come with me to the Jazz night at Celine's Saturday night?"

Maya's body went warm from the flush of excitement that passed through her. "You're asking *me* out? On a date?"

"I am, but I mean if you don't want to call it a date, we can call it a meet up. I can meet you at Celine's, after we work on the mural." Marcus said.

Maya raised her hand as she laughed. "Stop it. I'm just giving you a hard time." She watched a veil of tension leave Marcus' face. He stood up taller and his full, beautiful smile returned. "I would love to join you at Celine's on Saturday."

"Great. I will pick you up Saturday night." His smile illuminated under the streetlights. "Goodnight, Maya." He said before he turned and walked in the opposite direction.

Maya called to him. "Hey." When he turned back toward her; Maya pressed the key fob to her Volvo, its lights flashed once then a second time. "You haven't walked me to my car yet."

Marcus retreated back to her, grabbed her briefcase, then led her to her car. He opened the rear passenger door, set her briefcase on the back seat then opened the driver's side door. Maya kept her eyes on him as she slipped into the seat.

"Thank you." She said.

"You're welcome." His deep voice sent a vibration through her body. Maya gripped her steering wheel to keep her bearings.

No. She told herself.

Not yet. Not now.

Marcus' hand lingered at the top of the door before he closed it. Maya strained to see his face a second more behind the black tint.

Eight

It had been a unanimous decision, *Sterling, Turner and Associates* would launch Maya's Community Counsel Initiative. After the announcement, Robert embraced her like a proud father and looked at her with praise and excitement in his dark, brown eyes.

"That was one hell of a presentation." He told her. "Tim was blown away with all your insights and your plan for execution."

For the rest of the week, Maya kept herself composed and professional, but inside— and whenever she was behind closed doors, she jumped up and down like as if she had won the big showcase on *The Price Is Right*.

This was her moment. Her dream was coming to life.

When Maya arrived at her office Friday morning, Robert met her at the elevator with a wide smile. Maya knew that wide grin. When he had good news, his wide mouth would curl at the ends like the Joker and his eyes would narrow to the point where Maya could barely see them.

"There she is." Robert said.

"Umm good morning." Maya said as she stepped off the elevator. They walked in silence with Robert beaming. He wore a tailored, dark blue suit. The cuffs of his suit jacket were lined with a thin, silken burgundy braid and he had on a gold pair of cufflinks that had the initials RPT embossed on them. Maya recalled the cufflinks were a gift from Elena for one of their wedding anniversaries.

Their twentieth?

No, their twenty-second.

Robert only wore them for special occasions such as major cases or whenever he had to be on television. Maya stopped short of her office. The smile on his face didn't budge. "What's going on?" She asked.

"Tim called the local news stations." Robert said.

"For what?" Maya asked.

"For you to announce the Community Counsel Initiative." He said.

Maya's eyes widened and she felt her throat lock. She opened her mouth to speak but the words were dry on her tongue. Her face was a question mark, silently begging Robert to explain.

"Maya, the board believes this initiative could put us on the map. We're talking expansion, growth, revenue and partnerships. Tim wants you to talk about the initiative and share your timeline for launch." Robert said.

Maya gasped. "What." It was the only word she muster up. She glanced ahead; her desk was a few feet away and she needed to sit down. The world was spinning dangerously on its axis and Maya was losing her grip. She muttered, "I." Then stumbled into her office and dove for her seat.

Her breaths were short and labored. Maya braced her elbows on her desk as she looked at Robert; he was too drunk with excitement to notice that Maya had been stricken with a panic attack.

She felt small. The world around her was larger than life and when she looked at Robert his wide grin doubled in size. He looked like a circus clown-no, he looked like one of those manic clowns from *Killer Klowns from Outer Space*.

"I need some water." She said.

"Here." Nina said. As if on cue, she entered the room with a bottle of water. She set it down in front of Maya then stepped back.

Robert's smile slipped. "Jesus. Maya, honey. Are you alright?" He asked.

She nodded while downing the bottle, the plastic container collapsing under the pressure of her panicked suction. The world returned to its slow rotation and Robert's face transcended from sinister to familiar. Maya exhaled slowly then drew in a breath. She repeated the process three more times, ignoring Robert and Nina.

Once she was centered, Maya returned her attention to Robert. He stood at the threshold of her office; his face had taken on a serious scowl, but she could still see a glint of excitement in his eyes. "You want me to talk about the initiative, today?" She asked.

"Yes." Robert said. "The press will be here around 2pm. This will be live and the top story for the evening news, so make sure you're ready."

"Ready for what?" Maya asked.

"To be on camera." Robert's concerned face faded and his eyes glistened.

"I can't go on television." She protested.

Robert said, "You can and you will." He shifted his weight in the doorway then continued, "Maya, this initiative is spectacular. You know it and we know it. This is just the boost that we need to bring in more clients, more revenue. And this could skyrocket your path to becoming a partner quicker than we previously discussed." He stepped closer to her desk, his eyes fixed on her. "I know public speaking isn't your thing, but the people are. And this initiative gives you an opportunity to talk to the people. Let them know what you want to do for them and how you plan to do it. You are backed by us one hundred percent. This is *your* time."

Maya studied the high shine of her pink ombre nails. The *Community Counsel Initiative* had been a dream of hers before she joined the firm, and since then, it was all that she could think about. She recalled the long hours she spent drafting the idea leading up to her pitch.

Her dream was coming to fruition. Turning back at that point would have meant it was all in vain.

Maya looked at Robert. "What time will the press be here again?" She asked.

When he wasn't working in his home office, Marcus was at the small office that he and Darnell occupied just fifteen minutes from Downtown Cascade City. In their second year of business, when their clientele base entered the double digits, Marcus and Darnell decided that it was vital to have an office. Marcus wanted something small yet large enough to hold meetings and interviews with space for all of their equipment, but Darnell wanted something large that screamed "business."

They agreed on an upscale single story suite in Cascade's new industrial park. They were lodged between a home renovation company and an extermination company; both of which they worked with from time to time with tedious computer stuff.

"We're not an IT company." Darnell told him.

Marcus said, "We're not but we know computers and they're our neighbors. Plus, I would like to stay on their good side." When Marcus broke it down like that, Darnell understood. They had enough to deal with being a black owned business.

The term "black owned" was never something Marcus cared about, at least in the beginning when he was trying to get *InnovateCore* off the ground. He just wanted to be recognized as an entrepreneur; however, society was cruel, and they were labeled a black owned business, a category that felt like a badge of honor and a scarlet letter. Between Marcus and Darnell, they had over six degrees and a dozen certifications, yet despite it all, when people looked at them at tech trade shows or events, they were often judged then snubbed.

The evil eyes were the worst. Marcus became accustomed to the sneers and the "Thanks but no thanks" they would receive but it was the evil looks that really got under his skin. People would cut their eyes and scrunch their noses; those gestures cut him deeper than words could.

Marcus parked next to Darnell's Corvette then walked into their office. He could hear Darnell on the phone rambling off numbers which he followed up with a hearty laugh.

"See, it's not as easy as you think, Joe." Darnell said.

Marcus walked past the small reception area, sans receptionist and followed his business partner's voice to his office.

Darnell walked an invisible line in front of his desk while talking into his headset. He greeted Marcus with a brotherly hug and handshake. "Joe. Joe, I have Marcus here now. He's the man who can tell you all about this AI movement."

Darnell motioned for Marcus to pick up his matching headset. He covered his mic and said, "You remember Joe from that Accounting firm in Oakbrook that we were met with?"

"Yeah, we met with them months ago." Marcus said.

"Seven." Darnell said. "Seven months ago."

Marcus shrugged. "Why are you talking to them?" He asked.

Darnell waved a hand, disregarding Marcus' question. "Man, listen, they want us to come back out there with a new quote."

Marcus' brow shifted. "For?" He asked.

"They want us to develop that software we talked about." Darnell held up his left hand and swept the right one over it. He mouthed the words "Money, man." then covered the mic again. "They're ready to spend that money. I just need you to talk to him to seal the deal." He said.

Marcus exhaled hard. "I recall we gave them a good quote last time. And they still rejected us." He said.

Darnell rolled his eyes then said, "Man, come on. They're here now and that's what matters."

Marcus groaned. "And you want me to talk to him?"

"Yes." Darnell said. "Shoot the breeze and get him talking again about this program again."

The company, *Plante Adam Accounting* was run by Joe or Joseph Clark, their Chief Executive Officer, who, after loving Darnell and Marcus over the phone decided that the firm wasn't ready to advance after meeting them in person. Their proposal on the pitched project was declined. A few weeks later, Marcus learned that the firm took *their* pitch to another tech company, who declined the project because they weren't confident in their execution.

Marcus knew *they* could do it.

He looked at Darnell, he had returned to the call and laughed hard into his headset. "Joe, I'm telling you, AI is going to put a lot of y'all out of business." He said.

The voice on the other end spoke but Marcus couldn't make out his response. Darnell erupted with more forced, generic laughter. It sent a chill through Marcus as he watched Darnell dancing about the room. Marcus chuckled while watching his two hundred pound plus friend and business partner glide around his office like a ballerina.

He motioned for Marcus to pick up his headset again and he reluctantly did.

Marcus turned on the headset then patched himself into the call.

"Joe, my partner, Marcus is on the line. You remember, Marcus, right?" Darnell said.

"Of course. Hey brotha, how ya been?" Joe's voice vibrated through the airwaves.

Marcus laughed under his breath. They could code switch too, especially when they believed that it worked in their favor. "I'm good, Joe. How are you? I hear Plante Adam is ready to work with InnovateCore." He said.

"Yes. Absolutely." He said. "We have been throwing around this idea for."

"A bookkeeping system that you can monetize to your clients, right?" He asked.

"Right. Yes." Joe said.

"The same system that we discussed and pitched to you seven months ago, right?" Joe's end went silent.

Darnell glared at Marcus. His narrow eyes were pleading with him not to go there but it was hard for Marcus not to. He wanted to go there because Joe and the entire company that was *Plante Adam* went there with them.

Joe's laugh came through the headset; it shook before he cleared his throat and redirected. "Listen, our partners are ready and excited to move forward with InnovateCare." He said.

"Why?' Marcus asked.

"Excuse me?" Joe replied.

"Why?" He repeated. "Why all of sudden are you guys 'ready and excited' to move forward with us after you clearly declined our expertise *and* our offer?"

Joe cleared his throat again. "Well, we have been hearing great things about InnovateCore and your services. Plus, we hear that Wayne Carlson is backing your company with a huge investment."

And there it was. The catalyst for kindness.

Marcus shot a look at Darnell. He shrugged and shook his head, trying to silently claim his innocence. "Joe, who told you that?" Marcus asked.

Joe chuckled with more confidence. He said, "What? You're tech guys, you don't read blogs or tweets?"

Darnell pulled his cell phone from his pocket and went to work.

Marcus spoke again. "Joe, we haven't finalized that deal with Mr. Carlson just yet."

"Really? Well, he made the announcement a few days ago that he's investing quite a penny into an up and coming black owned tech company outside of Chicago."

"And you assumed it was us?" Marcus asked.

Joe's nervous chuckle returned. "It wasn't a tough search, Marcus. We want to work with a company confidently backed by Wayne Carlson himself." He said.

Marcus was speechless. His mouth was open, but his head was a tornado of thoughts.

"Oh shit." Darnell gasped. He turned his phone's screen toward Marcus.

It was a tweet from Wayne Carlson, his social media handle reading *G8WayneC* which was followed by a blue check mark to confirm that he was indeed Wayne Carlson:

Excited to invest in the next big thing in tech. InnovateCore, a #blackowned tech company out of Cascade City, Illinois. Me and these guys are going to change the world. #buyblack

A sea of people had gathered at the front of the Fremont building before noon. Their voices fused together, creating a dull roar that carried up into Maya's office. The drone of voices turned her stomach into a fury of knots. Maya peeked out the window; she counted three news trucks: Cascade City's local news station, *CC33* and two from Chicago.

A podium had been set up with a bouquet of microphones sprouting from it. This wasn't going to be like the speech at the art gala or even her presentation from days prior, this was going to be broadcasted for the world to see. At least as far as Chicago. Maya stepped back from the window and closed her eyes.

Find your colors. She told herself and suddenly wished that Marcus was there. She sent him a text message, letting him know about the scheduled broadcast.

He responded with an OMG gif then a message:

> I wish I could be there to support, but I know you're gonna be amazing!

He followed up the message with a heart emoji then mentioned that he was dealing with an issue at work and that he would fill her in on later on, which did nothing for her nerves, yet and for a second, Maya's world felt right. And she had faith that whatever Marcus and Darnell were dealing with, they could handle it.

"Maya?" Nina called from the threshold of her office. Maya looked at her but Nina avoided her gaze. "Are you ready?" She asked.

Maya slipped her phone into the pocket of her cream colored blazer then smiled at her paralegal. "I think so." She said.

With Darnell in his ear via his AirPods, Marcus pushed through the large crowd that gathered in front of the Fremont building. Near the podium, he saw Maya, Nina and the man who had introduced himself as Robert at the art gala. Robert was dressed to perfection in a dark blue suit while Maya stunned in a cream pants suit that accentuated her curvy physique.

Her dark hair was pulled back in a tight bun with a jeweled comb embedded in the right side; it glistened in the afternoon sunlight but not as bright as the smile she flashed when she looked out at the crowd. Marcus' eyes were fixed to her as she spoke quietly between Nina and Robert while a chorus of cameras shuttered, all aimed at her and the team on the platform. Marcus jerked forward, the result of him being pushed in the shoulder. He turned quickly to see Olivia grinning at him.

"What are you doing here?" His sister asked. Her eyelids were painted with a bold, green eyeshadow. It was the color of fresh moss or Oscar the Grouch yet somehow; Olivia made it look chic and beautiful. "I thought you and D were too busy fielding new inquiries thanks to Wayne Carlson."

Marcus groaned. "Jesus, you heard too?" He asked.

Olivia shrugged and said, "Anyone on social media and living in Cascade City probably heard about it by now."

"Right." Marcus huffed.

His sister studied his face intently. "What's wrong? You're not happy about all of this?" She asked.

Marcus pursed his lips together then said, "It was supposed to be a private investment."

Olivia nodded. "I see. Y'all make the deal, close the deal and he rushes to social media to tell every Wayne Carlson wannabe and gold digger the 'good' news." She said.

"Exactly." Marcus replied.

"Damn, I'm sorry big bro." Olivia's lips curved into a

grin. "And what brings you here in the middle of the day?" She asked.

"I was driving by" He said; his lips struggled to keep his smirk at bay.

His sister shoved him playfully. "Stop lying. I've been watching you two. I see it all." Olivia gestured with her two fingers aimed at her eyes then Marcus.'

"Whatever." He grinned.

"Don't 'whatever' me. I was hoping you two would hit off anyway."

"We haven't 'hit it off' yet." Marcus said and Olivia smirked.

"Yeah sure." She said.

"Did she say something about me?" He watched Maya step between Robert and another man who joined them on the stairs. The second man was a thin, white guy with even whiter hair and a long face. He wore a black suit; tailored like Robert's, with a white shirt and blood red tie. Marcus noted the Rolex on his wrist that almost blinded a few of the photographers when the sun shone on the watch face and laughed at the thought of Darnell drooling over the watch before looking up its retail value in a matter of seconds.

"She's mentioned you a few times, but I told her that since you're my brother I didn't wanna hear about all the nasty dreams she's had about you." Olivia said.

Marcus's ears perked up. "The what?"

Olivia laughed. "I'm kidding, man. She does think you're cute though. Said you're a good guy. I told her to give it a minute before you show your real self."

He glared at his sister but laughed. "Not funny." He said.

"Yes it is." Olivia laughed. "So, when are you gonna ask her out and redeem yourself for going out with her flaky coworker over there?"

A smile warmed Marcus' lips. "Actually, we're going to Celine's Saturday night."

"What?" Olivia's jaw dropped. "You asked her out?"

"I did." He said.

"When?" She asked.

"A few days ago. After the Summit meeting." He replied.

She shook his large shoulder and jumped up and down, disregarding the people near them. Olivia shrieked, "This is awesome. You gotta tell me how the date goes and you gotta tell me what you're going to wear." She said.

"What? Why?" Marcus asked.

Olivia's hands went to her narrow hips. She said, "Because I need you to look amazing for this date."

"Is there something wrong with the way I dress?" He

asked as he glanced down at his daytime attire of khaki cargo pants and *ICore* logoed polo shirt.

His sister opened her mouth to reply but stopped when the tall, white man stepped to the podium and spoke to the massive audience. "Oh it's starting." She said.

"Good Afternoon people of Cascade City. My name is Timothy Sterling of Sterling, Turner and Associates. On behalf of our firm, we thank you, the citizens and the media for coming out today as we are excited to share with you a new initiative coming from our firm that will serve our community immensely."

When he paused, the audience applauded softly. "Today, Sterling, Turner and Associates wants to remind our city that we are here for you. We want to be a beacon of hope and help for those who need it and provide the best legal counsel and services that we can offer. Today, one of our firm's top associates is here to announce a new project that will redefine how we as a legal entity support you. Ladies and gentlemen of Cascade City, please welcome Special Counsel, Maya Thompson."

Marcus applauded loudly, ignoring the short woman who stood less than a foot away from his clapped hands. He unmuted his phone to speak to Darnell. "She's about to talk. You watching?"

"I am, man." Darnell said. "And she is wearing the hell

out of that suit."

"D." Marcus said.

"Sorry, bro." He replied. "She looks good though."

"She does." Marcus marveled.

Maya stepped in front of the podium; she scanned the crowd for a second, looked down at the notes she jotted down in her office, then raised her head again. She smiled into the audience then spoke.

"I grew up in Cascade City. Born and raised here. My parents were imports from Chicago, but they always called Cascade City home. My father was a lawyer too. He worked for the Sterling's firm for almost thirty years and believed in giving back to his community so much that his pro bono caseload almost outweighed his retained cases. When he retired, my father handed me his office keys and a few cases, sort of like a rite of passage."

The audience chuckled softly along with Maya.

"Even though my father fueled my calling as a lawyer, it was the death of my brother Jerrod who inspired me to become the lawyer who stands before you today. Three men murdered my big brother in Cascade City. He took his last breath not even four miles from this very spot."

Maya paused. Marcus could see the sting of a memory triggering tears. She scanned the audience carefully taking in all the faces staring back at her. Then her eyes fell on him. In the mass of the crowd, Maya found Marcus. The corners of her mouth tightened into a smile and she felt the tears retreat. Maya stood a little taller and continued.

"My brother's murder went cold for three years before people started coming out of the woodwork with reports that they knew who did it. Eventually their tips triggered the second investigation and this time, they had names and faces. One of the men who was said to have killed my brother was just a Senior in high school, meaning that he had allegedly killed my brother when he was just a Freshman. He was arrested during his gym class and argued his innocence all the way to the police station then to jail. Imagine my family's surprise when we heard this."

The crowd was hushed; their faces sullen and eyes fixed on Maya as she continued. "The Cascade City PD swore that they had found the so-called 'ringleader' of my brother's murder in this... this child but something told me that they were wrong. You would think that it was a conflict of interest for me to serve as counsel to him or anyone related to the case but per the law it's not, and I decided to take him on as one of my first pro bono clients in order to clear his name. During that time, I learned a lot about my community when it came to the people of color and the legal system.

"People of color rarely get much help and distrust the

legal system in general. In fact, many fear the legal system because it hasn't been a system that can be trusted to do what's right by the people, *not* our skin tones. I won't bore you with the details, but I was able to get the kid's case dismissed and he was able to return to school with a clear name. It was at this moment that I realized that as an active member of this legal system I could do a service not just for the firm I worked for, but also my community.

The Community Counsel Initiative was born as a three-step process to aid, educate and support our community. Within the legal system, within our firm, we want to provide opportunities for lawyers and paralegals of color to find employment and internships for students of color studying law, along with making diversity training more than just a general topic but a daily integration.

In our community, we want to promote and provide equal access to legal representation and justice through the introduction of community legal clinics, extensive pro bono services and an outreach program that will educate and empower our citizens when it comes to their rights."

The audience exploded with praise. Maya's face lit up and Marcus saw her eyes well up again. She nodded in response to their cheers then said, "We may not be able to change every legal system in the country with this initiative, but I believe that we can create a legal system here in

Cascade City that upholds the principles of justice while actively working to address systematic inequalities and give a voice to those otherwise marginalized within the legal process. This initiative is not an ego boost for me or anyone standing behind me. This initiative is for the people."

Another roar of applause erupted from the crowd. Their claps and cheers ascended into the clear afternoon sky. Maya smiled out into the audience then leaned forward on the podium.

"Today, I dedicate this initiative to my brother and the community that we grew up in because I plan on living and thriving here for a very long time. Thank you." Maya stepped back from the podium while the crowd rejoiced. Marcus saw Tim and Robert rush to her side to usher her back to the podium where they each took a hand and raised it into the air.

It was very presidential, Marcus thought to himself as he watched cameras flash to the left and right of Maya and her bosses.

He was sure the moment, along with the images of Maya's beautiful face, would go down in Cascade City history. After the photo op, Marcus saw Maya slip away. She scanned the crowd and he stared at her until her eyes were on him again. She waved; he waved back then applauded.

The massive crowd was still on a high from Maya's

speech as she made her way through the audience toward him and Olivia. She obliged with grace when stopped to shake hands or snap a picture. Olivia chanted Maya's name and cheered like she was at a concert. "That was amazing." Olivia said.

Marcus agreed, "It was. Did you know that about her brother?"

His sister nodded. "Yep. They have a memorial at the high school for him. Retired his basketball jersey and everything. How did you not know that?"

Marcus shook his head, upset that he couldn't recall hearing about such a tragic death in Cascade City. The thought cast a black mass over his mood for the moment before remembering he still had Darnell on his phone. He tapped the left ear bud to unmute the line.

"Sorry, D." He said. Darnell just snorted playfully then Marcus asked, "Do you remember Jerrod Thompson?"

"Jerrod? Yeah! He played basketball. He was two years ahead of us, maybe three. They have that memorial every year at Cascade Park in his honor."

Another point missed but when Marcus thought about it long enough, he could recall a candlelight service or two mentioned on the local news and some local social media pages. He just hadn't paid attention to who the services were for.

"I had no idea that that was *her* brother that was shot." Darnell said. "That was a messed up murder too."

"You know what happened?" Marcus asked.

Darnell exhaled. "Kinda. I know he was murdered over some girl."

"What? Marcus said.

"Yeah, he was dating some girl whose ex was from Chicago. Ol' boy got pissed when he found out that she was with someone else." Darnell said.

"Damn." Marcus sighed.

Darnell shifted the conversation, "This is a great initiative, though. Hell, every community should have something like this." He said.

"She's asked us to help too." Marcus said proudly.

"Us." Darnell repeated. "Us as in ICore?"

"Yes." Marcus replied.

"Oh, she don't need to ask me twice." Darnell said. "I'm in."

"So am I." Marcus said.

Nine

♥

Despite the dense, pale gray clouds that threatened the early morning sun, it was a beautiful Saturday. Maya parked her Volvo in her designated spot outside the Fremont building, climbed out and followed the surge of voices traveling from the east side of the vine covered building. She was dressed for hard labor...and Marcus. She wore a tattered pair of Carpenter jeans that she managed to hold on to since her Freshman year at Northwestern and a black and yellow baseball tee bearing *Nirvana*'s classic logo. She braided her hair into two French braids and secured them with a bright yellow bandana. To keep the comfortable look going, Maya wore a matching yellow pair of low top Converse shoes.

Maya found Olivia huddled with some volunteers in front of the muraled wall, admiring the work in progress. She stopped just a few feet away, taking in the vibrant details of the mural.

"Wow." She breathed. The formerly exposed brick wall had been primed with white paint, allowing Olivia and her team of artists to get to work bringing their concept to life. From the rich shades of brown and cream tones that made up the hyper realistic citizens, to the bold reds, pinks and purples that made up the flowers that framed the bottom of the mural. Maya felt a lump build in her throat.

"What do you think?" Olivia asked. Maya failed to notice her best friend's presence at her side.

"It's amazing." Maya said. "Liv, this is even better than the sketches,"

Olivia laughed. "Of course it is. You know I don't play about my art."

"How much do we have left to do?" Maya asked with her eyes fixed on the mural; the paintbrush dripping to create the American flag was half finished yet so vivid it appeared to be waving in its own breeze. Maya's smile brightened.

"We have a ways to go," Olivia said. "But we're pacing ourselves since the Mayor decided that she wants to reveal it at the Summit."

Maya shot a look of surprise and concern to Olivia. "Is she sure about that? That's not 'til August and we still have a ton of work to do for that too."

Olivia shrugged and her off the shoulder tee shirt slipped further. She said, "I know but what the Mayor wants, the Mayor gets, right?"

"I guess." Maya muttered then both women laughed.

"Well, I'm no O-Mart but where do you need me?" Maya asked.

Olivia wrapped an arm around Maya's shoulder and squeezed her tight.

"We can work on some details in the flowers we finished the other day." She pulled Maya toward the crowd of artists then handed her an oblong piece of plastic that was covered in mounds of dried paint. Maya looked down at the object.

"What is this?" She asked.

"A paint palette." Olivia said.

"For what?" Maya said.

Olivia's eyes widened before she said, "To put the paint on."

Maya looked at the palette again; it was saturated with aged paint that had warped to the shape of it. "Won't the old paint mix with the new paint?"

Olivia and an artist with a high ponytail that looked like it had been dipped in green liquid highlighter laughed. "Can you tell she's not an artist?" Olivia said.

"Hey! I stay in my lane." Maya said.

"Clearly." Olivia picked up a large bottle of red paint then poured out a small pool of it onto the saturated surface of the palette. She proceeded to add small, wet blobs of pink, yellow and white.

Maya watched the paint spread and settle onto the dried hills and valleys of petrified pigments before Olivia dipped a large brush into the white blob. She swirled the brush around yet the dried paint did not budge.

"The old paint is dry." Olivia said. She was still humoring herself with Maya's silent ignorance. "We can start over here."

They sat on the ground at the corner of the mural where a collection of two dimensional flowers bloomed from the brick wall. Olivia held the paint palette and paintbrush like a server holding a plate of food. She pointed out a section on a set of red and yellow tulips, Cascade City's honorary flower and instructed Maya on how to fill in the sections that had faint, random lines that looked like chalk detail in and around them.

"I'm gonna have you work on the highlights for the tulips." Olivia said. "They don't have to be perfect because we want the highlights to look realistic."

Olivia pressed the paintbrush against the wall and made quick strokes from the base of a golden tulip, following the chalked lines. The results added depth to the yellow tulip.

She pulled her hand back then looked at Maya. "It's easy. Just follow the chalk lines in quick strokes. You press and pull up. Press and pull up." She repeated.

"Got it." Maya took the brush, dipped it back into the white paint then studied it. The paint was glossy and as thick as cake frosting. When the paintbrush met the wall, the application was smooth and unhitched. It was satisfying to watch the soft outlines disappear behind the white paint. After a few moments, Maya found a groove. Hypnotized by the quick motions of the paintbrush until her mind drifted and fantasized about the evening ahead of her.

Her date with Marcus was less than twelve hours away and she was a blend of nerves and excitement. She tunneled through her closet trying to find the right outfit after her shower that morning. And it was during her fashion frenzy that Maya realized, for the first time in a long time, she wanted to impress someone. She wanted to impress Marcus.

When Olivia's bony shoulder dug into Maya's, she yanked herself from the mental to-do list she had been drafting in her head. She surveyed her line work and smiled. The tulips were coming to life. When Maya looked at Olivia, her wide grin made her suspicious.

"What?" Maya asked.

"I heard you got a date tonight."

Maya hid her face; she didn't want Olivia to see her blush. "I do." She said.

"Ooh. I'm so proud of him. I told him I was excited to hear that you two finally connected."

Maya stopped painting and looked at her. "Finally?" She said.

"Yes. I have been trying to get you two hooked up forever. When he and his ex broke up I was so happy because that girl was crazy, then you and Derek split up right after." She laughed. "It was all God's timing."

Maya laughed softly.

God's timing. A phrase that she had heard all too often in her parents' home when she was growing up. A phrase that meant that what was meant for you was indeed for you and always arrived on time. She knew it to be true in various aspects of life but never in love.

"Are you excited?" Olivia asked.

"Very. And nervous." Maya said.

Olivia rolled her eyes. "Don't be. You act like you're not a catch and after that speech you gave the other day for the news, girl, my brother better act right or—"

"Or what?" Marcus had walked up on the two of them without warning. He held two large, white boxes, along with two coffee trays stacked on top of each other. Maya was impressed at his ability to balance it all and still look sexy.

He wore a dark gray set of joggers and a hoodie along with a pair of broken in black and white Jordans. In all the time they had spent together, Maya realized that she had never seen Marcus dressed so casually. He looked like he was ready for a weekend at home on the couch, instead of painting a mural outside.

"Do you ever show up for anything on time?" Olivia said. She grabbed the top tray of coffee, inspecting each one. "What did you get me?"

"Caramel hot chocolate because you're naturally caffeinated." He said. "It's the one with the white top."

Olivia cut her eyes at her brother. "Wow, segregating your own sister. That's low." She plucked the insulated paper cup with the white top from the carrying tray and took a long sip. Maya stood up and joined them.

Marcus handed Maya her cup without prompt. "Your usual." His eyes gleamed and Maya's face felt as hot as her coffee. Whenever he smiled, it was like an electric shock to her system.

"Thank you." Maya said.

"The usual huh?" Olivia grinned. "We already know each other's 'usuals'?" Olivia shifted her gaze between Maya and her brother.

"Can you mind your business for once?" Marcus said. His voice was playful with no hint of real anger.

"*You're* my brother and *she's* my best friend; therefore, you and her are in fact *my* business. And this." She passed her hand between Maya and Marcus. "I love this. Maya and Marcus. Marcus and Maya. See, it works so well. It's perfect."

Maya exchanged a look with Marcus.

"It does have a nice ring to it, doesn't it?" He said.

Ten

♥

I t took Marcus over thirty minutes in the shower to get all the paint off of him, then another thirty to groom, dress in an all black ensemble— approved by Olivia, and hype himself up before he was out the door. When he arrived in front of Maya's building, he stood at the passenger side door of his Land Rover with flowers; a collection of white peonies and blush pink roses wrapped in brown parchment paper and accented with Baby's Breath and Salal Lemon Leaves.

His heart ticked faster than the minute hand on his silver Invicta watch and for every second Maya didn't appear his mind thought the worst.

Tick! She changed her mind.

Tick! She said yes out of pity, and she was regretting it.

Tick! She.

His mind froze when he saw a pair of strappy, black heels

step into view.

Maya exited the building wearing a mid-length black dress and an embroidered kimono jacket. Her hair was gathered up in a messy bundle with soft, curly bangs framing her face. Marcus met her at the entrance, struggling to figure out his next move.

Flowers then greeting?

No, greet her then give her the flowers.

"You look incredible." He said. He kissed her cheek—an unexpected gesture and caught a subtle hint of her perfume. She smelled like a floral summer night, and he envisioned being wrapped in her arms, letting her perfume fuse to him. When he pulled away, he eased the flowers toward her.

"Oh my." Maya's voice fluttered with awe and laughter. "These are just beautiful." She buried her nose in the bouquet then looked at him. "Thank you." She said.

He nodded. "Are you ready?" He held out a hand; Maya placed hers in his, then led her to the truck. Once she was safely inside with her legs on full display. Marcus smiled nervously, closed the door then trotted to the driver's side. She watched him climb in; her smile glowing in the early evening.

"Are you a Jazz fan?" She asked.

"Can I be honest with you?" Marcus asked.

"I sure hope so." Maya said.

"I've never really listened to it." He said admittedly. They shared a laugh. When Maya shook her head the tendrils at her temples danced across her face. Marcus savored the view; she sat there laughing with the glimmer of the parking lot lights casting a soft halo over her.

She was ethereal.

"Are you judging me?" Marcus chuckled.

Maya giggled. "Not at all."

Marcus shifted the car into drive and headed out of the parking lot. "I feel like you are." He said.

"I'm not." She laughed.

In the heart of Downtown Cascade City, there was Celine's, the popular soul food restaurant that was a local favorite and a tourist magnet that fused southern cooking with urban opulence. The brick building could serve over seventy-five guests at a time, which meant that reservations were a must, yet no one complained about the wait, unless they were from out of town. The restaurant had an exposed kitchen, a bar, a large stage for live music and a lush flora backdrop made from real flowers and greenery that made the perfect setting for photo ops.

Celine's had a beer garden in the rear of the building that featured another stage, and outdoor seating that they offered year round. In the winter, the tables were encased in heated pods and by the spring, the pods were stored away so patrons could enjoy the fresh air and the wonderful river view.

The final gem of Celine's was their food truck that opened annually in the spring for lunch and special events through early November. Jazz Night was the signature kick off of their food truck season and the celebratory jolt that brought the city back to life after the winter slump.

Marcus and Maya entered the beer garden through an archway covered in ivy and twinkling fairy lights while a four piece jazz band performed on stage welcoming guests as they entered. Marcus helped Maya into her seat before he sat down across from her. "I love this place." She said.

"Me too." He said. "I just don't come as often as I'd like. You come here a lot?"

"Once or twice... a week." Maya smirked. "The office orders lunch from here for a lot. I think Robert would do anything for their blackened salmon." She said then laughed.

Under the lowlights, Maya's gold earrings and the small jewels in the initial necklace she wore sparkled. Marcus could look at her all night and he would.

Just in case it was his last time.

Marcus studied Maya's face discreetly. He wanted to remember every detail of her along with the moments to come.

Lord, take your time tonight. Marcus prayed to himself. *Please.*

"Good evening. Welcome to Celine's." Their server approached the table with a genuine, customer service led smile. Her name, "Nikki" was embroidered onto her black polo shirt underneath the trademarked Celine's scripted logo. Nikki smiled at Maya but her eyes lingered on Marcus for a beat.

They exchanged pleasantries with the young server as she set down drink napkins and small glasses for water. She explained the food truck's ordering process for the event then recommended that they give the Jerk Chicken Meatballs a try as well as the Sweet Potato Cheesecake. Before she left, Nikki reminded them that drinks could be ordered at the bar located behind them.

"Thank you, Nikki. We appreciate it." Marcus said.

"No problem." The girl rocked on her heels and her smile became a full grin. "It's my pleasure."

When she walked away, Marcus leaned over the table toward Maya. "Drink of choice? Wine?" The smirk on

Maya's lips distracted him. "What?" He asked.

"You're very." Maya paused and her eyes were lit up with amusement. "Oblivious." She finally said.

"Oblivious? To what?" Marcus said.

Maya said, "The girl."

"What about her?" A server approached their table with a carafe of water, already dripping with condensation. He pour water silently, they thanked him in unison then Maya leaned forward as if she had something private to reveal.

"She eyed you the second she came to the table." She said. "She barely looked at me."

Marcus chuckled, keeping his eyes on Maya. Her smirk was fixed and he noticed a shallow dimple in the apple of her right cheek. "Are you jealous?" He asked.

Maya sank back in her chair, still smirking. "I am the one sitting across from you." She said.

"I like that. Now about these drinks. Wine."

"Is that a question or an assumption?" Maya asked.

"A question." He said, unsure of himself for a brief moment. "It was a question."

Maya grinned. "I'm just messing with you. I'll have."

"Rum and Coke." He said. Maya's brow crinkled. "I'm impressed."

"At the mixer after the convention, that's all you drank. I didn't really take you for a wine girl after that."

"I can be." She said, "More so at home though. Rum and Coke is my signature. And yours? You strike me as an IPA guy." Maya's lips curled to taunt him, and Marcus erupted with laughter again.

"You're hilarious, but I'm sure you know the real answer." He said.

"IPAs are too preppy for you. I bet they make you feel like Carlton from *The Fresh Prince*."

Marcus' head tilted. "You know, I never thought about it that way." He said, "You're right though. I don't really have a type but if I see Stella on the menu, I'll get it."

Maya nodded as she glanced around the beer garden. She held her kimono jacket close to her chest while she watched people move throughout the lavish garden area. "Is something wrong?" He asked.

"What? No. No. I was just taking notes." She said. Her face held some concern. Was she nervous? If she was, it wasn't enough to make her get up and suggest they leave. *That* gave Marcus a small dose of relief in his already uneasy stomach. He touched her hand softly; the subtle movement redirected Maya's eyes back to him.

"Come on, let's grab a drink, order our food and enjoy our evening." Marcus stood up, taking Maya's hand to guide her up and out of her chair. The strain in her face faded and the brightness returned to her eyes. She cupped her free hand over their clasped ones; the warmth of her hands against his sent a jolt of happiness through him like an electric current and the contact intensified the smile etched into his face.

They ordered a feast of appetizers to share; Maya selected the recommended Jerk Chicken Meatballs, Mini Beef Patties and Crawfish Toast while Marcus chose Celine's infamous Macaroni and Cheese, Cajun Oxtail Dumplings and Red Velvet Beignets. Together, they critiqued each dish then selected their favorites. Marcus favored the dumplings and macaroni while Maya was partial to the beef patties and the crawfish toast. They agreed that the meatballs were perfect.

The beignets were unanimously delightful too.

Marcus crashed into his chair, exhaling hard while gawking at his plate. He still had half a beignet staring at him and Maya could see the determination painted on his face. "It's okay to tap out." She said.

He glanced at her over his beer bottle.

"Really it is." She grinned.

"Nope." Marcus grabbed the pillowy pastry and shoved

it into his mouth. A cloud of powdered sugar fell into his lap, but he didn't care.

Maya offered a slow clap and giggled, "Bravo Mr. Johnson. I am impressed."

He leaned forward, pointing at her plate. "So am I. I didn't expect you to eat all of that."

Maya grinned, "I take my love for food very seriously." She said before popping the last Jerk Chicken Meatball in her mouth, relishing its flavor.

The chicken had been minced finely; Maya could taste the roasted garlic, the sweet heat of the ginger then there was that kick of heat from the Scotch Bonnet pepper which was manageable thanks to the cilantro and tang from the pineapple glaze that coated them. She made a mental note to order them the next time the office agreed on Celine's for lunch.

Maya finished her second Rum and Coke and smiled. The liquor was coursing through her system at a good pace and a question that was dancing on her tongue worked its way to the edge. She folded her arms on the table and leered at Marcus.

"Can I ask you a personal question?" She asked.

Marcus matched her stance. He folded his large arms on the table then leaned forward.

"Sure." He said with amusement dancing in his eyes.

"Tell me about your last relationship." It wasn't how she had planned to open the conversation, but Maya let the inquiry go and waited.

Marcus sat back in his chair again, took a swig of his beer then leaned forward again; his eyes burned into hers. "I met a girl in the early days of ICore- the brainstorming phase I guess you would call it, and we hit it off quick. She was beautiful and..." He paused. Marcus' eyes fell to the table before returning to Maya. Upon his face was a steel veil. Maya knew that technique well; it was designed to hide the fact that he was seeking a better word choice than his initial choice.

In the courtroom, eyewitnesses' faces twisted in the same manner as Marcus' when they struggled to remember that they should never call a person a "victim". They were told to use their names. And defendants weren't "thugs" or "gang members"— words often used in their written statements, instead they were "he", "she", "they", or plainly recognized by their last names.

Behind Marcus' dark eyes, Maya could see him searching for another word to describe his ex that either wouldn't offend Maya or make her think that he still had feelings for her.

"She was *sweet*." He said dryly.

"So, what happened to you and this *sweet*, beautiful

woman?" Maya asked.

Marcus exhaled hard. "I proposed to her twice. Once after two years together and then again in our sixth year right at midnight on New Year's Day."

Maya scoffed. "And she said no?"

Marcus nodded.

"Twice?"

Another nod.

"Why?" Maya asked.

Marcus toyed with the paper wrapper on the neck of his beer bottle. "I wasn't enough for her. She hated the business and preferred I aim for a corporate gig. I think she stuck around as long as she did because she thought we were gonna be like Amazon or something."

"Ahh. I see." Maya said. "She wanted endless shopping sprees, handbags and a fleet of cars."

"Yes."

Maya leaned closer. "So why did you stay if *you* knew that?"

Marcus shook his head slowly. "I wanted to believe that she would be different. That she would come around and she would see that what I do is about way more than money."

"You really loved her." Maya said matter of factly.

He sighed, "I did."

Maya grabbed Marcus' hand and held it tight. His eyes softened when he looked at her.

"Thank you." Marcus said. "What about you, though? Spill the tea on your last relationship."

Maya let her hand slip away and return to her side of the table. The emotional weight shifted between the two of them and Maya felt heavy. "We lasted three years." She said.

"What was he? A doctor?" Marcus grinned. His dimples made a quick appearance then faded.

Maya laughed so loud the table next to them peeked at them. "You're funny." She said.

"Hey, it makes sense to me." Marcus said.

"I'm sure it does." She said, "He was a lawyer too." Maya stuck her tongue out at him. "But he worked for a law firm out of Chicago."

Marcus smirked. "So what happened?" He asked.

"Well." Maya breathed. "We had two different dreams."

Marcus tilted his head, waiting for her to elaborate.

"We met when I was in the depths of learning the ins and outs of Sterling, Turner and Associates. We started dating right away and I was advancing fast."

Maya thought that Derek had been concerned with her burning out, instead he was more concerned about meeting her in the courtroom one day and losing.

When he finally admitted that he hated the idea of Maya beating him in the courtroom, the distance between them extended. Then after six months of phone tag, canceled dates and refunded trips, Derek ended it. Six months later, Derek announced that he was getting married to a hair stylist and told the world, aka social media, he found his "true love." It was a punch to the gut for Maya, but it inspired her to work harder for what *she* wanted.

Maya blinked at Marcus; she felt the tears on the brink of coming through. "He couldn't deal with the fact that I was ambitious and independent."

"All great traits." Marcus said.

"Thank you, but for us, it wasn't. He wanted a stay at home wife, someone to birth and raise the kids while he went out to do God knows what. At the time, that wasn't on my agenda. Yes, I want a family too, but I have professional goals too and they are a priority in my life too." She said.

"You're doing a great job, Maya." Marcus said. He smiled again and Maya's heart thumped harder in her chest.

"Thanks." She said. "I guess when he moved on so fast, I started to question myself and my decisions."

"Why?" Marcus asked.

Maya shrugged. "I felt like I fucked up."

"Do you regret it now?" Marcus' hand grazed hers.

Maya glanced down at his hand covering hers then met his eyes again.

"Not at all." She said.

"Do you believe in love?" He asked. "I mean after all of that, do you believe that love exists in this world?"

"Of course." Maya said, "I still believe in love. I have seen enough good examples of love, I could write my own fairy tale. It's not rocket science."

"It's not." Marcus agreed.

"Do *you* believe in love?" Maya turned his question on him.

His full lips transitioned to a smirk. "I do. My parents are my favorite example. My mom was a real activist in her day and my father was a college teacher's assistant. He fell in love with my mom at a protest."

"Are you for real?" Maya asked.

"Yep. My mom was protesting something on campus and my dad was walking past, minding his business when bam!"

"He saw her and fell in love." Maya said.

"No. My mom threw a book and his face connected with it." They laughed hard as Marcus pantomimed the incident.

"That's adorable." Maya said.

"Yeah, it is now, but my dad said he was pissed when

it happened. Some people in the crowd pointed my mom out and my dad decided to confront her after the protest to tell her that she concussed him."

Maya giggled. "What did your mom say?

Marcus shook his head as he laughed softly. "She told him that that was God telling him that he needed a cause to believe in."

"And from there, they were inseparable?"

"Nope. It turned out my dad really did have a concussion. He was in hospital for a few days afterward. My mom did visit him at the hospital though."

"Oh my God." Maya said. "Wow. That's a good 'How I Met Your Mother' story."

"It is," Marcus said. "In fact, it was the last story my dad recalled before he passed away." Another round of somber stillness consumed the table.

Maya reached for Marcus' hand. She smirked at the sight of his open palm, awaiting hers. She placed her hand in his and watched it engulf hers.

"I know you lost your father too." He said. His voice was barely audible over the ambiance around them.

Maya nodded as she pursed her lips together to safeguard tears. "I did." She gave Marcus a warm, assuring smile.

"Damn, I think this conversation took a turn neither

one of us expected." Marcus said. He squeezed Maya's hand. She glanced up at him. "I'm really happy to be here with you tonight, Maya."

Maya's face went hot. She wanted to hide away from his gaze under the dim outdoor lights, but she couldn't resist him. She loved the way he looked at her. "Me too." She said.

The jazz band transitioned from a soft John Coltrane number to a melodic rendition of *Misty.* The soft snare drum echoed through the air while the piano's tune enveloped Maya. She started to sway and hum the song to herself softly.

"You know this song?" Marcus asked.

"'*Misty.*'" Maya said. "There's a lot of renditions of this song, but my favorite is by Sarah Vaughan."

Marcus nodded but she saw the name going over his head.

"I'll have to send you some songs to listen to." Maya said.

"Thank you." He replied. "Would you like to dance?"

Maya's throat tightened and her stomach flipped so hard, she thought their dinner would make an impromptu return. Marcus rose from his chair and moved to her side. Maya took his hand and followed him to the dance floor. They joined a handful of couples already on the dance floor; Marcus pulled Maya close to him, one hand held her close at her waist and the other guided her hand to his large shoulder.

Maya wanted to pull away; nervous that her heart would shoot from her chest like a love crazed cartoon character. She didn't want him to notice that, let alone feel that vulnerable around him. Despite her four inch heels, Marcus still loomed over her. As they swayed to the rhythm of the saxophone, Maya gave in. She rested her head on his chest. The warm scent of Teakwood was accented with the lingering aromas of Jerk seasoning and Stella Artois.

It was comforting.

Peaceful. She never imagined she would long for such a scent.

"I'm sorry." She heard Marcus's voice resonate in his chest. Maya looked up at him. "My heart is racing." He said.

Maya returned her ear to his chest and listened; his heart was beating faster than the snare on stage.

"It's okay." Maya said, looking up at him. "Mine is too."

"Why?" His voice trembled slightly. Their vulnerabilities were edging on their emotional horizons.

"You first." Maya said.

"Because, ever since I saw you, all I have wanted to do was be *this* close to you."

"Really?" She asked. "This close?"

"God yes." He smiled. "And since picking you up, all I have thought about is."

Maya pushed herself up on the tips of her toes until their lips met. Marcus sank down, returning Maya's feet to the floor but he held her tight in his arms.

Caught in the moment, like a movie, beneath her closed eyelids, Maya saw it all over again. Marcus' face in the crowd at the art gala and that ethereal shade of green, then his presence at the summit meetings to that very moment. When their lips parted, Marcus's eyes were locked on her. Somewhere in the lapse of time, the band had started a new tune that Maya didn't bother to recognize.

Marcus pulled her close again; their hearts were in sync, creating a soft, thumping melody. Maya placed a hand on his chest and looked into his eyes.

"Should we call it a night?" His voice was heavy with lust and for a moment, Maya considered the unspoken offer. The thought of being wrapped up in Marcus arms and tangled among sheets was tempting but she didn't—she couldn't go there just yet.

Her smile was soft, and she hoped that her eyes were letting him down much easier than her words could. "Not yet. Not tonight." She said.

They didn't call it a night after the kiss, they did agree to stay for dessert. Over Sweet Potato Cheesecake, Marcus studied Maya while she talked about the launch of her initiative with the law firm. He relished in the way her face lit up as she highlighted the key parts of the project. With every point made, her eyes sparkled and his heart swelled. Her joy reminded him of the excitement he exuded whenever he talked about InnovateCore. They were ambitious about their purposes but Maya's passion was contagious.

While she discussed the importance of family keeping up with their incarcerated loved ones, Marcus went to work mentally coding a program to help them locate inmates and create paperless communications.

When Maya stopped mid-sentence to study his face, she just smiled. "What's going on up there?" She asked him while motioning toward his head with her cheesecake ladened fork. "What are you thinking about?"

Marcus asked their server for a pen and a clean napkin from the bar. When she returned with both, he went to work shifting the concept from his head to the small napkin. In minutes he had the foundation for her pitched the program sketched out. "This." He said then slid the thin, inked napkin toward her.

Maya studied the napkin like an ancient text. Her jaw dropped and her eyes met his.

His breath seized his throat whenever her eyes locked on him. She could have seen into his soul for all he knew and if Maya asked for anything in that moment, he would have given it to her with no questions asked.

"This looks... Complicated." She said.

Marcus chuckled. "To the untrained eye, it does. But this is the groundwork for the program you just described." He highlighted the benefits of a database to help families locate and communicate with their imprisoned family and friends. His concept included paperless communication for inmates just processed in the system and advanced searches for inmates within the local courts in Cascade City and the Chicagoland area. "You would be able to connect it with the county's website with their clearance of course.

"This is brilliant." She said, "Could *you* do this for my project?"

"Absolutely." Marcus said without hesitation.

On the way home from Celine's, they rode hand in hand while listening to a Sarah Vaughn playlist. When Marcus walked Maya to the elevator inside her building, they shared another kiss. It was longer than the one they shared on the dancefloor and like that one, it left him breathless.

Eleven

♥

With most of his day spent at Cascade City's courthouse, Marcus knew there was no hope for the rest of his day. Darnell sent him a text confirming that he would be working from home and to "feel free" to reach out to him if he needed him.

Marcus knew better. He read between the lines of the message. Darnell had a date and did not want to be disturbed. And Marcus had no desire to. But he did want to get back to the office to finish up the last element to the website he created for Maya for the Community Counsel Initiative. He promised her that he would have it down in two weeks but he finished in less than five days.

Did some projects get delayed because he pushed her website to the forefront? Absolutely, but it was worth it and all Marcus could think about was the smile that would paint Maya's perfect lips when she saw the website and database completed ahead of schedule. That smile could save his life. It could change his life and make him do things that he never imagined.

Like delaying several paid projects.

After picking up a final payment from the clerk's office, Marcus walked down an empty corridor; his footsteps echoed on the marbled flooring and he could hear random voices behind the closed doors of a few of the courtrooms. When one of the doors opened and a man stepped out; he held a vibrating cell phone and answered it. Marcus peered through the door as it started to close and froze in his tracks.

"Maya?" He said softly. Marcus brushed past the man, caught the door and looked inside.

It was Maya. She paced the floor in front of a male judge with the name plate titled Judge Logan Ryan in front of him. The judge- Judge Ryan sat higher than everyone else. He was a plump man with a puffy red face and dark brown hair that was graying at his temples. He wore the classic black robe and and his dark eyes tracked Maya as she spoke. To his left, a bailiff stood proudly. He appeared taller than Marcus, who believed that at one point in time the man was the star quarterback of his college football team. He probably had dreams of going pro; however, like Marcus injuries sidelined him which made him really think about a future without football.

"In or out?" Someone asked.

Marcus blinked and saw a security guard inside the door. "What?" Marcus said.

"Are you coming in or out?" The male guard asked. "The door has to be closed while court is in session."

"Oh, sorry about this." Marcus slipped into the courtroom as quietly as he could, but a few sets of eyes were on him. He glanced at the guard again and pointed toward the front of the room. "Major case?" He asked. "It's pretty packed in here."

The guard shook his head. "I think it's about insurance fraud or some mess like that." He said. "Everyone's here for Miss Maya." He grinned feverishly while his eyes watched her walk the length of floor near the prosecution desk.

"Oh yeah?" Marcus said.

"Oh yes. There's not a man in this entire courthouse who doesn't want that woman." The guard whispered.

"Is that right?"

"Hell yeah. Look at her." The guard nodded his head toward her. "She's got this sexy, modern Clair Huxtable vibe that just..." He trailed off then shot a look in Marcus' direction. "Please take a seat." He said as if flipping a switch. He adjusted his holster and narrowed his eyes at Marcus.

Marcus slipped into the last row of the spectator area and looked ahead at Maya. She stood near the prosecution table with her eyes fixed on a woman who sat on the stand. The silhouette of Maya's curves were accentuated in a black blazer, matching pencil skirt and suede pumps. Her curls were detained in a sleek bun nestled in the back of her head and she kept her makeup clean. Minimal eye makeup with a brown ombre matte lip.

Damn. Marcus said to himself before glancing around and ensuring the coast was clear because his pants had started to tighten.

The security guard's eyes were glued to Maya too, so he adjusted himself stealthily and continued to watch her.

"Ms. Sherman, in your statement, you said that Mr. Donaldson properly filled out his insurance claims and that you found no errors when he submitted them, correct?"

The woman— Ms. Sherman, was rail thin with bright red hair. Curtain bangs framed her freckled face and her pink lips were turned down. When she responded to Maya, she forced a smile and the rest of her face went rigid. Ms. Sherman said, "Correct. He submitted three insurance claims. I reviewed them myself and I did not find any errors."

Maya swiped a piece of paper from her table then walked

to the stand. She set the paper down then walked away. "Your Honor and Ms. Sherman, I present to you copies of the three claims that Mr. Donaldson submitted to Landsman Insurance. Ms. Sherman can you please take a look at the dates for each claim and read them aloud?"

Marcus would have thought Maya asked the woman to put her hand in toxic waste. Ms. Sherman's head inched back before she reached for the paper. She read silently then her eyes swelled.

Maya turned to face the woman again. "Ms. Sherman, please read the dates."

Ms. Sherman's pink lips folded, she shook her head then read the dates aloud. "May second, two thousand twenty. July first, two thousand twenty and June first two thousand twenty."

"Thank you. And what was each claim for?"

Ms. Sherman looked down at the paper again. It felt like an eternity before the woman returned her gaze to Maya and answered. "They're all for theft. Home burglaries." She set the paper back down and her eyes lowered into her lap.

"Thank you, Ms. Sherman. Now tell me, what is Landsman Insurance's policy on claims?"

The woman's eyes didn't meet Maya's, she looked past her then she looked at Maya who stood poised and patient.

"We..." She paused. "Landsman Insurance states that a person cannot submit the same claim more than once within thirty days."

"How many days?" Maya asked.

Ms. Sherman sighed again. "Thirty days." She said.

"And don't these three claims go against Landsman's company policy?"

The woman chewed her bottom lip. "Yes."

"So three claims, all submitted within less than thirty days of each other and claiming home burglaries, yet they were still processed. Ms. Sherman, wouldn't you consider that a good sign to ring a few alarms?"

"Objection." A woman's voice bellowed for the table to the left of Maya's. She wore a pale gray suit that appeared to be at least one size too big. "Speculation." She said.

"I'm sorry?" Maya said. She turned toward her opposition.

The lawyer in the oversized power suit said, "You can't ask her that."

Maya smirked, then said, "She approved the claims."

"You can't..." The woman stopped then looked at the judge.

"Council approach." Judge Ryan said.

Maya and the Defense lawyer walked toward the judge and huddled together. Marcus watched the slender woman wave an arm while Maya maintained a level of cool, he had never seen in her. He even thought he caught her smirk again. When they walked away and returned to their desks, Judge Ryan spoke. "Clearly the defense was not ready for such evidence and needs some time to discuss with their client. Is this correct, Counsel?"

The Defense team, consisting of the woman, a man who wore a matching gray suit and another man who sat with his hands in his lap and barely looked around the room all nodded before they returned to whispering amongst themselves.

Judge Ryan continued. "Very well. This hearing has gone on long enough and I would like to wrap this up before my sixtieth birthday, so I am granting a two hour recess. Counsel, I advise you and your team to get your client together so we can conclude this. Am I understood?"

Another nod from the defense team. "Good. I'll see everyone back here in two hours." Judge Ryan banged his gavel, rose from his seat and exited.

The courtroom started to disperse Marcus heard the security guard whistle. "That woman is something else." He said. "I swear, we be fighting for a chance to sit in on her cases."

Marcus chuckled. "Oh yeah?"

"Hell yeah, man. That is a real woman in every sense of

the word." The guard exhaled hard. "Sometimes, it's hard to keep your composure around her."

"I bet."

"She's just incredible." The guard said.

"Yeah she is."

The guard looked at Marcus. "You know her?" He asked.

Marcus nodded. "Yeah, I do. We're working together."

The guard gave him a once over, eyeing Marcus' black cargo joggers and *ICore* Henley shirt. "You're a lawyer?"

"No. Entrepreneur. I own a tech company. Innovate-Core or ICore." He pointed to the logo on his shirt.

"Oh. IT." The guard said amused.

Marcus rose from his seat; the security guard surveyed his height for the first time then smiled nervously. "Excuse me." Marcus grinned. "I need to catch up with Maya real quick."

Maya glanced at the table to her left. Arthur Donaldson and his Defense team spoke in hushed voices while they collected their papers and shoved them into files and briefcases. "Did you pay attention to dates on your claims?" One of the two lawyers that teamed up with Donaldson asked. She was a leggy, blonde woman with muddled blue eyes. Arthur Donaldson sat in his chair; his face was frozen with fear and confusion. "Nevermind. Come on, we have two hours to figure this mess out." She snatched her briefcase and turned away from Donaldson. Her eyes met Maya's.

"Sylvia." Maya said.

"Maya." She spat her name like venom then she pushed through the swinging door and headed up the aisle.

Maya shook her head as she gathered up her paperwork, slipped it into its labeled folder then returned the folder into an accordion section of her leather briefcase. The rest of Donaldson's team— and Donaldson had slipped out quietly.

"I never thought that I would find a court case so exciting." His voice came to her before he came into view. Maya looked up to find Marcus standing on the opposite side of the swinging door.

She smiled. "What are you doing here?" She asked.

"I was in the building collecting a check." He said. " And

then I heard your voice and decided to come and watch you work." Marcus's eyes left hers to scan her frame before returning to hers.

Maya sat on the edge of the table. "And what did you think?" She asked.

"I'm glad I'm on your good side." He smiled and his dimples made an appearance.

Maya's body tingled but she pushed the sensation away as she cleared her throat. "Are you heading back to your office?"

"I am." He said. "You should come with me. I can show you what I've been working on for you."

Maya glanced down at the silver watch on her wrist.

"You have two hours and our office is not even twenty minutes from here." Marcus said. "I'll buy us lunch too."

She grinned. "You should have led with that." They laughed then Marcus' lips curved into a soft smile. He held his hand out. Maya looked down at it. "What?"

"Your briefcase, please." He said.

Without argument, Maya handed him her briefcase then hopped off the table. Marcus opened the swinging door and she led the way toward the double doors. She could feel Marcus's eyes scanning her body.

She made sure to saunter, not walk.

He kept checking for Maya's Volvo in his rearview mirror and despite the short distance, the drive back to his office felt like an eternity. He gripped the steering wheel when his mind remembered the way her pencil skirt clung to her frame or the way she commanded the courtroom with her voice. Watching her in her element was magical and a complete turn on. His erection resurfaced just as he pulled into his parking spot.

Calm down. Marcus told him. He cut the engine and saw Maya pull up beside him.

"Calm down." He said aloud. As if on command, his erection eased and his pants went slack. Marcus climbed from his SUV and Maya emerged from her car. She glanced ahead at the three suite structure then looked at Marcus again. "Welcome to the ICore HQ." He said.

She smiled at the middle suite with its large *ICore* logo plastered on the picture window. Their front door was painted a dark blue and within the window was a yellow and black sign that read "Black Owned Business." Maya beamed at the sign, after noticing the two other businesses that flanked *InnovateCore* didn't have the sign.

Marcus walked to Maya. He took her hand and said, "Come on. Let me show you around." He unlocked the door then directed Maya to walk in. She walked past him and took in the foyer first then approached a wall filled with photos and awards. She stepped toward the decorated wall and Marcus lingered behind her.

"That's our brag wall." He said. "Whenever we get a great testimonial, a review or even a photo op, we post it here. It's a great reminder to ourselves of what we do plus when clients come in, it gives them a peek into our success."

"A peek is an understatement." Maya said. He watched her take in every photo of Marcus and Darnell in various locations, alongside random people—their clients. Scattered amongst the photos were handwritten testimonials. She skimmed a few of them then smiled at Marcus. "I love this."

He beamed. "I picked up the idea from a college professor. He told me that everyone should have a brag file."

"Why?"

"Because every day as an entrepreneur isn't perfect and sometimes this journey gets lonely. You can get deterred really easily so having a brag file or in our case, a wall, helps us get back on track when we feel like we're failing."

Maya's eyes sparkled and her smile was soft, making her lips delectable.

He wanted to devour her.

"And just when I think I can't admire you anymore. You show me this." Maya pointed at the wall; her smile still glowing. "I imagine this is how Lois Lane felt when she learned the truth about Superman." She said.

Marcus's face went hot then he bowed it.

Maya placed a hand on his arm. "This is absolutely wonderful."

Marcus looked down at her hand on his arm then let his eyes return to hers. "Thank you." He said.

"Can I see the rest of the place?" She asked.

"Of course. Come on, I will show you the common areas first then my office." Marcus led Maya through the rest of the space, stopping to highlight the bathroom, equipped with hand soaps, hand sanitizers, lotions and even feminine hygiene products. "Liv would kill me if I didn't do that." Marcus laughed. He then directed her to the free vending machines for snacks and drinks and pointed toward Darnell's office.

"Where's Darnell?" Maya asked.

"Working from home...or playing hooky." He said as they entered his office.

Two matching dark Mahogany wood bookshelves flanked his work desk and were lined with books on coding and technology. Marcus saw Maya run a hand over a James Baldwin book before she examined the contents of a small desk in front of his picture window then stopped at a stainless steel refrigerator that completed his office décor.

"Feel free to help yourself to anything in the fridge too."
He said.

"What about the vending machines?" She asked. "You
said those were free."

"They are." Marcus said. He joined her by the fridge.
"But they don't have these." He opened the refrigerator
to reveal two neat rows of *Fiji* water and another row
of *Clearly Canadian* flavored waters. Maya's eyes swelled
with delight.

"Where did you find Clearly Canadian?"

He smirked. "I know a guy named Bezos."

Maya giggled; her infectious laugh was irresistible. Marcus stepped closer to her and pulled her to him. As she
stared up at him, Marcus remembered their dance and
their kiss. He bit his bottom lip then leaned in until his lips
touched hers. The spark returned and he felt Maya press
her body into his chest. Marcus wrapped his arms around
her waist and felt her tongue graze his.

Marcus' hands grabbed her ass, hoisted her up and carried her to an empty wall. Her heels fell to the floor with
a soft clunk while he buried his head into the warm val-
ley between her breasts. Maya's nails raked his back and
tugged at the hem of his shirt until she yanked it over
his head. Marcus held her with one arm while the other
hiked up her tight skirt and he felt the heat radiating from

her core. Maya's breathing hitched; she looked down at Marcus.

"Where do you want me?" He asked. His voice was fueled with passion. "Show me."

Maya nodded as she unbuttoned her blazer singlehandedly. Beneath her black blazer was a matching lace corset bra. Marcus licked his lips; he salivated at the sight of her bare flesh and the anticipation of what he would do next. He carried Maya from the wall to the empty desk in front of the picture window. Maya laid back while he pulled down her bra straps and kissed her neck. She moaned as Marcus planted kisses down her neck to her collarbone; his hand glided down the curves of her body, pulling away the cups of her bra and rubbing her nipple.

Her body arched beneath him while his erection throbbed against her thigh. Marcus's lips replaced his fingers on her nipple and his hand returned beneath her skirt. "Please." Maya breathed.

Marcus obliged. He slipped two fingers inside her; they gasped in sync. She wrapped around his fingers in a saturated warmth he had never felt before then slowly pulled his fingers out and rubbed on her clit.

"Yes." Maya cried out. Her hips rotated and bucked against him. Marcus' tugged on her nipple with his teeth and Maya's soft cry, followed by a moan made him grin.

She raked at his bare back before her moans became pleas. "Don't stop." She breathed.

Marcus peered at her. "I won't." He grinned.

Her dark eyes were soft and danced with anticipation. "I..." She said, "I want you."

In seconds, Marcus unbuckled his pants and discarded them alongside Maya's blazer and her skirt. He stopped then looked down at Maya. Her face fell. "What's wrong?" She asked.

"Hold on." Marcus retrieved his pants again and grabbed his wallet. He could feel Maya's eyes on him as he opened his wallet and pulled out a gold wrapper. The worry in her eyes faded. "Sorry." He chuckled nervously. He split the wrapper open and proceeded to sheath his erection.

"Where were we?" Maya asked.

Marcus lifted her legs onto his shoulders and let the tip of his tease her core. "Right here." He said, then slid into her and Maya's moans echoed throughout the office.

PART THREE | MAY 2023

Twelve

Marcus stared at the empty desk across the room. He couldn't shake the grin that spread across his lips as the memory of him and Maya played in his head like a highlight reel on *SportsCenter*. She set his soul on fire, among other things and in those moments of passion, they connected and unlocked a new level of passion. His mind recalled the pressure of her fingertips against his skin and the way her legs locked around his waist. He could almost replay the way her voice hitched when he slid inside and—

"I have had it with this damn accounting firm." Darnell's voice boomed from the other office, followed by the rustling of papers then his chair hitting the wall. The playback dissolved and suddenly Marcus imagined the large indentation in the wall behind Darnell's chair driving deeper into the wall, peeling the paint and breaking into the drywall.

His new thought, which felt like the hundredth one, was that they could kiss their deposit goodbye. When Darnell appeared in the threshold of his office, he had a yellow pencil wedged behind his ear and his headset draped around his neck. He exhaled loudly then shook his head. "What the hell were we thinking when we decided to move forward with these clowns."

"*We*?" Marcus said. "No, no. I told you after the way they dogged us out that we should have turned them down but no. *You* wanted to take this account. *You* wanted to build them 'the best damn database they ever had.' Remember that?"

Darnell rolled his eyes. "Whatever, man. All I know is that when they heard that Wayne Carlson was endorsing us and investing in us, they came running and *we* never run from money." He ran in place, pretending to catch falling bags of money then stuffing them in the pockets of his dark joggers.

Marcus chuckled as he sat back in his seat.

"What are you working on?" Darnell asked.

"This database for Maya." He said proudly. "I think I found that bug that you mentioned last week."

Darnell crossed the room to the small stainless steel refrigerator, opened it then retrieved two bottles of water. He offered one to Marcus who nodded in confirmation.

"We need to put some emergency beers in here." He said while opening his water bottle.

"No." Marcus' response was flat and final.

"Come on now. It's five o'clock somewhere. *We're* the business. There is no ICore without Marcus Johnson and Darnell Epps. That means that *we* make the rules and having beer in the office should be one of the rules."

Marcus replied, "And my rule, one of the few that I have, is no alcohol at work."

Darnell raised his hands to cease fire. He took another swig of water, clearly wishing that the alkaline water was a beer instead. "What's the latest between you and Maya? You've been pretty cheerful lately."

Marcus' lips twitched as he struggled to hide his ever growing smile. "We're cool." He said. "Been working on the summit and this project of hers."

"And blowing her back out." Darnell chuckled.

Marcus' eyes widened. He opened his mouth then paused, unsure of what he wanted to say and knowing that his best friend was waiting for the right moment—the right word to trigger what he really wanted to say. "What are you talking about?"

Darnell grinned. "You think I'm stupid? I know the smell of sex in the afternoon."

Marcus' head fell and he shook it. "You know?" His

question was muffled by his forearm.

"Sure do. Plus, I saw the condom wrappers in the trash."

Marcus groaned again.

"It's okay." Darnell laughed louder. "Hey, I'm proud of y'all for being safe."

"D." Marcus said. His voice was more playful than angry yet he still felt the heat of embarrassment lingering on his skin.

"Alright. Alright." Darnell said. "I won't hound you about it but..." He trailed off and Marcus stared at him.

"But what?"

"Three times, man? Y'all did it three times?"

"I don't think I should be listening to this right now." Olivia said over the speakerphone in Maya's Volvo.

"You did ask." Maya said matter of factly.

Olivia sucked her teeth on the other end which was amplified within the confinement of Maya's sedan. "You and my brother did it." She said, "At this point y'all go together." She paused then giggled.

"What?" Maya asked.

"Oh yes. First date. Check. First kiss. Done. First orgasm—"

"Three." Maya said.

"What?" Olivia asked.

"It was three orgasms. Maybe five because he did..." Maya trailed off as her mind detoured and she remembered her hands capturing every fiber of his flesh. Marcus' lips against hers and the way he—

"Hey, that's not my business" Olivia said, then added, "I don't think I'll be able to look at my brother the same way."

Maya rolled her eyes before she shifted her Volvo into Park. "O, I gotta go. I just made it to his office now."

"Give that table a rest too." Olivia cackled.

"Whatever. Bye." Maya ended the call, cut the engine then climbed out of her car.

She grabbed her briefcase then her phone and sent a message to Marcus confirming her arrival. He gave her a message a thumbs up which felt awkward and before she could dissect the reply, Marcus followed up with another message:

> Be right there!

Tension released from her body like air from a balloon

then Maya walked toward the door with her eyes fixed on her sable brown pumps. She didn't want to look him in the eyes, it would weaken her then the next thing she knew, she would be on top of his desk begging him to go deeper.

Oh god. Maya exhaled again.

Marcus opened the door dressed in his usual khaki joggers and signature, black work polo. Maya noticed the clean line up at his hairline and his beard along with his clearly oiled beard.

She swallowed her arousal then smiled nervously.

"Hey." He said. Marcus leaned forward and planted a soft kiss on her lips.

"Hi." Maya breathed. It was the best she could do because what she wanted to say would have led them to her car or maybe the bathroom in his office. "I hope I'm not late."

She wasn't. She knew she wasn't late.

"You're good." Marcus said, with both dimples on display when he smiled. He took her hand and led her in. When he closed the door, Marcus pulled Maya into his arms and kissed her deep. When they pulled away, Marcus held Maya tight and lowered his head until his lips grazed her ear. "You look good enough to eat." His voice vibrated inside her and made her shiver. His lips grazed her neck and his hands grabbed her ass.

Maya moaned. "Don't start something you can't finish." She said.

Marcus kissed her neck then returned her ear. "Who says I can't?"

Maya pulled away briefly to study his face; his eyes wild with excitement and his erection thumped against her thigh. She kissed again as her briefcase crashed to the floor.

"Yo! Marcus, I think—" Darnell entered the hallway, stopping abruptly.

Maya slipped out of Marcus' grasp. She adjusted the blazer while Marcus struggled to adjust himself. With his body facing her, he turned his head to meet Darnell.

Darnell stifled a laugh. "My fault. I didn't mean to interrupt y'all."

Maya smiled but felt her face flush with nervous heat. "It's okay." She said.

Marcus' husky business partner grinned at the both of them. "Well, welcome back to our home away from home." Darnell said.

Maya shot a look at Marcus, who was already staring at Darnell.

Darnell cleared his throat. "Make yourself at home." He said.

"Thank you." Maya smiled reluctantly as Marcus took her hand and ushered into his office.

Once he closed his door, he wrapped Maya in his arms again and kissed her. His hands returned to her ass while his tongue danced with hers. When he pulled away to look at her, they exhaled deep in unison. "Round two?" Marcus asked.

Maya grinned then said, "Two? Honey, it's like round four and I'm in, after we talk business."

Marcus lifted her chin and planted a soft peck on her lips. "Business first." He said. "Come on, I have so much to show you with this database. I think we finally got it cleaned and ready to launch." He pulled a second chair to his desk.

"That's great news." Maya set her briefcase beside his desk and took the seat next to him.

Marcus started clicking away at his keyboard.

"Oh, before I forget." She pulled her briefcase onto her lap, opened it and pulled a folder from it. "Sterling and Turner can be hard asses at times and *this* is one of those times." She handed Marcus the folder before she continued. "Those are NDAs and background check forms."

"Background checks." Marcus repeated the words as if they were foreign.

She nodded. "Yes. The NDA is standard as we want to make sure that anything related to this initiative stays in house."

"Understood and fair." Marcus said. "And the background checks?" He said again.

"A formality." Maya said. "Consider it like a part of the hiring process since I have hired ICore to work with me."

Marcus glanced at the papers within the folder; his face went blank then hardened. "I haven't worked for anyone else in over a decade."

"It's not an employment verification." Maya said. "It's a formality." She swallowed, feeling a rock of fear plummeting into her stomach.

He wasn't going to sign and all their hard work would be obliterated.

Gone.

She had warned Robert however, Sterling—not Robert, was adamant about the background checks. He was always adamant about them especially when it came to the "minorities" as Sterling called anyone who didn't look like him.

"We need to make sure that people are who they say they are." Sterling would say which ceased any future rebuttals from anyone. His stark words rang in her head like a bad song.

She trusted Marcus and Darnell too. She trusted their business; however, she knew that if she wanted to get this initiative executed, Maya would need to do the necessary song and dance with the law firm to bring it to life. Yet there was always an inkling in the back of her mind that often said: *You don't need them.*

Maya stared at Marcus as he studied the papers; his eyes searched the paperwork for keywords; as a businessman with intent and purpose. He knew what to look for. The words that screamed "lawsuit" or "termination."

Finally, Marcus grabbed a pen. And when he went from checking boxes to signing his name in a quick flourish, the lump in her stomach dissolved. She sat back in her chair feeling the short form tension dissipate. When he was done, he closed the folder and smiled at Maya.

"I get it." He said. "And I respect it. Besides, I know D and I are good. We have been in good business standing since day one."

Maya nodded. "I know." She said, "And you have the wall to prove it."

They smiled in unison. Maya said, "Thank you. Now show me this database. I am dying to see what you've done with it,"

Marcus motioned for Maya to move closer. "I don't bite." He said with a quirky grin.

Maya leaned toward him, her grin matched his. "Yes, you do." She said.

Marcus let Maya take his seat while she navigated with the database. He had asked her to bring in a few names to test the program; she pulled another file from her briefcase.

"I have some previous convictions here." She said before extracting a sheet of paper from the folder then typing in the information. Maya almost jumped out of her seat when she saw how successful her searches turned out.

"Marcus, this is amazing." She said.

"And that bug you found." He replied.

"I don't even notice it. It's so damn seamless."

"Good. And now that the database is done, let me show you this." Marcus leaned forward until his face was parallel with Maya's. Her floral perfume had a soft musk undertone and it radiated from her supple brown skin. He closed his eyes to savor her intoxicating fragrance then chewed his bottom lip to center himself and get his thoughts back on the job.

"Check this out." Marcus said. He took control of the mouse again and felt Maya's eyes on him. He wanted to meet her gaze. He wanted to kiss her again.

He wanted *her* again.

Marcus clicked the mouse twice and opened a new screen; Maya's mouth dropped, then she covered it with her hand. Elation flickered in her eyes.

"Oh my God. Marcus, is this the digital library?" Maya asked.

"Yes." He said. "I took your idea and tweaked it."

"Tweaked." She beamed. "Marcus, you amplified it times a thousand."

Her joy was contagious, and he smiled harder. "This is all you." He said.

"No. This is us. And this is for the community. This will not only help them understand the legal system but also find the resources they need to better equip themselves for legal matters." Maya spoke joyfully but her smile faded as she slumped back into the chair. The fire in her eyes was almost snubbed out.

"Maya? What's the matter? Did you find another bug?" Marcus asked. His eyes darted from the screen to her.

She shook her head. "My father would have loved this." Her voice was barely a whisper and when she looked at him, Marcus recognized the restrained tears.

Marcus sat on the edge of his desk and studied her face carefully. "Maya, can I ask you something?"

She dabbed the inner corner of her eyes and nodded.

"You are a dynamic woman. I mean absolutely wonderful. You understand the people better than anyone I know. Watching you in that courtroom blew me away. You were poised, knowledgeable and took no shit whatsoever."

Maya smiled softly.

"I wonder why you haven't started your own law firm?"

"W-what?" She looked at him as if he just insulted her.

"You've never thought about having your own firm? Those dudes, Sterling and Turner, they're old school. Hell, that Sterling guy looks like he still roots for the Confederates."

Maya laughed and a single tear escaped. She wiped it away quickly.

"And Turner, what's his deal?" Marcus asked.

"He and my dad were best friends. He helped me get my foot in the door."

Marcus nodded.

Maya's brow arched. "What?"

"It makes sense now." He said.

Her almond eyes narrowed at him.

"You're a token, Maya." Marcus said.

Her eyes swelled then she leered at him. "Did you call me a *token*?" She asked.

"You don't think so?" Marcus asked.

"Why would I?" Maya pushed away from his desk and stood up; she met his eyes with a subdued fury. "I worked my ass off to get where I am and for you to call me 'a token'..." She paused.

Marcus held up his hands. "I didn't mean it like that." He said.

She crossed her arms, and her arched brows sunk in deeper. "So, what did you mean, Marcus?"

"What I'm saying is that you're so intelligent. You're in tune with the community and you're a great advocate. You're not like them at that firm and it shows. They know nothing about this community. If they did, they would have started a project like this themselves."

Her brow softened but her arms were locked across her chest. "You have no idea what I go through." She said.

Marcus rose from the desk. "I bet I do." He said. "We are one of three Black owned tech companies in the state of Illinois. We are one of twelve in the Midwest. We have lost jobs just because of the color of our skin and today, we're a hot commodity because a white man announced online that he's doing business with us. So yes, Maya I know what you go through. They don't deserve you. I know you feel like you owe Robert your life because of your father, but you don't."

Maya's arms dropped to her side; tears broke through and left trails down the apples of her high cheekbones.

"I have been building this for years before I even landed

a job at Sterling and Turner." She cried. "I'm so close to bringing this to fruition that I cannot afford to walk away right now. I know that even *you* understand that much."

He nodded then pulled Maya into his arms. He held her tight and let her sob into his chest. She wrapped her arms around him as his chest absorbed her cries. Her body shook in his hold; Marcus rubbed her back and caressed her soft curls. "It's okay." He said. "I know how much this means to you, and I won't let you down either. I'm here for you, Maya."

Her sobs softened; Maya pulled away and looked up at him. Marcus cupped her face in his large hands and used his thumbs to wipe away the tears that clung to the rims of her eyes. Her makeup was muddled, leaving streaks like dark watercolor down her face.

She was beautiful.

"I'm here for you, Maya." He repeated then leaned in to kiss her.

Thirteen

♥

A cloud of pain hovered over Maya's left eye, and she groaned. It was too early in the day for a migraine yet there it was, along with no sign of going away. She sat back in her office chair, closed her eyes and massaged her temples. She wanted to snatch her hair from its snug bun but hated the idea of having to wrangle all her curls back up before her afternoon meeting and a quick visit to the courthouse.

Releasing the bun was out of the question, so she sat still, kept her eyes closed and daydreamed about Marcus and food. His text from earlier in the morning confirmed that he would stop by her office around one, then he called moments after to remind her again.

"You told me that already." She giggled and he laughed too. His laughter was just as addictive as his voice.

"I know." He said. "I just wanted to hear you laugh. It

makes my day."

Maya blushed and her cheekbones ached, she couldn't remember the last time someone made her smile so much. Marcus always knew the right thing to say and do. In a flash, Maya imagined Marcus in her bed. His slow and steady pace inching her closer to pleasure while he whispered in her ear, nearing the depths of her soul.

"I got you, baby." He said. "Just let go." And she would every time.

Maya exhaled hard, relieved that her migraine had downgraded to a dull headache.

Sex really was a powerful drug even when you were just thinking about it.

She laughed to herself then returned to her laptop.

"Knock knock." Nina said while tapping her knuckles on Maya's door. Maya smiled at her paralegal as she welcomed her in. Nina stood in the doorway with a pen and legal pad clutched to her chest.

"What's up?" Maya asked and motioned again for Nina to join her in the chair across from her. There was a time when Maya's office had been Nina's refuge, when she could just walk in, plop down in one of her chairs and start talking, venting or even sharing office gossip.

Each lawyer was assigned one paralegal; however, as Special Counsel, Maya was assigned two. Maya had interviewed Nina herself, noting her tenacity and determination, not to mention she was a poised, young black woman who had goals and understood her purpose. Maya loved it and the two of them hit off. Maya was eager to bring her on board, and Nina was just as excited and dedicated to helping her.

Two years of teamwork vanished after one unsuccessful date. Their informal greetings were down to a minimum and during meetings Nina kept her head down, avoiding most eye contact with Maya. Not to mention, the after work messages slowed down; their random phone calls and FaceTime sessions to talk about nothing had ceased too.

Nina sat down across from Maya; lately Nina rocked honey blonde hair that fell over her shoulders. The style complimented the burgundy pant suit she wore. Maya noted her fresh manicure, a pale pink hue that resembled her natural nails but were accented with gold flecks that caught the sunlight at random.

"I love the nails." Maya said.

Nina glanced at them and smiled. "Really? I got them cut down and I'm still getting used to them." Nina had kept her nails long, a little longer than Robert's liking, who made an appoint to complain to Maya about hearing her nails clicking away at the keyboards. He told Maya to talk to her about it, but she never did. Nina wasn't bothersome and neither were her nails.

"They look great. How have you been?" Maya asked. The question felt forced, but Maya did want to catch up with Nina and see how things were going on and offline. Maya knew the office was abuzz about her and Marcus. Yes, they maintained a professional relationship within the space; however, no one could ignore the sultry glances Maya gave him or how often she kept her door closed when he was there. Their budding romance was electric and hummed throughout the office.

There was a pocket of silence between them before Nina pushed forth a smile. "I've been good." She said.

Maya leaned forward to catch Nina's gaze. "Are you sure because things have felt off between us." She said, "Ever since..." She let the last portion of her sentence fall while Nina nodded her head. "Are *we* good?"

Nina inhaled deep and exhaled sharply. Never a good sign. She set her legal pad on Maya's desk before glancing back at the door.

The conversation was no longer casual, or business related.

Maya nodded toward the door and without another word, Nina stood up and closed it.

When she returned to her seat across from Maya, her eyes fell to her lap and when they returned to her, they were weighted with tears.

"Nina. What's the matter?" Maya pushed a decorative box of Kleenex toward her. "Is everything okay?"

Nina snatched a facial tissue to dab at the corners of her eyes. "I'm sorry." She said, "This isn't like me."

"I understand. Is there anything that you need to talk about?" Maya asked.

"I wanted to apologize to you." She said while choking back more tears.

Maya stared at her blankly.

Nina said, "I know that lately I have been a little short. Maybe even cold."

Cold wasn't the word that Maya would have chosen but she nodded.

"I got in my feelings and I shut down on you." Nina said.

"I thought that maybe you wanted to keep things professional." Maya said. It was a lie infused with truth.

The truth? Maya had in fact noticed Nina's behavioral shift, but she didn't want to create office tension because of a man.

This wasn't high school.

Nina shook her head. "No. You have been like the big sister I never had. I look up to you and I respect you so much, Maya. When you hired me, I knew that I couldn't disappoint you. You have had my back since the day I stepped foot in this place and when I felt like I didn't belong here, you always reminded me that I did, and I do."

Maya felt the corners of her mouth uptick, but she kept her face neutral, unsure of where Nina was headed with the conversation. "Working alongside you has been a dream."

A twinge of panic set in. Was Nina resigning? Maya sat up straight, she opened her mouth to protest, ready to stop Nina from speaking the words she didn't want to hear. But when she spoke, a different revelation emerged.

"I knew that Marcus asked you out that day after the convention." She said softly.

Maya closed her mouth and sank back into her seat. "What?"

"That night when we all came back from the convention. You climbed out of the front seat, and I went to grab the phone charger that was still plugged in up front. We were all so hyped up from the mixer, I guess you missed when Marcus looked at you."

Maya went back to that evening; she only had two Rum and Cokes at the mixer but she didn't pay attention to anyone else's intake. On the way back to Cascade City, Maya slipped into the passenger seat without any static from Nina because she and Darnell were comparing R&B albums from the early 90s to the late 2000s. She and Marcus joined in and the car was buzzing with conversation and laughter. Maya did steal a few glances at Marcus and he did too.

Nina continued, " I saw him look at you, but I guess you didn't."

"What?" Maya said. She *did* remember climbing out of the passenger seat to grab her gift bags from the back seat, but she couldn't remember Marcus trying to say anything to her.

How did she miss that? Maya looked at Nina and nodded for her to keep going.

"When he asked, it was instinct. I didn't want to leave his question hanging."

"So, *you* said 'yes' because *I* didn't hear him?"

Nina nodded but her head hung like a scolded child.

Maya chewed on her bottom lip. "Why didn't you just tell me that he was talking to me then?"

Nina shrugged as she said, "It's been a while since I went out on a date and that man *is* fine." They laughed in unison then Nina went on."I'm sorry I didn't tell you." Nina rambled on, explaining her version of events from their date. Nina told Maya she reached out to a friend from college while on the date and said that the wine choices "weren't that great."

Unsure of what to do with the information, Maya just

smiled. It was a stiff smile that she often gave to her opponents in the courtroom, but it was a smile and enough to assure Nina that their blistered bridge was in repair. Nina sat up taller in her seat and smiled softly. It was more genuine than Maya's, then again, the young woman just confessed her sins to her boss, so she was at ease.

"I just wanted to apologize because I didn't tell you that. I have been holding that in for too long. And I have been a little jealous, especially when I see him walk in and out of here, but I know he's always had eyes for you. Ever since y'all met at the art gala." Nina said.

"Thank you for telling me all of this, Nina. I really appreciate it." Maya said.

Nina popped up from her seat, her smile bigger and her face glowing. It was like the confession replaced a dead light bulb and she was shining bright again. "Thanks for hearing me out. I'll get started on that Casio case now." She picked up her legal pad then left Maya's office.

Maya felt like a balloon descending from the atmosphere. The dull ache was transforming into a migraine again.

"Everything alright in here?" Robert Turner filled her doorway; his hands were shoved in the pockets of his black suit pants, and on his round face, he held a subtle smile.

"Yeah. Yes, Nina was just briefing me on some information that she thought I would find valuable and insight-ful." Maya said.

"Hmm. Nice." Robert crossed the threshold into her office, but he didn't sit down. He rocked on his heels and scanned her office as if it was his first time visiting. "How are things coming with the Community Counsel Initiative?"

"Things are progressing well. I have a meeting this month with the county clerk and Marcus and Darnell are in the process of reviewing the databases for additional bugs. Were you and Tim able to take some time and look at them?"

"Oh yes. I love them. They're helpful." There was something in his voice that made Maya uneasy. Robert said that *he* loved them but what about Tim? Did *he* not like them?

"Did Tim give you any feedback?" She asked.

"Not yet." Robert said. "But he is happy with the publicity. The city is loving this initiative, Maya. I'm so proud of you." He looked at her, his brown eyes glimmering. "I know if your father was here, he would be proud too."

"Thank you but it's not just me bringing this to life now. Marcus and Darnell are really helping to..." Robert raised a hand and shook his head. Maya was so jilted by the move; she sat back in her seat.

He moved closer to her desk, planted his palms on it and

stared into her eyes. "Maya, this is *your* project. This is *your* baby, and I refuse to let you give someone else credit for your creation."

Maya said, "I'm not giving—"

Robert cut her off again. "This is *your* project." He repeated. "This project is not only big for the firm but you too. When this project takes off, you could find yourself being the youngest partner here. Think about that." He grinned. "Sterling, Turner, Thompson and Associates. That has one hell of a ring to it."

Thompson and Associates sounds better. Maya thought.

That had been her father's dream. To become a partner, to stand alongside the man who took a chance on him and his best friend. The idea of bringing her father's dream to life was beautiful; however, *that* wasn't Maya's dream.

Robert stared at her, awaiting her response.

Maya brought forth another stiff smile and felt a bolt of pain shoot behind her eye. "That sounds great." She said. Another lie laced with truth.

"I know, right? Listen, Elena wants to have dinner with you and, what's your boyfriend's name?"

"Marcus." Maya said. "And I don't like the term *boyfriend* for a grown ass man."

Robert shrugged. "Your partner then. She wants us to have dinner this weekend at our place. I thought I could fire up the grill and we could talk more about this partner venture."

"I need to make sure that Marcus is free." Maya said.

"I'm sure he is. Saturday at seven. Don't be late or I'm starting cocktails without you."

And without another word, Robert was out the door. Maya collapsed in her chair, grabbed her phone to check for a message from Marcus. He should have been on his way.

He had sent a text, letting her know he was twenty minutes away.

Maya sent a reply:

Are you free for dinner this Saturday?

Fourteen

T he transition from Spring to Summer was never subtle in the Midwest and in the middle of May, dusk held on to the dry heat of the day. Marcus turned on the A/C in his Land Rover before he pulled into the parking lot of Maya's building. When she climbed into the passenger seat, she leaned over to kiss him. He grinned while his face and the rest of him warmed up at the sight of her.

Maya was dressed in white linen, wide leg pants, a white camisole and the kimono jacket she wore on their first date. Her textured combination of loose and tight coils, created an abstract crown on her head. Her soft Summer look complimented his pale khaki shorts and matching button up shirt; they both finished their looks with gold accents. Maya chose dainty hoops and a few rings while Marcus wore a thin Cuban link chain.

The GPS projected a fifteen minute drive, so Marcus and Maya filled the time catching up on their day to day antics, despite talking and texting each other every hour on the hour. Maya shared a story about the free legal counsel she gave her manicurist earlier that day then showed off her shiny, French manicure. In exchange, Marcus told Maya the tale of Darnell's recently failed hook up.

"You mean to tell me that he didn't tell the woman he had a kid." She laughed.

"He said that it slipped his mind." Marcus said.

"I'm sure." She said.

Marcus rested his hand on Maya's thigh as he drove, and she stroked his knuckles with her thumb. The subtle contact relaxed him. Unsure of what to expect at dinner, Marcus had spent time during the day wondering exactly *who* Robert Turner was.

He looked up Maya's boss and family friend online and found that Turner and Sterling had been working together for over thirty years. Robert graduated at the top of his class at UIC, where his wife studied too. Together, they invested and launched a wine company. *True Blends Wine* had nearly two years of success before it went under. Their business partner, a man named Shawn Locke, made off with over a million dollars. The Turners never recovered the lost funds, but they didn't experience a heavy financial ruin thanks to his partnership with the law firm. Robert appeared to be a good man which supported the influence he had on Maya, yet Marcus had his reserves.

He peered at Maya; her eyes were already on him. Her lips curved into a soft smile. "What can you tell me about Robert ahead of dinner?" Marcus asked.

Maya said, "Well, I've known him all of my life." She said. "He and Elena were high school sweethearts. He and my dad grew up together in Chicago and went to college together. They might as well have been twins." Her smile returned and transcended to her eyes as he watched her recall something in silence. "When I made the decision to study law, I couldn't tell who was more excited, my dad or Robert."

Marcus chuckled. "He seemed cool at the art gala, but at the office though, he's a hard ass."

"Oh God yes." She laughed. "He's no nonsense when it comes to the firm. My dad was the same way."

"Now it makes sense." Marcus said.

Maya stared at him.

Marcus replied, "Where *you* get it from."

"Get what from?" Maya asked.

"That no nonsense attitude of yours." Marcus chuckled.

Maya snatched her hand away and playfully hit him in

the arm. "Hey, don't abuse the driver, ma'am."

"Ma'am? Ma'am? I got your ma'am." They laughed as Marcus turned onto a private street, stopping in front of a large, wrought iron gate. To the left of the gate was a stone sign reading *Cascade Glen* in bold, legible script.

Cascade Glen was a small, gated community just west of downtown. It was known for its mini mansions and since the community was less than twenty years old, it was highlighted as a place where "new money" resided.

Marcus pulled up to the gate where a security guard checked them in. Upon confirming them, the iron gate creaked then slid to the right as it opened.

"Damn." Marcus sang.

"I know." Maya said.

"When are *we* moving into this place?" He grinned.

Marcus drove slowly with his GPS directing their way. Each home was as immaculate as the last one, with pristine cars overflowing from the multi-car and lush, freshly cut lawns. When the GPS confirmed that they had reached their destination, his jaw dropped at the gorgeous view of the large, two-story home ahead of them. They pulled up behind a pearl white Mercedes C-Class that was parked in the first of three spaces for the home's attached garage. In the second spot was a black Mercedes G-Wagon.

"I feel like they're calling me 'broke' without even saying

it." Marcus said.

"That was Elena's Glam-Ma gift." Maya nodded to the G-Wagon while Marcus cut the engine.

"Glam-Ma gift?" He repeated.

"Yep. Robert and Elena's son had a baby about a year ago and Robert bought her the G-Wagon as a way to surprise her with the big news."

Marcus whistled then smiled at the vanity plate attached to the rear of the truck. "When you meet my mother, please don't tell her about this. I can't compete with *this*." He said.

Maya laughed and climbed out of the truck. "Come on." She walked around to meet him, took his hand and led the way up a black brick laid path lined with bright solar lights. Large rose bushes lined the perimeter of the house, two stone columns covered in moss and ivy framed the main entrance that led to a set of black, lacquered French doors, flanked by frosted sidelites etched with slim abstract black lines.

Maya rang the doorbell, and a chorus of shrill chimes echoed from the house. A figure took shape in the frosted glass of the sidelite before one of the doors opened and a woman beamed at them.

"Maya." The woman said before her eyes gravitated toward Marcus. Her smile was infectious and warm. "And

Marcus." Her brown eyes glistened as the outer corners of her almond eyes crinkled. "Please come in you two."

She pulled the both of them into the foyer then closed the door. When she came face to face with Marcus again, her deep red lips shifted into a full grin that told him she knew a thing or two about him. Maya squeezed his hand and introduced him. "Marcus, this is Elena Turner. Robert's wife."

He remembered her face from the art gala but had failed to retain her name. Elena was a petite woman with a sharp jawline and high cheekbones. Her brown skin was so rich and velvety; had it not been for the soft laugh lines near her mouth, Marcus could believe that she was a woman barely out of her thirties.

Elena wore a silk headwrap in a black and ivory mud-cloth pattern, complimenting her black pants and tunic of a similar scheme.

Marcus extended a hand, but Elena pulled him in for a hug. "Oh, it's so nice to see you again, honey." Despite her slim figure, Elena's embrace was strong and tight. When she pulled away, Elena looked from him to Maya before she swooped Maya into a hug just as quickly as she had him.

"You look stunning." Elena told Maya, looking over her.

"Thank you. So do you." Maya said.

Elena giggled and playfully swatted away the compliment like a pesky fly.

"How's RJ?" Maya asked.

Elena raised an eyebrow and beamed at the both of them. "Just the absolute best. Robert and I can't get enough of him."

"Plus, we don't have to keep him full time." Robert Turner's voice boomed down the hallway. He stood a few feet away from them and to Marcus' surprise, Robert wasn't in a suit, instead he wore sand colored linen pants and a matching short sleeve button up shirt. The top three buttons were left undone, revealing a gold chain. He had a glass in his hand which he raised toward Marcus and Maya. "Come on you two, let's celebrate this beautiful evening while we have it."

Dinner was held on the Turners' temperature controlled, covered patio. When Marcus made a joke about the patio feeling like a small house, Elena shared that she wanted the space to be utilized year round, so she had the original screened frames replaced with a solid structure and tempered glass. The patio was carpeted in a soft shag the color of speckled, white sand and plants overtook gold shelving installed throughout the space. At the center of the room, an intimate round table sat with seating for the four of them.

Beyond the patio was half an acre of land which could have easily supported an inground pool, but, the Turners transformed the backyard into a serene oasis with ornate lawn furniture, a brick fire pit and an outdoor kitchen, equipped with a massive gas grill and stone oven.

"Robert has been dying to open the outdoor kitchen and get on that grill." Elena told them. "*This* was his perfect excuse."

By default, Marcus assisted Robert on the grill with lamb chops that Elena had seasoned with Jerk spices, honey and citrus and bundles of asparagus wrapped in bacon. Elena made rice and peas and fried plantains to accompany the lamb. Maya helped Elena prepare a salad made from kale and a savory citrus dressing that complimented the chops perfectly.

Robert opened a bottle of Syrah, a red wine. "I'm not a wine drinker." Marcus said.

"You are tonight." Robert retorted. By their third bottle, Marcus came to enjoy its bitter, bold flavor.

"I wanna make a toast," Robert said.

Everyone picked up their glasses; Marcus stole a glance at Maya, her wine stained lips curled into a smile.

"To family old and new." Robert said and directed his attention to Marcus who sat across from him. Robert's bald head gleamed under the soft lighting on the patio as he smiled at him. Marcus raised his glass.

"To family." They said in unison then drank. Marcus savored the sip then returned to his second lamb chop.

Elena looked at Marcus; her smile was still pleasant and bright. "Marcus, I hear that you're helping Maya with the Community Counsel Initiative." She said.

Marcus chewed quickly and nodded. "Yes. I'm helping with the technical logistics to ensure that Maya has everything she needs to get this off the ground efficiently."

Elena went on. "Has tech always been your thing?"

Marcus wiped his mouth with his linen napkin then spoke. "I've always loved computers and coding since I was a kid. I think I fell in love with technology before I even touched a football."

Elena and Robert laughed; much to Marcus' relief and Maya smiled at him admirably. She placed a hand on his and Marcus' entire body flushed.

"And how's my husband treating you at the firm?" Elena asked.

"Really well. Robert— Mr. Turner has been nothing but wonderful to us." Marcus replied.

"Please, call me Robert." He said. "At least in *this* setting."

"Yes, sir. I mean, Robert. Thank you."

Robert waved one of his large hands before he poured

himself another glass of wine. After a large gulp, his eyes watched Marcus again over the rim of his glass. When he finished the glass, he set it down slowly and said, "You know, this project that Maya is working on is important." He said matter of factly.

Marcus bobbed his head. "Absolutely. And I know how hard she's worked to bring this project to fruition." He stole a look at Maya.

"Good. Then you also understand that this project is *hers*." His voice took a turn, and Marcus felt a sharp edge of concern in it.

"Robert." Elena said softly. Her smile was as delicate as lace but her eyes had hardened while they shifted from Marcus to Maya and back to her husband. "Easy now, honey."

"Hey, I just want to make sure that Marcus knows how special Maya is, not just to the firm but to me too. And this project, this initiative that she has been birthing is all hers. Furthermore, she doesn't need anyone coming in trying to mooch off of her greatness."

Maya's eyes narrow in Robert's direction. "What are you talking about?" She asked.

The air at the table had transcended from warm and peaceful to cold and venomous. Marcus felt Robert's icy stare while he watched Maya and Elena speak only through their eyes. Maya returned her gaze to Robert.

"Robert, what are you talking about?" She said again.

Robert's head lofted to the right then left. His eyes fluttered then popped open as if he was suddenly surprised by something.

Marcus eyed the third, empty bottle of wine then remembered the glass Robert had in hand when they arrived. Robert had also enjoyed two highball glasses half full of Johnny Walker while they were at the grill.

The man was drunk.

"Maya, listen to me." Robert's voice came in a wave. "Listen. You are a great lawyer. I told you that all your hard work would pay off, and now." He stopped and threw his arms up. "Look at you." His arms came down fast with his hands hitting the table with a loud bang. The substantial quake rattled the glasses and plates. Robert leaned over his plate, disregarding that his short sleeve button up was suddenly saturated in the lamb chop's marinade and citrus dressing. His wide eyes were on Maya. "Look at you, special counsel for almost three years with the possibility of becoming a partner."

Maya's eyes shot to Marcus; he saw an aura of tension around her that he had never seen before. It glowed white hot beneath the dim lights.

"Maya." Elena smiled. "Is that true?"

"Of course it is." Robert said. "I told Tim that we need you as a partner. Of course, he argued me down and said that there were others waiting in the wings for the opportunity. Naturally, Tim wants another white man, but we can't overlook you."

"Robert, please," Elena begged. "Honey, I don't think this is a good time to discuss business."

"Why not?" His voice ricocheted off the glass panels. "It's perfect. Right Marcus?"

Marcus opened his mouth to respond but when he saw the distress on Maya's face, he paused and withdrew into his seat. Robert chuckled; he was the only one at the table laughing at a silent, private joke. Elena and Maya stared at him like two lost souls while Marcus kept his eyes on the half-eaten lamb chop on his plate. When he thought about taking a sip of wine, one look at Robert Turner, Esquire made him think otherwise.

The drive back to Maya's place felt like an eternity. Marcus drove in silence while Maya kept her lips pursed together and stared out the window. The heat of the evening had vanished, and Maya wrapped herself tighter within her kimono jacket. She peered at Marcus; he was already staring at her when he pushed a button and Maya felt her legs warm up quickly.

"Heated seats." He said. His eyes found hers in the darkness. "Are you okay?"

Maya nodded. "I should be asking *you* that."

"Why? Because your overprotective boss tried to accuse me of mooching off of you?"

"That part." Maya sighed. "I'm sorry about Robert and everything he said tonight."

"Don't be. But why didn't you tell me that this project could help you become a partner?" He asked.

Maya bit her lip. "Because that's not why I'm doing this." She said, "And besides, it's not important."

It wasn't important for *him* to know. She wanted to add that part, but felt like the conversation was already on shaky ground.

Marcus said "That's *very* important. That means that Darnell and I need to make sure that every database is in tip top shape and I—"

"It's not about you." Maya said. The words shot out like bullets and Marcus took every single one. Maya sank down into the warmth of the passenger seat. Marcus gripped the wheel, but his face remained neutral. When he finally smiled at her, she saw the strain at the corners of his mouth.

"Marcus..." She trailed off, unsure of what she could say to ease the sting she just delivered.

When they pulled up to her building, Marcus helped Maya out of the truck; their silence serving as a third wheel. When they approached the elevator; Maya turned to Marcus and smiled.

"I'm sorry that I..." She trailed off again then reached out to touch his face. She held his chin in her hands and felt the resistance in his shoulders radiating like a fever. "I'm sorry. You have been such a lifesaver through all of this. I couldn't have brought this to life like this without you." She said. Maya pulled his face to hers for a kiss.

Maya felt his restraint melt when she pulled away to look into his eyes. "I'm not used to someone showing genuine concern let alone support for me. Outside of Robert and Elena."

Marcus smiled, the strain erased from his lips. "I got you. I promise." He said.

Maya hoisted herself upward and kissed him.

Marcus pulled her into his arms and Maya let herself fall deeper into his hold. He pressed her back against the marbled wall that separated the lobby elevators; their lips parted, and Maya's tongue brushed against his bottom lip.

His hand ran the length of her leg before he cupped her breast; his thumb grazed her nipple and it hardened against her camisole top. Maya pulled away with her heart ready to eject from her chest and her body aching for more. Marcus stood out of breath too, his eyes wild with anticipation.

The elevator chimed and the tension slipped away.

Saved by the bell.

"I should go." She said softly. "I have to start reviewing documents for a new trial next week."

"Yeah." Marcus' voice had deflated. "I'll call you tomorrow, okay?"

"Of course." Maya stepped into the elevator but turned to give Marcus one last kiss. Her lips bloomed on his again, but she retreated again with a gentle smile. "Goodnight."

"Goodnight, Maya." He said.

On the ascent, Maya cursed herself; she mentally kicked herself as she walked into her condo and closed the door behind her.

She had completely forgotten about make up sex.

Fifteen

♥

Marcus felt like he would throw up. He sat in his office chair, jaw unhinged and mind whirling as he stared at his computer screen, displaying their business bank account. Wayne Carlson had made good on the investment; however, that morning, their angel inventor made another deposit, followed by a message to him and Darnell:

> I am loving what I see at InnovateCore and so do a few of my business associates. They have asked me to invest on their behalf. Congrats fellas. Oh, and I will be in Chicago at the close of Q3. I would love to schedule a dinner for us to sit down and talk about the future of ICore in person. Let's make it happen.
> -WC

Marcus gawked at their account while Darnell hovered over his desk. "Holy shit." Darnell said. "We've touched six figures before but *this*. We have never seen it all at once like this. Never like this."

"I know." Marcus refreshed the screen three times out of fear that the numbers he saw would fade into the ether of the world wide web but they didn't. He took a picture of his screen then forwarded it to Maya:

> I guess we can call this a "bonus".

Maya responded to the photo with their usual Black Panther salute and a message:

> So, dinner on you tonight?

He chuckled to himself and agreed to her message.

"You tell, Maya?" Darnell asked.

Marcus grinned. "Just did."

Darnell said, "Things cool between you two after her boss accused you of using her and her project for clout?"

"That's not what he said, man. He actually accused me of 'mooching' off of her."

Darnell moved to perch on the edge of Marcus' desk. "Damn. But who is he to say some shit like that to you?"

"He's like a father figure to her. He helped Maya get into the firm."

His partner scoffed. "So what? She thinks she still owes him for that? I'm sure Maya has brought in bank for that firm since she started there."

"He also co-signs the checks for our work as well." Marcus said.

Darnell tilted his head. "On second thought, maybe he *was* right about you." He laughed.

Marcus chuckled. "Go to hell."

"Not without you." Darnell winked. He slipped into his office just as their front door opened. "Liv's here." He announced.

Marcus stepped out of his office to see his sister close the door behind her then smile at him.

"Liv, what are you doing here?" Marcus asked.

Her smile vanished after she hugged him and looked into his eyes.

Marcus said, "What's wrong? Something up with Mom?"

"No. That woman is an ox. Did you read any of my messages?" She asked.

"What? No. I was busy." He said with a lighthearted

chuckle, but when he looked into his sister's eyes. They were weary and heavy with concern. Marcus picked up his phone and went to Olivia's text thread.

She had sent him a screenshot from her Instagram direct messages.

He recognized the handle and face associated with it.

Kiana had reached out to Olivia.

Marcus' stomach dropped. "What the hell is this?" He asked.

"Kiana found me on social media." She said.

"I thought you blocked her." Marcus hissed.

"I did, on my personal page but look again, that's my art page." He checked the screenshot again and saw Olivia's *O_Mart_Art* handle at the top. "She asked for your number." She said.

"Why?"

Olivia crossed her arms. "She said that she wanted to talk to you. My guess is that she heard about your big investment."

Investments. He wanted to say with some pride, but his chest tightened when he looked down at the small photo of his ex-girlfriend.

Marcus remembered the last time he saw Kiana, a few days after his doomed New Year's proposal-when he decided to move out of their condo and end their relationship. Kiana had been far from heartbroken, in fact, she argued that she keep the espresso maker because *she* picked it out. Marcus didn't argue though.

"Keep it." He said before he left with the last of his things.

Marcus looked at his sister. "Did you give her my number?"

"Hell no. I told her that you are happy, thriving and in a great relationship. Why the hell would I give her your number when you and Maya are together?" Olivia leered at him, her large eyes reading him. "Marcus, did *you* block her?"

"What?" He asked.

"Did *you* block Kiana?" Olivia repeated.

"Yes." He said.

Olivia asked, "Everywhere?"

"Everywhere?" He mimicked.

"You know what I mean. Everywhere. Social media *and* phones?"

He paused and peered down at his phone before he looked at her again and smiled. "She's been blocked for damn near two years and I don't need to see her *or* talk to her."

Olivia's shoulders dropped and her eager smile returned. "Good. Because I think she's up to something. It's best if you leave her in the past and focus on what you're building with Maya."

Marcus beamed. "You're right." He said. "Thanks for having my back."

"It's my job." Olivia said. She hugged Marcus then moved to the other side of his desk.

"Wait. You came all the way over here to tell me *that*?" Marcus sensed an additional motive behind his little sister's visit.

"No. I also came to see if you and Darnell were free to help with the vendor application page for the summit?"

Darnell's deep cackle echoed from his office. "Sorry, I'm busy." He said.

"Liar." Olivia shouted. "What about you? I know you're busy with a hundred and one projects."

"So, what's one more, right?" Marcus said.

Olivia grinned. "That's why I love you. It doesn't need to be fancy. I already sent you the guidelines and the logo to your email."

Marcus sighed, "Damn. So, you just knew I was gonna say 'yes'."

"*Hoped*. I *hoped* that you would know how important this summit is for me and that you would see my email and have pity on me." Olivia's purple hued lips poked out. Her younger child syndrome still ran rampant when she wanted it to.

Marcus laughed. "Alright." He said. "I will work on it this week. I'll have something for you by Thursday."

"And this is why I have the best big brother in the whole wide world. I love you." Olivia blew Marcus a kiss then slipped out of the office. Marcus listened to her footfalls until he heard the front door close.

He stared down at his phone, studying the screenshot of the brief exchange between his sister and Kiana.

Kiana opened the conversation by asking Olivia how she was doing and after a few lines of small talk, Kiana went in for the kill. She asked Olivia for Marcus' phone number, citing that she had deleted it after the breakup. Olivia didn't hesitate; she told Kiana that her brother was happy, had a girlfriend and advised her to leave him alone.

Kiana read Olivia's message, but she didn't respond.

Marcus exited the inbox then went to his contact list; he knew exactly where to go. He scrolled to the bottom of his digital rolodex, down to the letter X.

After their breakup, Marcus did consider blocking Kiana completely; however, he questioned if and when he would need to reach out to her again. A personal reference for an apartment or a job maybe? He could never be sure so he changed her name in his phone, believing that changing her name would reduce the temptation.

Out of sight. Out of mind.

Or so he thought.

Marcus tapped the contact labeled *X-Kiana* then tapped the icon to send her a message:

> Hey! I heard you were looking for me.

He sent the message then set his phone down as a notification pinged:

> Hello stranger!! How have you been?

Marcus peered over his computer into Darnell's office. He had his headphones on and was deep into work behind his curved monitor. Marcus responded back:

> I've been good. Business is good. And you?

He chose to keep it short and sweet. There was no need to show any excitement after all.

Then came another ping. Another message:

> I've been alright. I would really love to see you and catch up. When are you free?

Shit. Marcus thought to himself.

Kiana went straight to the point.

He and Maya had dinner plans in the evening, but he had time in the afternoon for a quick cup of coffee and a meet up. Marcus assured himself that it would be short and harmless as he sent the confirmation message, adding that he would be free within the hour.

Kiana responded with a heart eyed emoji.

Just before Marcus left the office, Kiana decided they should have a "quick lunch" at Celine's. Marcus protested the suggestion as he felt a level of sanctity with the restaurant where he and Maya shared their first kiss.

It was sacred ground to him, but Kiana argued that it was *her* favorite spot in town, and refused to take 'no' for answer.

When Marcus walked in, Kiana met him at the entrance. She almost knocked over the hostess when she threw her arms around him and hugged him tight.

"Oh my god. It's so good to see you." She said in his ear. Her arms tightened around his neck but Marcus pulled her away to restore some distance.

Kiana wore a bright orange, long sleeve maxi dress with tan heels. She had long, thin braids that cascaded down her back and her face gleamed with bronze makeup and nude glossed lips.

"It's so good to see you." She said again. "I already have a table for us." Kiana snatched Marcus' hand then pulled him toward their table; a large booth next to the picture window that donned Celine's scripted logo.

Kiana loved to be seen and when Marcus looked out the window, he had a clear view of the Fremont building less than two blocks down. His heart raced and wished he tried harder to persuade her to meet for just coffee.

After a disagreement on how to sit; Kiana wanted to sit next to him, but Marcus objected and asked that she sit across from him. She pouted but obliged his request. Marcus sat facing the door and a hot wave of alert washed over him.

This is a mistake. He told himself.

Marcus stared at Kiana, imagining Maya in her place

with that warm smile that set her brown eyes ablaze and the allure that radiated from her body. He wanted it to be Maya looking back at him and reaching for his hand.

Instead, it was Kiana and when she touched him, the memories came rolling in like an unruly tide and flooding his emotions. He looked at her again, she was smiling at him but it didn't reach her eyes. It never did. It was like she was always wearing a mask. Hiding something or holding something in. Kiana was emotionally handicapped, but she was still beautiful.

A huge mistake. He thought.

"You look great." She said. There was a key of surprise in her voice but she giggled it away. "Seems like your business is going well."

"It is." Marcus said. "D and I have been doing well."

Kiana nodded and grabbed a menu. Marcus exhaled slowly before reaching for a menu too. He wasn't hungry; his stomach was in knots but the menu made a great shield against Kiana's lustful gazes over her menu. Paranoia gnawed at him. It was the lunch rush at Celine's and all he could think about was running into Maya or someone from the law firm.

He had sat in Maya's office for weeks and he had learned a few faces and names, so it was inevitable for someone to walk in and see him at a table with another woman and assume the worst, right?

"Marcus?" Kiana's voice bled into his mental spiral.

"What?" He said.

"I said everything looks so good, right?"

He looked down at the menu again.

"Do you know what you want to—"

Marcus cut her off. "Why are you here, Kiana? What do you want?"

Her smile didn't fade but she put down the menu and leaned forward on her elbows. "I've been thinking a lot about us." She said, "I realized that I didn't treat you the way that you deserved, and I have never been able to forgive myself for it."

She closed her eyes and shook her head.

Marcus recognized the move. He sat back in the booth and prepared himself for the next phase. Kiana was about to put on an excellent show.

She looked out the window then looked back at him. Her eyes were suddenly welled with tears. "That night when you proposed to me, I said 'no' because I was scared."

"Scared of what?" Marcus asked. His voice came out rougher than it needed to.

Kiana exhaled hard. "Scared to really be loved by you, Marcus."

"Kiana? You were scared to be loved by me when all I did was love you unconditionally despite the way you dogged me *and* my business out at any given chance." Marcus stopped once he felt his voice rising.

"Marcus, you know that I always believed in you and your business." Kiana's voice rose then fell. "I knew that you would make InnovateCore into something big." Her hand returned to his, but he withdrew himself. Kiana sat up straight.

"Is that why you're here?" He asked. "You heard about the investment deal, and you wanted to see if I was still hard up on you?"

To his surprise, Kiana smiled. "Aren't you though?" She asked. The tears she had worked to produce were gone. Her eyes were ice cold as she stared at him.

"What?" Marcus said.

Kiana leaned forward as if she was about to cue him in on a secret, but her voice was far from hushed. She said, "Why are *you* here, Marcus? You want to pin me as some gold digger—"

"Are you not?" He spat. "Not even a month after we broke up, you were already on the arm of someone else. Wasn't he a doctor or something?"

Kiana tilted her head then said, "And still, you came to me almost instantly. Something tells me that despite that thriving romance Olivia made sure to mention, there's something inside of you that wants that old thing back."

Marcus chuckled. Hearing his own laughter made him laugh a little harder but Kiana's eyes were glued to him. The humor in her arrogance dissolved and was replaced with his own malice.

Why had he come?

Did he still want Kiana?

What part of him still desired her?

No part of him desired her and as she sat across from him, unable to read him but hoping that her usual tactics were working, Marcus grinned. He said, "I reached out to see if I was still a fool for you. To see and prove to myself that I could sit across from you and not give in. Not fall for the fake tears or your fake concern."

Kiana sat back in her seat.

"I wanted to come, look you in your eyes and tell you I'm doing much better now."

Kiana studied her clasped hands atop the table. She said, "Marcus, I know that I hurt you when I rejected your proposal."

"Twice, Kiana." Marcus said. "You said 'no' to me twice and you never even told me why."

"You weren't ready to marry me, Marcus." She said. "We both knew that. I needed more than you could give me at the time."

"And now I can?" He said. "Now that you know that me and my business are thriving, you believe that I can give you what you want?" The reality of that statement rip through Marcus' heart yet cleared the remnant haze in his head.

Kiana sat up tall. "I won't apologize for wanting more for myself, Marcus." She said.

"And wanting *me* to take care of you." Marcus shot back.

Kiana's eyes avoided his as she folded her arms on the table. "When you and I first met, I imagined you with a great tech job with a Fortune 500 company. I saw you excelling with a great company, even becoming a CEO."

"Imagine how long *that* would have taken, Kiana. Especially for me, a Black man in a predominately whitewashed industry."

Kiana pursed her lips together.

"You think that these people would choose *me* as a CEO of *their* company?" Marcus chuckled softly. "Yeah right."

"You don't know that, and you didn't try either. And the second you and Darnell started putting all your money into that damn business..." She trailed off when Marcus' laughter interrupted her.

He said, "'That damn business' huh?"

"You could have played the game, Marcus. Keep your head down and do the damn work they asked you to do." She said.

"Is that what you do, Kiana? Keep your head down and do the work *they* ask of you? Are you still writing those 'ethnic' articles for that Chicago housewives magazine?"

Kiana shrank in her seat. Her allure tarnished.

Marcus pushed the menu toward her. "This was a mistake." He slipped from the booth and Kiana grabbed his arm.

"Marcus, wait a second." Her grip softened and she smiled at him. Maybe she had a little allure left in her after all. "I'm in town for a few weeks and I know that this didn't turn out the way that we— well, *I* expected, but we could try again and do dinner." Her nails raked at his forearm playfully; Marcus snatched his arm away.

"No thanks, Kiana." He said.

PART FOUR | JUNE 2023

Sixteen

Maya downed the last of her iced coffee but she couldn't remember if it had been her third or her fourth. Nina had dropped it off to her before calling it a night, leaving Maya waist deep in paperwork and website links. She sat at her desk, her orchid pink blazer slumped over the back of her chair and her white pumps tucked in a corner under her desk. She had made herself as comfortable as possible and committed to living in her office until the sun came up or at least until she made a substantial dent in her work—whichever came first.

The office had cleared out quickly thanks to the bright sunshine that called to everyone from the floor to ceiling windows surrounding the office building. Maya watched them file out in groups until the building hummed with silence. Bouts of jealousy nipped at Maya from her desk. She wanted to be outside too and daydreamed about her and Marcus driving to Chicago for the weekend to go to the beach. They would relax and she would forget about the Community Counsel Initiative for just a few moments.

But that was just a dream.

Timothy declared that the project had to launch by the close of their third quarter, so that meant that Maya had to review, test and finalize everything sooner than later because Sterling could and would pull the trigger at any moment.

"I know it's daunting, but you can do it." Robert assured her after Timothy gave her the news. "This is your baby. Remember that."

How could she ever try to forget it? Maya had held onto the dream for nearly a decade. She imagined all the people she would be helping, and all the lives that she would be changing. If the initiative was successful then Maya would make her move toward starting her own firm.

That reality gave her a bigger boost than her last sip of coffee. Maya returned to her laptop and went to work reviewing the initiative's website.

"Knock knock." Marcus stood in her office doorway. He held a large, brown paper bag spotted with grease stains and a drink tray holding two Styrofoam cups.

"What are you doing here?" She asked. "I thought you

and Darnell were working late too."

"We were then D's mom called him and said that his son wasn't feeling well so we cut our work day short. I thought we could have dinner together while spot checking the website again."

Maya breathed a visible sigh of relief then motioned for Marcus to come closer with the food. She could almost hear the French fries still frying in the bag. "Rudy's Red Hots?" She asked.

"Naturally. Only the best for my girl." Marcus grinned. He kissed her then set the food and the drink tray in a chair. He organized Maya's papers into their color coded folders; she smiled and her heart fluttered as she watched him handle her files with meticulous care.

"For tonight's gourmet feast, I have selected the finest double cheeseburgers and natural cut fries in all the land, along with a Cherry Coke for my queen and an Orange Fanta for yours truly."

"Thank you." Maya moaned. All her manners went out the window when she snatched up a burger, ripped it from its parchment paper and took a large bite. In mid-chew, Maya grabbed some fries. She closed her eyes, savoring the sea salt from the fries that complimented the brine of the pickles and natural spice of the red onion. When she opened her eyes, Marcus was staring at her, his deep dimples prominent.

"I'm so sorry." She said. "I haven't eaten—"

"Since lunch, I know." He said. "Remember, I was the one who sent you lunch and reminded you to eat."

She nodded while sipping her Cherry Coke.

Marcus looked back at her entrance then at Maya again. "Where is everyone?" He asked.

"Gone." Maya said then took another bite of her burger.

Maya noted a flash of delight that covered his face then disappeared when he asked, "How's it going?"

"It's going." She sighed. "I was about to test the website again."

Marcus said, "Great. Let me see it." He bit into his burger then moved toward Maya. He knelt down beside her and kissed her cheek as he chewed.

Maya giggled and turned her laptop for Marcus to view beside her.

The page loaded then suddenly went white. A gray dinosaur appeared on the screen alongside a message stating that the website could not be found. Maya's chest caved into her back and her stomach dropped.

"Wh-what the hell is this?" She typed in the web address again. The page loaded with the dinosaur and the error message once more. Maya's breath caught in her throat as she turned to Marcus; he had already abandoned his food and stood hunched over her laptop. His fingers started flying across its keyboard. "Marcus, what happened?"

"Hold on, honey. Give me a second and let me sort this out." He said.

Marcus' voice became a dull drone in Maya's ear. As she watched him type, her vision blurred, and she could hear her heart beating in her head like a ticking clock. Maya felt the tears rising to the surface, stinging her eyes and she couldn't stop them.

Maya said, "No. No. No." She fell back in her chair with hands over eyes. "No. We have to fix this." She said, her voice elevated and frantic. "Marcus, please tell me that you can fix this."

"I can fix it." He said. "I promise. I have to check something on the back end."

Maya rocked back and forth nervously while she watched Marcus access another website. In a few keystrokes, he was logged in and typing vigorously. The screen was black with a collection of numbers, letters and symbols. Marcus typed, stopped to read, typed again before pausing to look at Maya.

"It's okay, baby. I got it." He said then resumed typing. He mumbled a few words to himself before the typing ceased. "I got it."

Maya's head throbbed and her stomach flipped. She

forgot about her double cheeseburger.

Marcus typed in the web address again, the page loaded and there it was. The white, blue and gold motif that she and Marcus set for the website appeared.

"Oh my God." Maya exhaled. "You did it." She wrapped her arms around Marcus' waist and hugged him tight. "Thank you. I thought I was done for."

"What?" Marcus laughed as she released him. He knelt down again beside her chair then pointed to the laptop screen. "It looks like there was a coding issue with the webpage." He gave Maya a reassuring smile, cupped her chin then looked into her eyes. "No big deal." He said, "I got you."

Marcus leaned forward and kissed Maya softly. His full lips were plush against hers and when his tongue explored her mouth, Maya's core throbbed. His large hand crept up her thigh while planting hot kisses on her neck.

Maya exhaled softly and her breathing quickened. Marcus' grip on her throat was forceful yet sensual; Maya could feel her arousal spilling from her as he kissed her neck. He growled against her ear. "Let's relieve some tension. Okay?" He said.

Maya nodded her head quickly and he responded with another passionate kiss. She could feel Marcus unclasping her pants and without tearing away from his lips, Maya raised herself up from the chair. Marcus pulled her pants from her rounded hips then down her legs.

Marcus pulled away, his eyes shifted down to her snug bodysuit and smiled again. "This is perfect." He plucked her bodysuit closure open.

"Wait." Maya said as she glanced at the door. "Someone may still be here."

"We're alone, baby." Marcus said. "And I'm very curious to test out the acoustics in here."

Before Maya could argue further, Marcus pushed her legs open wide and kissed her inner thighs. His massive shoulders served as a wedge to keep her legs open and the warmth of his breath against her bare flesh made Maya shudder. When his tongue collided with her fluid warmth, Maya gripped her chair and leaned back. His tongue danced up and down her aching opening before it tapped on her clit.

"Marcus." She breathed. She glanced down and her eyes met his immediately while his tongue circled around her throbbing clit. "Fuck." She cried out.

His eyes lit up with delight as a hand snaked beneath her bodysuit and bra. His fingers latched on her nipple; he massaged the hard nub of sensitive flesh with his thumb and index finger.

Maya grinded her hips against his face while his tongue

twirled and flicked against her clit. All her senses were in overdrive and she could feel her release inching to the surface.

"Baby." Maya said. Marcus was purposely oblivious to her cries. She moaned louder and gripped his head. "Oh god." She moaned. Her body burned bright as his tongue worked double time. Her legs shook and her heart drummed hard in her chest as Marcus twirled and massaged.

Massaged and twirled. His pace steady and hypnotic.

Massage.

Twirl.

Then, Maya let go.

Her body rose and fell in a rush of passion that Marcus consumed like a glass of water. When he finally pulled away, his beard glistened against the glow of her desk lamp.

Maya collapsed in her seat; her legs silently vibrating as she tried to close them.

Marcus smirked, then said, "Sorry, I've been thinking about that all day. I couldn't help myself."

Maya sighed. "No qualms here." She said.

Marcus helped Maya slip back into her dress pants then rose from the floor.

"I have an idea." The corners of his mouth twitched with excitement and Maya was intrigued.

"What?" She asked.

"Why don't we spend the weekend at my place? Let me take care of *you* for the weekend and *we* can take a break from the Community Counsel. We'll put our phones on Do Not Disturb and unwind."

Maya sighed, "Marcus, I can't afford to..." He kissed Maya to muffle her objection. When he pulled away slowly, his eyes scanned hers.

"You need to take a break." His voice was barely a whisper. "We're gonna stay in, watch horrible scary movies and eat whatever you want."

Maya grinned. "Will there be wine?" She asked.

"And ice cream." Marcus said.

She laughed. "Let's do it."

Marcus waited in his truck while Maya packed for their staycation. He grabbed his phone and sent a check in message to Darnell. His best friend responded:

This kid deserves an Oscar.

Marcus laughed as he replied, then his phone vibrated. A new message arrived in his text inbox.

Kiana sent him a photo.

His heart dropped to the depth of his stomach. Marcus glanced ahead at the double glass doors to Maya's building. No sign of her; his eyes returned to his phone and he tapped the message to open the photo.

Regret washed over him.

In the photo Kiana wore a white lace bra with matching panties. Underneath the photo, she said:

> Can't figure out what to wear. Any suggestions?

Marcus' stomach turned. He returned to his message inbox to delete the message thread when three more photo notifications appeared.

Kiana was naked in every single one. Following the third photo, she said:

> This is what you could have had after lunch.

Marcus punched in his response to Kiana, demanding

her to stop but before he could press the blue arrow to send the message, Maya emerged from the double doors and walked eagerly toward his truck. He slipped his phone into his pocket, rubbed his face to clear off the shame and smiled at her.

Maya opened the back passenger door and tossed a black leather duffle bag and a purse in the back seat. When she climbed in beside him, Marcus grinned. "Damn. I said a weekend, not a week."

"You're not funny." Maya laughed.

Marcus kissed her. "Are you ready to be pampered?" He asked.

Maya smiled, "Of course."

By the time they were en route to his home, Kiana's messages— her photos, were in the rearview of his mind. He looked at Maya; her eyes shined in the afternoon's glow.

"You okay?" She asked.

A jolt of nervousness struck him like a bolt of lightning, but Marcus smiled harder. "Of course. Why?" he asked.

Maya shrugged. "I don't know. I thought you would be nervous. I mean this will be our first sleepover." The flirtation in her voice made his pants tight.

Marcus glanced at her, his smile beaming. He said. "We've been overdue."

Maya turned her head, but he could see the swell in cheekbones as she tried to conceal her smile.

"Are we blushing over there?" He asked. Maya peeked at him from over her shoulder. Marcus grazed Maya's thigh; she turned toward him then looked down at his hand. "Don't worry." He said. "I'm gonna take good care of you this weekend."

Maya's electric gaze met him and it took his breath away. "Me too." She said.

Her words vibrated throughout his body, a contrast to the vibration against his thigh.

Once.

Twice.

And a third time.

Marcus knew it was Kiana. And he knew he had to block her as soon as he could.

He should have blocked her after he left Celine's.

No.

She should have been blocked two years ago but Marcus refused to. The justification to keep the contact was always easier than admitting the truth.

What was the real reason?

Was it fear?

Or longing? Had he at one point still wanted her?

Did he still love her?

No. He didn't.

He had fallen for someone else. And he was happy again.

Marcus parked in front of his brownstone building. Maya climbed out of the truck first; she had swapped out her lively, pink work suit for a bright yellow tank top and black leggings. Her hair was gathered in a messy bun with strands framing her face and neck.

Marcus enjoyed the view while he retrieved her bag. She glanced up at him.

"Are you coming?" She asked.

"Are you?" Marcus grinned seeing the innuendo catching them both off guard.

Maya smirked. "Do you want me to?" She asked.

Marcus nodded. "Every time. Again and again." He said as he took her hand and led the way to his front door. When he opened the door another vibration surged through his thigh. Marcus carried his phone to a docking station in his living room.

Maya set her purse beside it then slipped out of her black Converse high tops. She let her bare feet sink into his rust colored shag area rug. "Oh, I am so ready for this weekend." She sighed then collapsed on Marcus' black sectional couch.

Marcus joined her, he knelt down beside her and caressed her face. Maya closed her eyes and her full smile widened. His body went stiff when she looked into his eyes and pulled him toward her. He slipped his hand under her tank top. His thumb grazed her bare nipple; the stout mound of flesh and nerves was already alert as if waiting for him.

Maya' body arched against the couch while her sounds of pleasure echoed through his home.

Marcus moved to her other breast but pulled away to look into her eyes. Her surrender was beautiful, and he loved to watch it all unfold to the point of climax. "Maya," he said, his voice encased in arousal. "Show me where you need me."

She nodded slowly but her hand was already guiding him to her leggings. When he slipped his hand between the fabric of her leggings and satin panties, his fingers glided along the thick, warm folds of her center. Another pleasurable moan escaped Maya's lips when Marcus' fingers met the hard nub of her clit. Maya shifted under his touch; she begged him to keep going.

He rubbed at her clit slowly, drawing circles around the small bud while studying her face. Her hips bucked when he tapped it; when he'd glide a finger inside her then retreated back to her real pleasure zone the loudest moans escaped her lips.

Marcus lifted her shirt and latched onto her nipple; Maya gasped before her body went into a frenzy. She reached for him, her manicured nails raked at his back ravenously. Marcus pulled away from her long enough to get his shirt over his head.

Maya stopped and he froze too.

"What's wrong?" He asked.

Maya shook her head, and her lips curved into a smile. "Where are your condoms?" She asked.

Marcus grinned but the amusement faded.

Fuck.

He didn't want to disturb their groove; his erection throbbed and he knew going down the hall, into his room then to his bathroom could slow things down. Marcus sighed.

" Don't worry." Maya said, "I do." Shirtless, Maya walked to her purse; she plucked a long, black leather wallet from her bag and opened it. When she pulled two red foiled squares from it then set her wallet down next to his docking station. Marcus sat down on the couch relieved and felt his erection recharge.

His phone lit up. From his distance, Marcus recognized the text notification. His stomach did a quick flip before leaping into his throat as he saw more notifications come in.

Please don't be her. He said to himself. *Please don't be her.*

Maya giggled. "Jeez, someone's popular."

"I can check it later." He said.

His phone vibrated two more times. Then once more.

Maya disconnected the phone from the docking station. "You better answer these before..." Her voice trailed off when she glanced at the screen. Her eyes were fixed on the notifications on his phone and when she looked up at him, all the joy had already drained from his face.

Maya stared at the bright screen of Marcus' phone. She blinked in hopes that her eyes and her head were playing some weird, sadistic trick. It was bad timing, but she hoped that it was indeed a trick.

It wasn't.

Her shaking hand clutched Marcus' phone with her watery eyes glued to the notification bar on his screen informing him *and* her that he had six new messages from someone named *Kiana*.

Her lips curved into a shape, but the words didn't come out. When she did speak, her voice shook. "Who is Kiana?"

Marcus stood stunned. His mouth wide open but his words were on a delay too.

Maya repeated the question. "Who is Kiana?" She moved closer to him, closing the gap between them.

The phone vibrated in her hand again. Another message. From Kiana.

Maya scoffed and then tossed the phone to Marcus. He fumbled to get a grip on it before he finally clutched it to his chest. Her eyes burned into his forehead while she anxiously waited for him to speak. The silence between them was thick as heavy as the humid air outside. Marcus glanced at the phone, his shoulders fell and he sighed.

"Marcus." The voice that came out wasn't Maya's. It was foreign and searing with pain. Fight or flight was triggering her while every red flag that she could imagine flooded her brain, sending warnings to her heart to abandon ship. But Maya stood there, half naked and boiling from the inside out. "Who is Kiana? Another girl you're talking to?"

"No." Marcus said. His mouth turned into a straight line across his face while the silence between them was setting her inner rage ablaze.

Maya asked, "Who is she, Marcus?"

Marcus bowed his head.

"Answer me." She snapped.

His eyes met hers again.

"My ex." His voice was exhausted. "Kiana is the ex that I told you about. Last month, she reached out to Olivia and asked about me."

Marcus crashed onto his couch, his phone slipped from

his hand but he didn't recover it. When he looked up at Maya, she saw fear swimming in his eyes. "I reached out to her to see what she wanted. She said that she wanted to catch up and asked me to lunch."

Maya held up a hand in protest and Marcus pursed his lips together. "You had lunch with her?" She asked.

"We were supposed to meet for coffee."

"And that turned into lunch?" She spat.

Marcus sighed and said, "I ended up leaving though. I just wanted to tell her that I was over her."

"Clearly she doesn't think so if she's still messaging you." Maya said. She paused a beat then asked, "Have you been talking to her since then?" Maya asked.

"She'll send random texts but I never respond." He said.

Maya swallowed hard. "Does she send you nudes?" She asked.

Marcus' eyes shifted away from her.

Maya scoffed. "Why would you even entertain any type of conversation with her?" She bit her lip. The physical pain kept the tears at bay, so she bit into her bottom lip harder until the metallic taste of blood coated her tongue. "This was a bad idea. I need to go."

Maya slipped her tank top back on. Marcus jumped from his seat. "Maya, wait a second. I can explain this." He said.

His words, his pleas were muffled against the rage that burned between her ears. Maya grabbed her duffle bag then her purse. When Marcus grabbed her wrist, his voice broke through the white noise in her head.

"Maya, I can explain this." He said.

Maya shook her head. "Don't. I knew that this was a bad idea." She said.

Marcus' hand fell and his face shifted like she punched him in the stomach. "Maya, you don't mean that." Regret hung in the air between them.

Maya hurried to the door with Marcus at her heels. "Maya, wait a second. Can't we talk about this?" He asked.

"No." She said, "I-I can't talk about it right now. With everything that I have going on..." She paused then pointed past him to the phone Marcus had abandoned on the floor. "I don't need this right now."

"Maya please." Marcus reached for her arm again, but Maya opened the door and stepped into the early evening. "Maya, wait a minute. You don't have to leave."

She wanted to stop, turn back and yell at him *then* talk about it and make up all at the same time, but she couldn't. The pain was outweighing the opportunity.

Maya ordered an Uber instead.

Seventeen

Rain had threatened the skies over Cascade City, and it felt like perfect timing when a heavy rainfall consumed the city on a gloomy Friday morning. Maya kicked herself for deciding to come into work instead of working from home another day, but some files she needed were in her office, plus she realized that she couldn't hide from Marcus for too much longer.

She had kept their virtual interactions via the office's messaging system professional and even swapped the wallpaper on her phone from a cozy photo of them to a scenic photo she took on a trip to Italy last year. She needed him out of her head, so she braved the cold rain to drive to the office only to find that most of the staff had decided to work from home.

"Great." She mumbled as she tossed her briefcase into an open chair in front of her desk then peeled off her gold blazer, saturated in rain. She went to close her door when Robert appeared in her doorway. Maya squealed and jumped.

"Oh Jesus. I'm sorry, Maya. I thought you heard me coming." He said.

"I didn't." She gasped.

"Sorry." He said. "What are you doing here anyway? I figured you would be working from home again."

Maya shook her head as she walked around to her side of the desk. She sat down, grabbed a few Kleenex from the acrylic box on her desk and dabbed the rain off of her face. "No. I was getting cabin fever."

"I bet. You know your guy was moping around here all week. Looking like someone kicked his puppy." Robert grinned at his own jab.

"I'm sure he's fine." She said.

Robert's brow arched. "Trouble in paradise?"

"No." Maya responded so quickly that she knew retracting her statement would only make matters worse. She cleared her throat and forced a smile so hard it triggered a mild headache. "We're good. This project has just taken a toll on us." It was a good cover but when Maya watched Robert take the other vacant chair alongside her briefcase, she knew he didn't buy a single word.

"Maya, you seem to forget that I know you damn near

better than I know my own son." She nodded but kept her eyes low. "So you know that I know when you're bullshitting me, right?"

"Yes." She said softly.

"Good. Now why don't you tell me what's really going on."

And she did. Maya told Robert about the flood of messages that came to Marcus' phone; she left out the fact that they were about to have sex when it all happened— he didn't need to know everything. When she was done, she exhaled hard and dabbed at her eyes with a fresh Kleenex.

Robert sat back in the chair, one leg over the other with his hands in prayer in front of his mouth.

Maya recognized that look; she studied it for years in and outside of the courtroom, but to see it firsthand— to be on the other end of Robert Turner's contemplative gaze made her feel like a defendant on the stand. He blinked slowly then lowered his hands to his lap. He studied his cuff links but spoke directly to Maya.

"I know that I may have been rough on Marcus the last time we sat down face to face, but you know what?"

"What?" Maya asked.

"I actually like the guy. Here I was thinking that he was like that dick Derek you dated. Arrogant, emotionally detached and just an all-out ass but he isn't. He's smart, hardworking and Elena and I can see that he's head over heels for you."

More tears stung her eyes. Maya tapped the inner corners of her eyes with more Kleenex. "Head over heels yet still talking to his ex?" She scoffed.

Robert leaned forward and asked, "Did you give him a chance to explain?"

Maya sat up straight as if she was struck by a rod of lightning.

Robert chuckled. "You know if Elena was here right now, she would pop you for being so damn stubborn. You didn't even give the man a chance to explain himself."

"Why would I?" She asked. "He admitted that he did text her from time to time. What more did I need to know?"

"Since when do you accuse someone without proper questioning? You're Special Counsel and *you* know how to cross examine a defendant."

Maya grinded her teeth then said, "This isn't a court case, Robert."

He shook his head. "It's not and yet you're treating it like one."

Maya opened her mouth to object his statement but Robert's raised, open palm stopped her. "You think love makes a relationship bulletproof?" He sat back in the chair and chuckled.

"Who said I loved him?" She asked.

Robert grinned as he said, "You do. You're in love but a roadblock came and you detoured."

Maya glared at Robert. She pursed her lips together and crossed her arms. Robert leaned forward again. "You are stubborn as hell." He said. "Your father would be proud but now is not the time for you to be a bull in a China shop."

"I'm not." Maya said.

Robert cut her off again. "Yes you are, and you refuse to admit that the only reason why it hurt you to see another woman's name on that man's phone was because you love him. If this was, what do y'all call it now? A booty call?"

"Hookups, Robert. We just call them *hookups* now." Maya said, struggling to hide the amusement in her voice.

Robert smiled. "Whatever you call them, if it was just that then who's on his phone wouldn't matter, right?" He asked.

"Yeah."

"See! Now what you need to do is call Marcus. Talk to him and most importantly listen to him. He deserves that much."

Maya let the tears fall freely and she watched Robert's smile soften. "You know what you need to do. I'll see you on Monday." He said and rose from the chair.

"Are you leaving early?" Maya asked.

Robert glanced at her from the threshold of her office. "*You* are. Enjoy your weekend, Maya." When he disappeared from her door, Maya snatched up her leather briefcase and grabbed her phone from a side pocket.

She looked into the dark screen; she needed a reason to call him.

A good one.

Olivia gave the summit team a break while she took a trip to New Orleans and all the technical elements for the Community Counsel Initiative were completed to ready to run.

Maya unlocked her phone and sucked in a deep breath. She'd play it by ear.

Her phone vibrated in her hand.

It was a message from Marcus.

Maya scrambled to get to her message inbox. He had sent a picture. She opened the attachment; in the photo he held a long, black leather wallet.

Maya's wallet.

In addition to the photo he sent, he sent a message:

> How have you managed to survive an entire week without your damn wallet?!

Maya erupted in laughter then responded:

> Who waits an entire week to tell someone they left their wallet at their house?

She watched the three dots dance at the bottom of the screen, then Marcus responded:

> Touché

Maya typed back:

> Return what is mine for a hefty reward.

Marcus clutched Maya's wallet to his chest like a newborn baby. When the elevator doors opened to her floor, he hurried down the long corridor with his heart drumming. The week snaked by at the slowest pace he had ever felt and despite their workload increasing by the day, Marcus could not focus. Instead, he studied the innards of Maya's wallet.

After her abrupt departure, he found it abandoned alongside his docking station.

The scene of the crime.

He studied her Driver's License, noted her library card and a punch card for Java Peak that he considered snatching because she was just two punches away from a free drink. Behind two twenties, he found a photo. The frayed photo had a little girl, an older boy and a tall man. On the back of the photo, Marcus recognized Maya's neat, slanted handwriting:

Me, Jerrod and Dad, 1989.

Younger Maya had a rounder face and chubby cheeks, but those almond shaped eyes were the same. They shined despite the age of the photo. She and her brother were dressed in Sunday best, just like their father. Marcus imagined Maya carried the photo as a remembrance of her brother and father. She needed those memories back which served as the perfect excuse to hear her voice again.

Two birds. One stone, right?

But once he made the plan, fear consumed his last ounce of courage.

"Just tell her how you feel." Darnell told him. "Don't sugar coat it. Own up to your shit."

"But she hates me." Marcus said. "I fucked up. I shouldn't have even entertained talking to Kiana."

"But you did and now you gotta play Keith Sweat and beg yo' ass off." Darnell then went into his own rendition of Sweat's *I Want Her* which made Marcus chuckle harder than he wanted to.

Darnell was right; he had to tell Maya how he felt and what he wanted.

Marcus wanted Maya.

He stood in front of her door; her wallet still affixed to his chest. Marcus wrapped his knuckles on the door melodically then waited. There was a beat of silence, then the door opened. Maya stood in the doorway, barefaced with her hair tied up in a bun. Marcus could see every feature in her face and when she smiled, he thought of the little girl in the picture.

"I think this is..." She stopped him with a kiss. Marcus wrapped her into his arms and carried her back into the apartment. When they pulled away to breathe, Marcus said, "Maya, I'm sorry that I didn't tell you about Kiana. I should have told you right away." He paused to study her face. "When we met for lunch, she asked me why I came too. I told her that I had to prove to myself that I was over her."

"Are you over her?" Maya asked.

"Yes." His voice cracked and he felt tears burning the rims of his eyes. He held Maya's face in his hands. "I'm sorry." He said. "I love you, Maya."

His heart raced but when Maya looked into his eyes and smiled, Marcus felt his world resetting. The jagged edges of life were coming together to create something new.

"I shouldn't have walked away like I did but I was hurt. And it hurt because I love you." She said. Tears reflected in her eyes. "I'm sorry."

Maya fell into his chest; her sobs absorbed by his t-shirt. Marcus wrapped his arms around her and held her tight. He cupped her chin then raised her head to see her face again.

"You think, we can pick up where we left off at your place?" She asked.

"Before the fight?" He grinned.

Maya nodded.

"And where did we leave off again?"

"*I* was headed to you on the couch, but we can start in the bedroom this time." Maya toyed with the hem of her black V-neck shirt.

"Or we can start right here." Marcus picked Maya up, her legs locked around his waist like magnets as he pressed her back against the door.

When Marcus woke up, the soft neon LED clock alongside Maya's bed notified him that it was just a few minutes shy of four a.m. He glanced down and smiled at Maya in the darkness. She laid on his chest, her nude body flushed and warm against his. Somewhere between the couch and the bedroom, her top bun unraveled, and her soft, unruly curls were all over the place. He ran his hand over her smooth skin; his fingers lingered over the curve in her shoulders to the dip in her lower back. Her body fluttered underneath his touch, and she nestled deeper into him.

After he slipped out of the bed to go to the bathroom, he returned to find Maya awake and staring at him. "What are you doing awake?" He whispered.

"Why are you whispering?" She whispered back playfully.

He returned to bed and kissed Maya's forehead. Her hand caressed his chest while she kissed a trail from his neck to his collarbone.

Marcus moaned softly. "You're going to start something." He said.

Her lips pressed against his chest while her hand slid beneath the sheet. Her fingers grazed his thighs before brushing against his awaiting erection.

"You act like I'm scared." She said. Her breath was warm against his skin and sent a sensual chill through his body. She held him firmly then started a steady motion; slow strokes while she praised him in a hushed voice.

"Good boy." She said. "That's it. Just like that."

Marcus's body became an instrument under her instruction. Her words ignited pockets of ecstasy while she edged him to the point of no return. His moans became grunts.

"Baby." He moaned. "W-wait."

"No." She said. "Enjoy it."

Marcus groaned and Maya giggled. "Good. Let it out, baby."

With every word of praise, she stroked a little faster, a little harder. "That's it." She said, "Don't hold back, baby.

You deserve this."

He was losing control; the more she praised him, the quicker she stroked him until Marcus felt himself explode from the inside out.

"Shit." He hissed. Beneath the veil of darkness, he saw stars burst beneath his eyelids and his body tingled. Marcus reached for Maya's face; he held her chin and looked at her. "I love you." He breathed. "I fucking love you." His kiss was feverish and passionate. "Come here." Marcus pulled Maya onto him, his erection still aching and anticipating more of her.

The night wasn't over just yet.

PART FIVE | JULY 2023

Eighteen

♥

The annual Sterling, Turner and Associates Fourth of July cookout was hosted by Robert and Elena. Next to their Christmas parties, it was one of the events that everyone in the office looked forward to the most because it meant great food, unlimited alcohol and Maya's infamous desserts.

For the year's event, InnovateCore was added to the guest list, so Robert resigned as the grill master and asked Marcus to man the grill instead. "You proved yourself with those lamb chops." Robert said to him when they arrived ahead of everyone. "And I trust you. Consider this the passing of a torch. From a father to a son." The two made a big spectacle of the moment; Robert passed his grill tools to Marcus ,who kneeled before him to accept them.

Maya and Elena laughed at their dramatization. "He can be so dramatic sometimes. I apologize in advance for him,

Marcus." Elena said.

"This is an honor." Marcus said. He added to the drama when he wiped away invisible tears. "Thank you, Mr. Turn- Robert. Thank you."

While the men were at the grill, Maya and Elena worked diligently in the Turners' picturesque kitchen.

Their kitchen was bright with white, marble countertops, white birchwood cabinets and gold accents on everything. The large island in the middle of the kitchen could serve as a dining room table and a bar alongside a dual sink. Their range stove was restaurant quality with six burners and a double oven. A large, stainless steel exhaust system glistened under the range lights. A breakfast nook made of white birchwood completed the look of the space, surrounded by windows that looked out into their massive backyard.

"So what decadent desserts are we having tonight?" Elena asked. "When I asked you to send me a list of items to pick up, you were pretty hush hush about the final results."

Maya nodded with a grin. "I was because I wanted it to be a surprise even for you." She set a rectangular cooler on the large, marble island then opened the lid. "I'm making my lava cakes too, but I made these." Maya set three large, air tight sealed glass bowls onto the table and smiled.

Elena stared at the frosted containers before she clasped her hands together and squealed. "Did you make home-made ice cream?"

"And a sorbet for the vegans." Maya said.

"Oh, my goodness." Elena picked up one of the containers and opened the lid. She stared at a bright yellow, frozen mixture in amazement. "The sorbet?"

"Yes. Limoncello." Maya said.

"I gotta try this." Elena said. "I have to try this right now." She pulled a small spoon from a drawer in the island then scooped up a sample serving. Maya beamed when she saw the exact moment the sorbet met Elena's tongue.

Elena's eyes fluttered behind their lids and she did a little dance. "Oh Maya. This is heavenly. I'm not vegan but I could eat this all day." She said.

"Thank you. I caught Marcus indulging in some early this morning." Maya said. She glanced outside to Robert and Marcus. She beamed while she looked at Marcus. He was using his hands to explain something to Robert.

"You're glowing." Elena said.

"No, I'm sweating." Maya said.

Elena asked, "He makes you happy doesn't he?"

"Absolutely." Maya said.

"You look..." Elena paused, then said with a smile, "Refreshed."

Maya blushed at the underlying notion.

"I know the feeling." Elena said, "Robert gets me like that too."

Maya's brow shifted up. "Is that right?"

"Of course." They giggled then Elena asked, "How's the initiative going?"

Maya exhaled as she made her way to the large sink to wash her hands. "There's been another delay." Maya said.

Elena leaned on the island; her head tilted and eyes full of concern. "Another? Since when?" She asked.

"I have no clue." Maya said. "But you know how Tim is."

Elena rolled her eyes. "I do." She said, "And what did my husband say?"

Maya rested her elbows on the island and looked at Elena's beautiful, round face. "He told me that Tim had more questions, and he wanted to address them before we moved forward."

Elena carried two bunches of Romaine lettuce to the sink, Maya intercepted and started to clean them. "What are you doing while Tim makes you sweat it out?" She asked.

"Marcus and Darnell have been sweeping the website for bugs again." Maya replied. "And I have been visiting local colleges to introduce myself and the program. And we're wrapping everything up for the Community Summit next month."

"Oh yes. Robert and I are excited about that. I can't wait to see that mural." Elena said.

"It's been hell keeping it under wraps." Maya said. "Just last month, Olivia had to hire security guards because people have been trying to sneak photos or vandalize it."

Elena shook her head. "That's horrible but I know all this hard work is going to pay off tenfold. Trust me, I know it."

An hour before dusk, guests arrived and ushered themselves into Robert and Elena's backyard. Marcus had wrapped up a round of lamb burgers that Robert instructed him to guard with his life. Marcus hid them in the oven, away from guests' eyes and alerted Robert of their whereabouts when the coast was clear. Robert approved with a single thumb up and a promise to share his "private stock" with him after the party.

When Darnell arrived with his son, Quentin, the little boy raced toward Marcus and threw his arms around his neck squeezing with all his might.

"Uncle Marcus." Quentin sang his name and Marcus

locked him in his arms.

When they pulled away, Marcus eyed the young boy's clean bald fade. "Look at you. Ya Daddy took you to the barbershop today?"

The little boy's head bobbed up and down. "Daddy said we had to be clean today because he said that there would be lots of pretty women here and—"

"Hey boy!" Darnell appeared beside them. "Don't be repeating what I said. I said that in private."

Quentin giggled then looked past Marcus; he turned to see what he was focusing on. Maya was waving at him from a few feet away. "You know her?" Marcus asked.

Darnell's son shook his head.

"You wanna meet her?" Marcus grinned. "Come on. Let's show off this fresh cut then."

He carried Quentin to Maya. She greeted them with a warm smile then raised an eyebrow.

"Party crasher?" She said, winking at Quentin.

"Lil' dude said that he wanted to meet the most beautiful woman here tonight, so I brought him straight to you." Marcus said.

Maya's smile blossomed into her eyes before she planted a soft kiss on his cheek. She looked at Quentin. "And what's your name, party crasher?" She asked.

"Quentin Epps. You can call me 'Q'." He said.

"Well, it's very nice to meet you, Q. I'm Maya."

Quentin grinned and said, "Hi Maya. I'm not a party crasher. I came here with my dad."

"Oh yeah? What's your dad's name?"

Quentin's round eyes swelled. He looked at Marcus, then Maya and back to Marcus. "I can't say it." He whispered.

Maya stepped closer. "Could you whisper it to me? Don't worry. I won't tell." Marcus beamed as he watched their exchange. Maya and Quentin whispered back and forth and giggled between glances at each other.

"You know, I know your dad too?" Maya said. Quentin shook his head. "Yep. He's pretty cool."

"Not as cool as Uncle Marcus." Quentin said. "But don't tell my dad I said that."

"Secret's safe with us." Marcus said.

"Quentin, are you hungry?" Maya asked.

"Yeah." He said.

"How about I show you around while Uncle Marcus and your dad have some bro time." Maya said. "And then we can raid the table over there." Maya pointed to a six foot long table ahead of them, filled with a buffet of foods.

Quentin's eyes widened; he smiled, showing all of his teeth except for a missing one at the top.

"Let's go!" He pushed away from Marcus, signaling

his release. Marcus obliged and released Quentin to the ground.

Quentin took Maya's hand.

"We'll be back." Maya said then trotted off with Quentin at her side. Marcus watched them until a crowd of guests obstructed his view.

"That's the quickest I've ever seen that boy take to a woman." Darnell said. "There are times when he can't even stand his mama."

Marcus laughed then hugged Darnell. "Glad you made it, bro."

"Hell, when you said free food and drinks, I knew I couldn't miss this. Plus, I've always wanted to check this area out." Darnell's eyes scanned the lawn, his face was a little harder than Marcus wanted it to be but he knew what Darnell was doing.

He was looking for bugs. People who would be a potential problem for him, Quentin and Marcus. Darnell whistled. "Jeez, this place is packed. All these people work for the firm?"

"Yep and their guests." Marcus said. "Robert is around here somewhere." Marcus scanned the crowd. "Come on, let's get you a beer then we can socialize."

Darnell nodded. "Lead the way."

Marcus and Darnell walked through the crowd and

stopped at a galvanized tub filled with ice, beer, hard seltzer drinks and bottled water. He grabbed two bottles of Stella— a request he forwarded to Robert days before, then handed one to Darnell. They opened the bottles in unison. "Cheers." Marcus said.

"Happy Fourth." Darnell said. Their bottlenecks clinked then they drank. "So, *this* is where you've been spending most of your time when you're not in the office?"

"Or Maya's place. Or mine." Marcus grinned.

"You and Robert buried the hatchet, huh?"

Marcus was mid-swig when he nodded. "Yeah, we're cool now. He's a good dude." He said.

Darnell didn't say anything. He took another drink and scanned the lawn again. "And you and Maya? Ya'll good?"

"Better than good." Marcus smiled harder than he intended but he didn't care, "Things are great."

"I'm glad you didn't let—"

Marcus cut him off. "Please don't say her name," he said. "I don't wanna hear *her* name ever again."

Darnell shrugged his shoulders, but Marcus saw the corners of his mouth upturn. "Now tell me the truth." The smile that Darnell had preserved transformed into a full grin. "Is Maya it for you?"

"Is she what?" Marcus asked.

Darnell shoved him playfully. "Stop playing. You know

what I mean. Is Maya the one? You two have been going pretty hot and heavy for a few months now. Y'all had your first big fight. Her boss and his wife seem to love you, and y'all do look good together." Darnell said.

"Thanks, D." Marcus said. Marcus stared across the lawn at Maya; she waved at him and smiled before she and Quentin toasted with cupcakes. "She's all I need."

Marcus, Maya, Darnell and Quentin made their way throughout the backyard. Maya introduced Darnell and Marcus to members of Sterling and Turner's IT team and some part time paralegals. In between random conversations, Marcus watched Elena snap photos of guests with her instant film camera. When she caught him and Maya, Marcus wrapped Maya in his arms and grinned.

Elena said, "Hold it." There was a quick flash then the camera ejected the photo. Elena fanned the photo, took a look at it then smiled. "This is my favorite of the night." She handed the photo to Marcus. "See."

Marcus said, "I love this. We look good, don't we, baby?"

Maya looked at the picture and said. "Oh yes." She snatched the photo from his fingers and slipped in the back pocket of her olive green shorts. "This is mine." She giggled.

As the evening moved on, Marcus and Darnell grew comfortable alongside the staff of the law firm. Marcus's grill skills were praised, Darnell talked sports with a few paralegals and people begged Maya for her recipes. "I haven't perfected them yet." Maya told a woman who Marcus recognized as one of the receptionists.

"She's cute." Darnell said. Darnell then winked at Quentin; his son's cue to move in and he did.

Quentin approached the slender, dark skinned woman with two-strand twisted locs and showed her an action figure he had tucked in his khaki cargo shorts. Marcus and Maya watched Quentin's performance play out before he took the woman's hand, leading her to the food table.

"Oh, he's good." Maya laughed.

"My boy." Darnell chuckled. "I'll be right back." He slipped out of the circle, looked around, then called for his son as if he hadn't watched him lure the receptionist to the table like it was home base.

Marcus looked at Maya. She peered at him through lowered lids. "I swear I had no idea that he was doing that." He said and held up his hands in surrender.

Maya laughed. "That's *your* friend though." She said.

"Wait a minute." He chuckled. They argued playfully

until Marcus noticed a tall white man approaching their circle carrying a glass of wine and donning a broad smile. Marcus recognized the man from the photos in the office and at the press conference where Maya announced her now delayed initiative.

It was Timothy Sterling in the flesh.

The lanky man wore dark blue Bermuda shorts and a Hawaiian shirt in the same hue, covered in white flowers. Timothy had been absent in the office but his presence was always felt. And when he needed to say something to Maya or anyone, he sent his partner aka his lackey, Robert. In private, Marcus joked with Maya; calling the two "Ebony and Ivory."

This was his first time meeting Ivory.

As Timothy smiled at Maya, Marcus noticed his dull, uncapped teeth and his crooked, bottom row. His cold, blue eyes stole a glance at Maya then his thin, pink lips became a formidable sneer. His uncomfortable gaze and smile sent a chill through Marcus. He imagined Timothy watching Maya's every move in the office or calling her into his office for private meetings, where he could be alone with her.

"Marcus, right?" Timothy asked. Marcus blinked only to realize he had missed some form of an introduction. Timothy's icy eyes were set on him and he had his free, large hand extended toward him. Marcus studied the awaiting, open palm. He felt a moment of hesitation run down his back like a bead of sweat.

Marcus grabbed Tim's hand and shook it vigorously. "Timothy Sterling?"

"Yes. Just Tim though." He said. With their hands still clasped, Tim gave Marcus' hand a squeeze. "It's so great to finally meet you in person." Tim said.

"Likewise." Marcus said. The grip and the relentless gaze felt personal to Marcus. The small crowd around them resumed their side conversations and the soft jazz that flooded the Bluetooth speakers around the backyard faded in his ears.

Marcus released his hand and Tim's laugh boomed through the air. "I have heard some great things about you and your team. I hear you work for a great tech company." He said.

"Actually, we own it." Marcus said. He bit back a snide remark, for Maya's sake and mirrored Tim Sterling's pained smile. "InnovateCore has been the number one tech company in the Chicagoland area for the last four years now."

"Good for you." Sterling's tone was more condescending than celebratory "And Maya chose you to work with on this big project."

Marcus said, "She did." He straightened up.

"You know, I recommended that she go with Tech Sphere. We have a great history with them, and I think *they* are one of the top tech businesses in the Chicagoland area too. Do you know Chris at Tech Sphere?"

"We know Tech Sphere and Chris." Marcus said. "And they fell out of the top ten two years ago when they were found using artificial intelligence to draft codes."

Tim shrugged off Marcus's comment. "Isn't AI the next wave for tech anyway?"

Marcus said nothing.

"Nonetheless, I trust Chris and his team." Tim said.

Marcus' brow tightened. "You don't trust ICore?" He asked.

Tim finished his wine, it was red.

Marcus laughed to himself. What was it with these stuffy lawyers and red wine? The stuff was like a truth serum for them.

Tim peered at his wine glass as if staring at it would manifest another full glass on its own. After a brief pause, he returned his attention to Marcus. "It's not that I don't trust your business, son."

Son. The word felt like a hot fire poker to Marcus' ribs.

Tim said, "I would just prefer to keep ties with—"

"With who?" Marcus's voice boomed.

Tim smiled again, unfazed by Marcus but his eyes were glazed over. Marcus could smell alcohol oozing from his pores.

"Whoa now, Son. No need to."

"I am not your 'son'." Marcus said. "My name is Marcus. You owe me that much respect."

The music died down and Marcus could feel everyone's eyes on them.

"Babe." Maya's voice cut through the anger that was clouding him. She tugged at his arm. "Babe." Her melodic voice soothed him.

Marcus saw Darnell and Quentin rejoin their circle.

Tim's shit eating grin spread over his narrow face as if he knew something that no one else did. "I see it now." He said, looking at Maya then Marcus. "How long has this love connection been happening?" He waved a long finger between the two of them. "This is how you got the gig, huh?"

"That's enough, Tim." Robert's voice spliced the tension as he approached them with Elena in tow.

Tim stared at Robert but pointed at Maya and Marcus. "Did you know about this, Robert? Huh? Did you approve of *this*?"

"Approve?" Maya stepped forward. Marcus used his arm as a barricade. Her eyes were so dim Marcus thought that she was on the verge of tears. He grabbed her hand and squeezed it tight; the pressure grounded the both of them.

"I think you've had enough to drink for the night, Tim." Robert said.

Elena said, "In fact, I think you should call it a night." Her round face was stiff and her smooth brow rippled. "Call yourself an Uber and get home."

Tim spun in a small circle to smile at every face he came in contact with until his glassy eyes stopped on Marcus and Maya again. "I had a full background check completed on you and your partner." He scoffed. "I'm looking forward to discussing the results with you when they arrive."

Marcus pursed his lips together to hold in the rage that was boiling over inside him. He squeezed Maya's hand tighter as they watched Timothy Sterling, Esquire stumble out of the backyard just as the first round of fireworks shot into the dark, night sky.

Nineteen

♥

Maya stepped onto the fourth floor office space of Sterling, Turner and Associates feeling excited. After Sterling's behavior at the Fourth of July party, he released the hold on the Community Counsel Initiative and blessed Maya to move forward at her own pace. She decided that she would roll it out the same day as the Summit.

"Baby, we have to celebrate." Marcus told her earlier that morning as they drank coffee and dressed for the day. "I'm making dinner for two tonight." He said.

Maya said, "Oh yeah?" She slipped into a black, pleated skirt then tucked her v-neck t-shirt into it.

"Yes. A three course meal with wine *and* dessert." Marcus pulled Maya onto his lap. Her skirt spilled over his legs, and she felt him throb against her bare thigh.

Temptation ignited.

Marcus kissed her neck then let his lips linger on her collarbone as he spoke. "Just me and you. Celebrating this wonderful moment." He kissed her neck again.

Maya swooned, "That sounds." She stopped.

Marcus' lips returned to her collarbone and his hands massaged her lower back.

"Oh God." She moaned. Maya kissed him hard, pressed her body against his bare chest and Marcus let them crash onto the bed.

Maya savored the playback, but her joy burst like a balloon when she saw Robert and Timothy in her office. Robert sat on her office loveseat while Timothy sat in a chair at her desk. "Jesus." She said, setting her briefcase down but not taking her eyes off her bosses as if they were two gunmen ready to pull their triggers. "A heads up would have been nice." She said.

Robert was the first to speak but his voice felt distant. "Sorry, Maya. We didn't mean to startle you." He said.

"It's alright." She said. Maya examined both men closely. They were polar opposites; Robert sat deflated while his partner sat upright and exalted. Maya noticed a hint of delight on Tim's face and his eyes were electrifying. Maya had never experienced them in such a stark tandem. At least not before the Fourth of July party.

Maya spoke, "What's going on?" The words came slowly but her heart had picked up a frantic pace and her stomach churned with nervous disgust.

Robert pursed his lips together and the soft smile on Tim's face went into full bloom. "Is anyone going to say anything?" Maya asked.

Tim shifted to the edge of the chair. He said, "Maya, we just received some news from Human Resources that we wanted— no, we need to share with you."

Human Resources. What the hell could they want with her? She sat down in her chair, her eyes darting between the two partners. Robert's eyes never met hers, they were focused on the swirls within the area rug on her floor as if they were ancient artifacts.

Tim spoke again. "It appears that ICore is connected to some unethical business transactions."

Maya blinked hard and said, "What kind of unethical business transactions?"

Tim pulled his phone from the breast pocket inside of his suit jacket. His thumbs moved feverishly over the large screen, then stopped. He turned his phone to Maya. "ICore took a large sum of money from Wayne Carlson."

Maya looked at Timothy. "Why should *we* care about their financials?" She asked.

"Well, it appears that Carlson has been outed." Tim said. His wide grin stretched further and Maya imagined his face splitting in two.

"For what?" Maya asked.

Tim's grin went sinister and rigid. He said, "Maya, Carlson launders money for drug dealers in Mexico."

"What?" She said.

"Looks like your boyfriend withheld some very important information from you." Timothy said. "Now the real question is, what do *we* do?"

Marcus ignored his phone as it vibrated against his thigh; he lost count of the number of times the soft vibration surged up and down his leg in the last half hour. He had hailed the day an off day which meant that there was no such thing as an 'emergency' for the next twenty-four hours and if someone really needed a member of ICore, they could always contact Darnell.

From his truck to the door, his phone vibrated four more times. Whoever it was, they would have to wait and if they couldn't, there was always *Tech Sphere*.

That thought made him chuckle.

With his duffle bag pressing into his shoulder, he juggled a cluster of plastic and paper bags in both hands while unlocking the double locks on the door to his townhouse. Marcus slipped out of his black Jordans then let his duffle bag drop to the floor. He passed through his living room, entered his kitchen, disarming the bags on the granite counter. Marcus glanced at his watch; it was almost noon and a notification on the digital watch face told him that he missed a dozen calls from Darnell.

Marcus pulled his phone from his pocket; the notification on his phone's screen also mentioned that Darnell left five voicemails and one urgent text message:

CALL ME ASAP

Darnell's message was accompanied by the two red exclamation points emoji.

This was serious. Darnell only used the red exclamation points whenever he was in over his head on a date and he needed Marcus to call him so he could give his date an excuse to leave.

Since when did Darnell go on dates during the week and before eight p.m.?

Marcus grinned then punched in a quick message:

You're on your own today, D. I'm off.

He considered setting his phone to *Do Not Disturb* but reconsidered it just in case Darnell really needed to be bailed out. Instead, he checked that the ringer was off and set his phone face down on the counter. Marcus pulled groceries from the bags; his mind recalling the grocery list he logged into his silenced phone. He promised Maya a three course meal that morning and as soon as he climbed into his car, he started planning his menu.

Marcus chose Italian for dinner: Caprese Salad, Italian Braised Beef with Parmesan Polenta and Roasted Broccolini. For dessert, he chose Vanilla Bean Panna Cotta—store bought of course but it was the thought that counted, right?

He added two bottles of red wine and a white to a corner wine rack and heard his phone vibrate against the countertop. "Not now, D." He said. Marcus snatched his phone, stormed into his living room and set it on the docking station.

Out of sight. Out of mind.

Marcus looked around the living room; the space felt stale and neglected. He pulled a cordless vacuum from its charging post in the kitchen and returned to the living room when he heard three knocks echoing from the hallway. Marcus peered at his front door from the living room's archway. The frosted sidelights were free of obstructions, but he held his breath and stood firm. If he didn't move, maybe whoever it was would go away.

They didn't.

Another round of knocks came from the front door. Marcus sighed and shuffled to the door. Whoever it was on the other would have to leave immediately. He unlocked both locks then swung the door open and froze.

"Kiana?" He said.

She stood on the other side of the threshold smiling with her eyes hidden behind a pair of oversized sunglasses. "You're home. Thank goodness."

"Kiana, how the hell did you find my house?"

She removed her sunglasses; her eyes were wide with concern; her lips were just a straight line across her face. "Are you okay?" She asked.

"I'm fine." Marcus said. "How did you find my..." He stopped as Kiana stepped closer to him.

She stood inches away from him. Kiana looked up into his face. "Can I come in?"

"No. You're not welcome here."

She smirked then frowned. "I think you'll want to hear what I have to say if you don't already know." "No." Kiana stepped past Marcus, pressing her body against him then strutting down the hallway. Her voice trailed behind her.

"I knew I had to check on you and make sure that you were okay."

Marcus closed the door then hurried down the hall. Kiana stood in his kitchen as if she had been there before. She held one of the stainless steel refrigerator doors.

"I'm fine. How did you know where I lived?" Marcus asked again.

Kiana pulled a black takeout bowl from the refrigerator. She pulled back the clear lid on, raised it to her nose the wretched. She tossed the bowl on the counter. "When was the last time you cleaned your fridge?"

"Kiana." Marcus's voice bellowed.

That smile returned and Marcus hated it. She knew something that he didn't and she was loving it. "Well since you blocked me for real this time. I had to do some recon to find you and talk to you."

"We have nothing to talk about." Marcus said.

Kiana scoffed then dug into the pocket of the cropped pink vest she wore as a top. She pulled out her cell phone but said nothing.

Marcus kept his distance but watched Kiana swipe through her phone. She paused then walked toward him. "It looks like ICore is connected to money laundering." She said. Kiana held up her phone for Marcus to view.

He stared at the screen. There was a picture of Wayne

Carlson, dressed in a black tux with the headline above him silently screaming the end of ICore.

Marcus' mouth was dry; he tried to speak but he only repeated the words he read just seconds before. "Money laundering. Money laundering. This is a joke." He said.

Kiana shook her head. "Afraid not. It's been trending all morning. You didn't know?"

Marcus glanced at his phone nestled in the docking station; a pit was widening in stomach and his heart jackhammered in his chest.

All those missed calls from Darnell. He heard the news first and tried to let Marcus know. Instead, he had to hear it from his narcissistic ex-girlfriend who arrived on his doorstep at the worst time. Marcus returned his gaze to Kiana; she sat on the arm of his sectional, legs crossed and beaming at him. Her smile was turning his stomach; he wanted her to leave.

She needed to leave because if Kiana knew, Maya had to know which meant that the firm knew. The pit in his stomach became a boulder. Marcus collapsed into a stool at his counter.

"Fuck." He breathed. Reality was shattering before him; jagged pieces of his life were floating through his brain. Marcus thought of Maya again. She knew everything about the deal. What if Sterling and Turner questioned her about the money they received? What if they accused her of being in on the deal?

Marcus rubbed the back of his neck then glanced over to his phone. The screen was dark, but it was just a matter of time before it was ringing again. Who would it be then?

Darnell?

Maya?

"Kiana, you gotta go." Marcus said.

Kiana rose from the end of the couch, her smile was still fused to her face as she inched closer to him.

"You look stressed, Marcus. I can't imagine what you're going through."

His voice went flat. "Kiana."

"I'm going." She said but her steps were advancing to him and not the hallway. Her eyes smoldered and Marcus could feel the heat radiating from her. She moved closer and closer until he could feel her breath on his bottom lip. Kiana's eyes flicked up. "But I can't leave without saying goodbye."

Kiana's arms snaked around Marcus's neck then she pressed her lips to his. It was the electric shock that he didn't need. Her arms locked around him, but he pulled away. "Kiana, what the fuck."

Her lips crashed into his again.

Marcus pursed his lips while using an arm to pry her off

of him. "Kiana." He mumbled beneath her lips.

Kiana pulled away. Her eyes danced wildly into his.

"Stop acting like you don't want me, Marcus. You know you never stopped wanting me." Kiana peeled off her pink vest then slipped out of the long skirt she wore. She stood there in just sandals and a lace thong. "You can't tell me that you don't miss me, Marcus."

"Do you miss her, Marcus?" Time split and Marcus's heart stopped when Maya's voice entered the room.

Maya's heart echoed in her ears and muffled Marcus' voice. She saw his lips move as he rushed to her side, but she was focused on the half-naked woman standing in his living room with a look of pleasure and delight on her face.

"Maya? Maya, wait." Marcus' voice materialized before she saw him in front of her.

He held her hand—her free hand; the other hand gripped her briefcase. His eyes were wet and searching hers. "Maya, baby. Baby, listen to me." He said.

Maya shook her head. She couldn't listen to him. She couldn't even see him clearly, all she saw was the naked woman. And without confirmation, just intuition.

Maya knew *she* was Kiana.

"Maya, baby." Marcus grabbed her hand.

Maya snatched it away.

"Maya?" His voice shook. "Maya, wait a second. I can explain this."

Maya blinked then scoffed. "*You* can explain." She kept her voice steady, refusing to let Kiana hear her break but Maya was already broken. She stepped backwards into the hallway.

"Maya. Hold on." Marcus said. He held up his hands like he was a cop trying to talk down a gunman with their weapon aimed at him. He inched closer to her; his arms extended and palms wide open. "Baby, let me explain this." He pleaded.

Maya shook her head. "There's nothing that you can say to me that will justify why you have a woman, half naked in your living room." Her voice broke.

Marcus said, "Maya, I told her to leave."

"And that translated to this?" She motioned to Kiana still in the living room, naked and unfazed in her lace thong and sandals.

Maya laughed dryly. "I'm done, Marcus. This is over."

Maya turned on her heels and stormed to the door. Marcus scrambled to catch up with her.

He grabbed her arm then positioned himself in front of

the door.

"Marcus, get out of my way." Maya hissed.

Marcus said, "Maya, this isn't."

She held up her hand. Tears stung her eyes but she didn't blink them away. "Don't tell me this isn't what it looks like, Marcus because *you* let her into *your* place. You." She paused, leaned forward then inhaled. He hadn't showered yet, but he smelled like amber. "You smell like her." She whispered.

Marcus' head fell.

Maya forced a smile and said, "Yeah, this is definitely what it looks like."

Maya reached past Marcus and opened the door. The slab nudged him in the back, but he refused to move. He had started to cry.

"I came here to tell you that despite the news about Carlson, Robert fought to keep ICore on board to complete this project. For me *and* you because Robert said that you were 'a good man'." The corners of her mouth trembled. "But I think it's best we sever ties immediately. For good."

Her words felt like serrated knives in her own heart. Maya looked up at Marcus; the tears flooded his eyes, and she wondered if he could even see her face. Could he see the pain in her eyes? Did the hurt of her heart reflect in them? Of course he couldn't. How could he when he had a half-naked woman waiting for him in his living room.

Marcus didn't need Maya. And he sure as hell didn't want her. His eyes burned into hers, but she refused to fold.

"Maya." His voice was hushed. "Baby."

"No." Maya said. "Goodbye Marcus." She slipped past him, then out of the door and out of his life.

Twenty

♥

M aya could hear the vacuum just a few doors down from her office. She glanced at the clock on her laptop; the office had been closed for nearly four hours, and she didn't want to go home. Going home meant that she would be alone with her thoughts and within her thoughts she could see Marcus. Her mind would play back every single time he made her smile then her mind would rip through those happier moments like sinister wrapping paper to reveal her last memory of Marcus and Kiana, half naked in his living room with a smug smile on her face. The moment was branded in her brain, and a new terror had been unlocked.

But she had to keep going. Maya couldn't afford any more distractions. Her relationship with Marcus had been a major distraction but it felt good. Being with him made Maya feel alive; she shed her workaholic skin and felt renewed. Their connection and the relationship gave her something else to believe in aside from her work and the Community Counsel Initiative.

Then it ended.

Maya comforted herself with the closure. Despite the pain of seeing Marcus and Kiana in the same room together, despite the way her heart crushed under that reality that *that* was what he wanted; Maya told herself that it was okay and that it was what was best for the both of them.

It was an easy yet agonizing way to say, "This is over."

Then it was back to work. Maya rolled up her sleeves and dove head first back into her work. Between court cases, preparing for the Community Counsel launch and the Community Summit, she hoped that the more she worked, the less space Marcus could occupy in her mind.

It didn't work.

Each new day brought forth another memory or a flash of Kiana's flawless frame. Maya believed Marcus when he told her that Kiana was in the past. She believed him when he looked into her eyes and assured her that she was the one he wanted.

Because she wanted him too.

She loved him.

Maya fell for Marcus the moment she saw him. That beautiful shade of green that her eyes fixated on when she looked out into the crowd at the art gala. He had calmed her quivering spirit when she stood on that podium. There was a peace that Maya experienced when she was with him that she never knew existed.

Marcus was smart and sexy; he could carry a conversation about damn near anything and he was charming. He was enthusiastic about his business and the community too. Together, Maya believed that they could elevate their community. They could have been that power couple she dreamed of.

Had it all been wishful thinking?

What red flags had she overlooked? What big issues had she masked as little ones?

None.

There were no red flags. She didn't spot any until Kiana came into the picture.

Maya gripped her pen tight then heard the thick plastic snap. "Shit." She hissed. She tossed the broken pen into a wastebasket beside her desk and reached into her briefcase for another. Her phone vibrated against her fingertips then her heart pounded at the idea that Marcus was calling her but when she looked at the lockscreen, Maya sighed.

Olivia's face filled the screen.

Maya swiped the screen to answer. "Hey O." She said.

"Hey honey, how are you?" Her voice was soft and

syrupy.

"I'm." Maya paused, unsure of how she wanted to respond. She could tell Olivia that she was "fine" but that would be a lie, or she could tell Olivia that she was "miserable," which would be the truth but just a fraction of it. "I'm alright." She said and prayed that it would be enough for her.

"That's good to hear." She lost some of the sweetness in her voice. "The shirts for the Summit arrived this morning and I wanted to drop yours off and see if you needed anything."

Maya smiled. It felt good to have a friend in her corner, even if it was her new ex-boyfriend's sister. It felt odd, but Maya had to remind herself that she knew Olivia before she knew Marcus. And hurting Olivia because Marcus hurt her was out of the question.

"Umm yeah. I mean, no. I'm still at the office right now but I'll be home tomorrow. You wanna swing by then?" She asked.

"Yes. We can make a girls' night of it." Olivia's voice was hopeful.

"Sure. Sounds good." Maya said.

Her and Olivia said their goodbyes; then Maya slipped her phone back in her briefcase and returned to her quest for a new pen.

A short janitor appeared in her doorway; he wore dark blue coveralls and pushed a vacuum cleaner across the threshold. "Ms. Thompson?" He said her name like a question.

"Hey Richie." She said.

Richie glanced at the silver watch on his wrist then looked at Maya. "It's late." He said.

"I know." Maya gave up the hunt for a pen, closed her laptop then shoved it into her briefcase. Richie watched her gather up her blazer and briefcase in silence. When Maya walked to the door he smiled at her.

"I read about your project in the paper." He said. "My wife said that this could help us possibly get my brother the legal aid he needs."

Maya nodded. "That's wonderful, Richie!"

The janitor smiled and his hazel eyes brightened. "Oh yeah." He fished in one of the deep pockets of his coveralls and pulled a bent polaroid photo from it then handed it to Maya. "I found that in your wastebasket the other day. I don't think you meant to throw it away."

Maya looked at the crumpled photo of her and Marcus at the Fourth of July party. Marcus had Maya wrapped up his large arms, his chin on her shoulder and they smiled into the camera. Her heart knocked in her chest and the corners of her mouth twitched; Maya could feel the tears surfacing again.

"Thanks, Richie. Goodnight." She said.

2 a.m.

Marcus' eyes opened to darkness; he had been suffocating in two ways. Once from the heat that lofted through the open window and secondly from Kiana. She had him in a death grip with her arms draped over his neck. If he moved, she moved then her arms would constrict like snakes wrapped around its prey.

But it wasn't the heat or Kiana's death grip that was killing him.

It was his heart.

Marcus looked at his phone, sleeping on his bedside docking station. He tapped the dark screen feeling hopeful to see a message or a missed call from Maya, but the only notifications he found were from social media and business emails.

Yes, ICore had been roped into the mess with Wayne Carlson, so much so that Marcus and Darnell spent most of their work days dodging reporters and Twitter mentions, but whenever his phone rang he hoped it would be

Maya.

Marcus pried Kiana's arms from his neck then slipped out of bed. He grabbed his phone and padded into his living room. He sat down on the couch, staring at the black screen of his phone. A glint of reflection stared back at him. He was not the same man he was weeks ago. He barely knew himself again.

With Maya, he was himself. Free of judgment and brimming with love.

Marcus tapped his phone's screen, the lock screen appeared, displaying the InnovateCore logo. He punched in his PIN, then his lock screen became his home screen which was a picture of him and Maya. He ran his thumb over the image of her smiling and his eyes burned with tears.

He wanted to call her. He wanted to hear her voice and he tell her that he was sorry and explain that Kiana being there had been a mistake.

But how could he explain Kiana's current presence?

After Maya left, Kiana stayed. Brokenhearted, Marcus let Kiana stay and let her help him feel something other than the pain that was festering in his chest. When they were done, Marcus' flesh crawled. He took a hot shower while sobbing and cursing himself.

Marcus clicked to his message inbox. The last message

he received from Maya had been a photo. A selfie of her getting ready for the day. She was bare faced with her full mane of hair framing it. Maya was dressed in a black and white satin kimono robe.

A short one. That was his favorite.

She blew a kiss into the mirror with her pouting lips. Marcus touched the image; he smiled then reality sucker punched him.

Maya was gone.

Within his messages, Marcus selected Darnell's name and sent him a "You up?" text. Knowing Darnell, he was wide awake either watching movies or...

Marcus didn't want to think about what else he could be doing.

His phone vibrated. Darnell and Quentin's face appeared on his phone screen.

Marcus answered. "Dry night?" He chuckled into the phone.

"Dry what? Man, whatever. You alright over there?" Darnell asked.

Marcus stood up and paced the perimeter of his area rug in the dark. "I'm not." He said.

"She hasn't called you?" Darnell asked.

"No."

"Damn. Is Kiana still there?"

"Yes." Marcus sighed.

He heard Darnell exhale hard and he could practically see his best friend shaking his head. "Why?"

"What?" Marcus asked.

Darnell spoke clearly. "Why is she still there?"

"Because she never left. After Maya walked out Kiana stayed." Marcus said.

"She should have never been there at all." The usual wit in Darnell's voice was gone. "You should have never let that chick into your house. She's like a vampire and you never let them suckers into your crib." He paused. "Man look, I love you. You're my brother but I gotta be real with you for a second."

"Okay."

"Why did you even let this chick back in your life? The door was closed, shit, I thought you bolted it shut but here she is. Back again and ruin your life."

Marcus signed and massaged his left temple. "You're right. I fucked up." He said. "I thought I could prove to myself that I was over her."

Darnell grunted on the other end. "Why? You don't have to prove shit. You knew you were over her."

Marcus nodded in the dark. He said, "I made a mistake. And her being here now is an even bigger mistake."

"Exactly." Darnell said. "You love Maya, don't you?"

Marcus sighed again. "I do. I love her but D, she doesn't want anything to do with me. If she saw me right now..."

Darnell cut him off, "She would beat yo' ass because you playin' house with your ex."

"I'm not playing house." Marcus said.

"Well, whatever it is that you're doing over there, you need to stop it because if you want to win Maya back, you gotta let go of the past once and for all."

Footsteps cut the moment of silence and Marcus saw Kiana's silhouette before he heard her voice. "Marcus?" She called.

Darnell scoffed into the phone. "You know what you need to do, man." He said then ended the call.

Twenty-One

♥

The first summer rainfall in Cascade City was a monsoon and Marcus was caught in the midst of it. After detouring to avoid high flood areas and drivers trying to qualify for the Indy 500 in the mess, Marcus arrived at the InnovateCore office dripping wet and clutching his thankfully waterproof computer case.

Darnell poked his head out of his office. "You made it." He said.

"Of course I did." Marcus huffed. "You said '911' in your message so I knew it was urgent." As he walked toward his office, his soaked black and white Jordans squeaked against the gray linoleum flooring before the sound was absorbed into the flat carpeting of his office.

Darnell entered and he tossed Marcus a towel. He propped himself against the doorframe and waited.

Marcus scrubbed at his rain drenched arms and face.

His black logoed polo was saturated, and his khaki joggers were spotted from the rain in all the wrong places. He sat down in his chair, powered up his monitors then glanced at Darnell.

"Which accounts did we lose?" Marcus asked. His heart had been ready to jump out of his chest ever since Darnell's message yanked him from his sleep.

More news about Wayne Carlson had been released and the media outlets were buzzing. The millionaire had been arrested, charged with money laundering and awaiting trial. He was denied bail after being deemed a flight risk.

In the midst of the scandal, the lowest hanging fruits— InnovateCore was the first to be picked off. Not only were the funds Carlson wired to them seized but their client list started circling the drain too.

Darnell and Marcus worked together assuring their clients that while Wayne Carlson did invest in ICore, he had not been a part of the company. They released a statement on their website, their Instagram, Facebook and even their barely active Twitter account.

"How many today?" Marcus asked. He pulled his laptop from the rain splattered bag and powered it on.

Darnell looked down at his phone. "Three so far." He said.

"Which brings our grand total to nine." Marcus turned

in his chair to the large whiteboard behind him. He started tracking their losses after the first client pulled their contract as he was anticipating a domino effect. He logged their names, along with the date they separated from ICore, their reasoning, which they knew was bullshit, but they had to make it as professional as possible. And for good accounting, Marcus noted how much each contract was worth.

Darnell dictated as Marcus logged the information about their latest losses. With a red dry erase marker, he tallied up the sum of the contract totals.

"Is that right?" Darnell asked, pointing to the red number Marcus underlined and circled. "That can't be right."

It was. Thanks to Wayne Carlson, InnovateCore had lost over an additional twenty-five thousand dollars. Darnell bent at the waist, put his hands on his knees and sucked in a deep breath.

Marcus turned away from the whiteboard. "We can't lose our heads over this." He said.

Darnell shot up, his round eyes bulging. "Marcus, not only has over two-hundred thousand dollars been snatched from us, we've also lost another twenty-five grand— oh and let's not forget the fact that our reputation as a reputable business is tanked. Fucking tanked."

"We are not tanked." Marcus said. His voice was steady;

however, his faith was shaken. "We are fine. We have reserves. We have savings."

Darnell punched the door frame and yelled. "What about our rep, Marcus? You think that after all this blows over, we're going to be good? We are a Black owned business now connected to money laundering. We will never recover."

Marcus rose from his seat; fueled by an assault of anger from every aspect of his life. Darnell's attitude set off the last alarm. "I did not make it this far to give up, D. I'm not giving up because *that* is what they expect us to do. That's what they want us to do. When I came to you with the idea of InnovateCore, what did I tell you?"

"You said that you would always root for this business. You said that no matter what, you wanted to give your clients top notch service."

Marcus nodded. "And I still stand on that. I'm not gonna lie and say that it's gonna be easy to overcome this but we will. I promise."

"Alright, man." Darnell said, rubbing the back of his neck. "But isn't there some legal action we can take to get the funds that the feds took back?" He asked.

Marcus shook his head. "I'm not sure."

A slight grin took over Darnell's lips. "Damn, if only you knew some fine ass lawyer who could give you some advice on the matter. Oh wait, you do."

"I can't." Marcus said.

Darnell walked toward him and planted his hands on Marcus' desk, his smile growing. "You can." Darnell nudged Marcus' phone toward him. "And you can apologize."

Marcus chuckled as he glanced down at his phone. It felt good to laugh but his smile dropped when he saw a message had come in from his sister, Olivia:

> MAYA'S PROJECT HAS BEEN DROPPED!

Maya couldn't say that was she surprised when Robert came in and delivered the news. Of course, she was stunned that Tim hadn't been delighted to deliver the news himself because she knew that deep down he never liked the project.

"That's not true." Robert said after Maya shared her thoughts. "Tim believed in you."

"Just not the project." Maya said.

Robert avoided her eyes as he cleared his throat. "Maya,

there will be more opportunities like this." He assured her.

Maya nodded her head slowly. "Thanks." She said solemnly.

Robert rose from his seat across from her and made his way to her door. When he opened it, he appeared startled by a mystery on the other side of it. "Umm, I think your next appointment has arrived."

"Next appointment?" Maya asked.

Robert opened the door wider and motioned for someone to step in.

Maya's eyes swelled as Kiana entered her office.

"Kiana." She said the woman's name softly while Robert glared at her.

"Do you need me to..." Robert trailed off. "Nevermind. Excuse me." He slipped past Kiana but kept the door open behind her.

"What are you doing here?" Maya asked. Her heart was rattling in her chest and her hands tightened to fists.

Kiana's cropped denim jacket was spotted with raindrops despite the pink umbrella she held and dripped onto her floor. Her long, thin braids were pulled back in a low ponytail; Maya studied her face for the first time. She was pretty, radiant even with soft features and a doe like eyes.

"We never formally met." Kiana said.

"I had no desire to." Maya retorted. "What are you doing

here?"

Kiana toyed with the braid cord attached to the base of her umbrella. She watched her hands for a second before she looked at Maya again. "I came to apologize and tell you what really happened that day."

Maya sank into her chair. "Why?" She asked. "You won, Kiana. You got Marcus back. You both deserve—"

Kiana cut through the start of Maya's rage fueled rant. "He didn't want me." She said, "I lost that man a long time ago." Her dark eyes darted around the room. "Did he tell you what happened at Celine's?"

Maya nodded slowly and the woman laughed nervously.

"He blocked me right after that."

"Why are you here, Kiana?"

She ignored the question again then said, "Before he blocked me, I went through his social media, you know. I wanted to see if he was as happy as Olivia had said. I saw you and him and..." Kiana paused. "I got his address from an old classmate some time ago. I had planned on visiting him before. To surprise him but something just didn't feel right."

"Until *that* day?" Maya said.

Kiana sighed. "The money laundering mess was trending. I wanted to check on him and see if he was alright."

"And that meant stripping down to next to nothing, knowing that he had a woman."

Kiana chewed her glossy, bottom lip.

Maya said, "You played on his vulnerability but then again, it looked like you didn't have to play too hard."

"He loves you, Maya." Kiana said. "I can tell because he used to look at me the way he looks at you. I just came here to say that he's all yours."

Maya scoffed and Kiana's face wrinkled. "I'm good."

"What?" She asked. "I just told you that you can have him and you'll never see me again."

"I should have never seen you at all." Maya said. "But I did and I can't unsee it. You and your body are embedded in my brain. Whenever I see him, I see you."

Kiana's lips trembled but she managed to speak. "I'm sorry, Maya. I really—"

Nina entered the room and her eyes were set on Kiana like lasers. "Okay! Your time is up, homewrecker." She opened the door wider for Kiana to exit.

"Homewreck..." Kiana stopped. She looked at Nina then Maya. "Maya, I said—"

"I heard you." Maya said. "And like I said, I should have never seen you at all."

Nina crossed her arms over her chest; her professional demeanor was slipping away by the second.

Kiana exhaled softly. "I'm really sorry, Maya." She turned on her heels then exited her office.

Nina closed the door and Maya collapsed on her desk.

Twenty-Two

♥

With her initiative canned and a surprise visit from Marcus' ex-girlfriend, Maya decided to give herself a half day.

On the way home, she reached out to Olivia. She sent her a simple text:

The initiative has been cancelled.

She didn't bother to wait on Olivia's reply; she tossed the phone in her briefcase and continued her drive home in an emotional daze. Once she was home, the daze transcended into a fog as she moved about her bedroom. She wasn't sure what she wanted to do. She thought about taking a shower to wash the residue of rejection and rage off of her. She contemplated pouring a shot of bourbon for herself.

Or a double. Hell, she could have cleared the entire bottle if she really wanted to.

Then there was the third option.

Cry.

Tears streaked the apples of her cheeks, and her eyes burned when she closed them. Maya drew in a deep breath then exhaled slowly. She grabbed a pair of black biker shorts and a gray, oversized Chicago Bears t-shirt then headed to the shower to begin another round of grieving.

The shrill bell of her intercom echoed through her living room and down the hall toward her bedroom. Maya hurried to a silver speaker box next to her door as she struggled to pull her damp coils into a bun. She engaged the 'TALK' button and spoke. "Yes?"

"It's me." A slightly distorted version of Olivia's voice came back.

Maya stared at the speaker box then pressed the 'AC-CESS' button and minutes later, Olivia was at Maya's door.

She said nothing, when she pulled Maya into a tight hug and held her for what felt like forever.

"Honey, I am so sorry. I can't believe this." Olivia said. Her breath was warm against her ear. She pulled away then closed the door behind her. Olivia was dressed in paint splattered denim overalls, a pale pink tank top and brown sandals that were also saturated in dried paint. Her gray hair was pulled back from her face, secured by a pink bandana.

She carried a large slouchy, canvas bag slung over her shoulder. Maya noted the soft cling that chimed whenever Oliva moved.

She knew the sound of a wine bottle when she heard one.

The corners of Maya's mouth curled on instinct. "You didn't have to come by Liv." Maya said.

"Yes I did.There was no way in hell I was gonna let you sit here and think about what happened today." She said and crossed into Maya's kitchen.

Olivia set her canvas bag on the black granite countertop of her island.

Maya said, "Kiana stopped by my office today too."

Her best friend's eyes enlarged. "What? What the hell did she do that for?"

"To tell me that Marcus was all mine."

Olivia's face puckered like she swallowed a lemon. "What the hell does that mean?"

"I don't know and I didn't care." Maya said.

"Well, it's a good thing I bought two bottles of your favorite red and ordered some sushi for us. It should be here..." Olivia pulled her cell phone from the bib pocket of her overalls. She glanced at the screen and smiled. "In twenty minutes." She then pulled the two bottles of wine from her bag, opened a drawer on the island and she cheered when she retrieved the corkscrew from it. "Let's get this party started."

By the time they made their way through the California and Dragon Rolls and half way through the Godzilla Rolls along with the second bottle of wine, Maya was laughing alongside Olivia as she shared her latest dating horror story.

"The man looked nothing like his profile picture." Olivia giggled.

"You mean to tell me that you didn't exchange more photos once you two had each other's number?" Maya asked.

Olivia downed her half glass of wine and shook her head. "I sent him pictures, but he didn't send me shit." She said.

"Red flag." Maya said. She finished her glass then reached for the bottle. "So, what happened?" She asked.

"Well, I decided that I would tell him that I was running

late so when I got to Celine's, I went to the bar and sent him a message. I scanned the room looking for someone on his phone." Olivia said.

Maya topped off Olivia's glass then hers. "Did you catch him?" She asked.

Olivia's wine stained lips poked out. "I caught his cat-fishing ass. He looked like a Jodeci reject."

Maya cackled. "What?"

"Maya, not only did he look nothing like his picture he was also wearing a full leather outfit." Olivia laughed.

Maya pulled her glass away from her lips and said, "You're lying."

"I wish I was." Olivia took a long sip then set the glass down. "I got out of that place so damn fast. I sent him a text and told him that my dog was sick." She said.

"O, you don't have a dog." Maya said.

"He didn't know that." Their boisterous laughs filled the living room. Olivia shook her head and chuckled softly. "I tell you the dating pool is a shit show."

"I'll drink to that." Maya raised her glass then took a full gulp. The alcohol was jetting through her bloodstream, making her lips tingle. She had let Olivia's stories distract her, but the alcohol was conjuring up the suppressed emotions. Maya pushed her glass around her coffee table. She kept her eyes low and away from Olivia when she spoke again. "Have you heard from Marcus?"

Olivia pursed her lips together then said, "Every once in a while. I told him what happened too."

Maya nodded. "Thanks. I thought about telling him myself. I mean he and Darnell helped out with so much of that initiative, but I wasn't sure if I wanted to hear..." She stopped. Maya could feel the lump in her throat expanding like a balloon.

"He did tell me that he didn't invite Kiana over." She said. "He said that she just showed up."

Maya nodded again. "Kiana told me that too." She said.

"I also told him he was stupid for letting her just walk into his place like that." Olivia said.

Maya took another drink. Her glass was more than halfway gone. Tears clung to the rims of her eyes and the mass in her throat felt like a jagged piece of smoldering coal. Olivia shifted closer and pulled Maya into her arms as she sobbed.

"Maya, listen to me, okay." Olivia's voice was soft and muffled as she cried into her friend's chest. Olivia held her tight and rocked slowly. "I can't speak for my brother, and I won't, but I can tell that he loves you just as much as you love him." She cupped Maya's chin and lifted it to look into her tear filled eyes. "I may not be lucky in love but you two are blessed and I think that you both need to talk about what happened."

Maya opened her mouth to protest but Olivia shook her head, and a gray curl slipped from her bandana. "No. I refuse to let the both of you run away from each other."

"O, it's over. I told him, "I was done."

"Are *you* really done though?" Olivia asked.

PART SIX | AUGUST 2023

Twenty-Three

♥

Maya slipped into her office and closed the door behind her before collapsing into her chair. She sat forward and peeled off her cream colored blazer. Her sleeveless, olive green, silk blouse was spotted with sweat, and she shivered when a bead of it slipped down her back. Maya grabbed a file on her desk and used it as a makeshift fan.

A soft knock sounded off on the other side of her door. "Yeah?" Maya said as she continued to fan herself.

Nina poked her head in; her latest hairstyle was an auburn brown bob that complimented her oval face perfectly. She smiled then frowned as she stepped into the office. "Damn. Is the AC still out at the courthouse?"

"Yes." Maya said. "It's been out all week, and it feels like it gets hotter every time I go."

Nina said, "I heard you won the case though." Her smile

returned but her eyes reflected concern for Maya's sweltering face.

Maya grinned. "I did. All charges were dropped and his
record will be cleared."

"Another win for Maya Thompson." Nina replied.

"No." Maya's grin slipped into a grimace. "Another win
for Sterling, Turner and Associates." She closed her eyes
and fanned herself harder. "You got something for me?"

Nina's gentle smile turned into a full grin. "Actually,
you're holding it. You're three o'clock is here." She said.

"My three." Maya stopped fanning herself then looked
down at her watch.

It was almost fifteen minutes after five. "They're still
here?" She asked.

Nina nodded her head. "I told him that you were running late after you called me and told me that the verdict
was running long—"

Maya cut her off. "He?"

Nina said, "Yeah. He said that he was willing to wait."

Maya looked at the folder fan in her hand and passed
a hand across her sweat coated brow. She said, "You can
bring him in."

Nina smiled then exited.

Maya laid the manilla folder on her desk then flipped it
open. The file was filled with photocopies of documents.

There were nine documents in total and when Maya examined them closer, she realized that they were in fact business contracts. She inspected the first page of one of the photocopies closely.

She recognized the capital I in the business logo.

"Oh my God." Maya breathed.

"Maya?" Nina's voice snatched her from her revelation and when she looked up, her heart plunged into her stomach.

"Marcus." Maya said his name as if she had witnessed a divine miracle.

He stood in the threshold of her office dressed in black cargo joggers and a white t-shirt. The sides of his hair were faded and tapered. Maya could see that he was letting the crown of his hair grow out; it was a mass of soft curls and swirls. When Marcus smiled at Maya, her breath seized in her chest.

Nina cleared her throat abruptly. "I'll just close the door. Oh, can I get you anything Mr. Johnson?"

Maya watched Marcus; his eyes never left hers, but he shook his head. "No, thank you. I'm good for now." He said.

Once the door closed, Maya snapped out of her trance. She blinked hard then smoothed out the front of her blouse. "You want to sit down?" She asked.

Marcus stepped closer to her desk, but he didn't take a seat. He set his leather bag down in a chair. His eyes still fixed on her.

A layer of tension kept them apart and as Maya stared at Marcus, everything came flooding back to her. His presence was like a crashing wave pulling her into him.

Marcus said, "I asked Nina not to tell you it was me."

Maya shifted in her seat and her hands moved from her desk to her lap then back to her desk again. Her French manicured nails tapped on the open file while she gnawed on her bottom lip.

"I'm sorry if this makes you uneasy. I could just find another lawyer." Marcus said.

"No." Maya said. "It's fine. What can I do for you, Marcus?" Her voice was sharp, but Marcus felt a warmth lingering behind her words. Her jaw clenched then released when he made a move closer to her.

Marcus walked around the desk, toward her. Her eyes darted away from him but not for long. Maya inched her chair back until the wall locked her in place. He closed in the space between them and savored her perfume.

She smelled like orchids and summer heat.

Maya looked up and at him; her eyes were red rimmed and weary. He looked at her hands then took in his to lure her from her seat. When she looked up at him, Marcus couldn't help the smile that spread over his face. "I heard that love can make you do some crazy things."

"Communicating with your ex isn't one of those things." Maya retorted.

Marcus agreed. "You're right. I should have never let her in. I broke your trust. I hurt you." His voice fell but he held Maya's hands tighter. "I messed up and I thought that I could just let us fade but I can't. Maya, I need you in my life and I'm sorry. I'm so damn sorry."

He stared into her eyes and recognized a familiar glow behind her darkened eyes.

"You hurt me, Marcus." Maya's voice rattled but she stood firm. "Seeing her in your place like that. I can't forget that. I can't even close my eyes without seeing her."

"Maya, I told her to leave. I was trying to get her out of there." Marcus' voice retreated. "I didn't use my better judgement with Kiana. I know that and I also know that I have never been more sure about you and I in all my life."

Tears flooded Maya's eyes. "What do you want me to do, Marcus?" She asked.

"Forgive me. Let me be the man that you need me to be

and love me."

Marcus lifted Maya's face to meet her gaze again. He said, "Love me because I know that I love you and I want you. I want this."

"Marcus." Her voice shook as more tears fell, creating small pools between his index fingers and thumbs. "Marcus." She said his name again and again.

He leaned in until his lips were grazing hers. When he closed his eyes, his tears collided with hers. "I'm sorry, Maya." He whispered in between his sobs. "Please, Maya." He said. "Forgive me. Tell me that I am yours." He opened his eyes and stared into hers. "Tell me you love me."

Maya's breathing hitched; she was crying harder and nodding her head. "I." She said. "I love you, Marcus. I love you."

He exhaled slowly. His entire body went limp, but he pulled Maya into his arms as she locked hers around his neck, and they cried together.

A chorus of crickets pulled Maya from her sleep. She blinked at her balcony door, cracked open and pulled in the summer's late night lullaby. The dark sky sparkled with stars and the sounds of the city were somber. Maya shifted then felt a strong arm pulling her close.

Marcus.

She beamed while studying his silhouette in the darkness. His bare, solid frame was tangled beneath a white sheet they shared. His breathing was soft and steady. Maya placed a hand on his chest; his heart drummed rhythmically against her palm.

"I love you." She said softly into the darkness.

Marcus said, "I love you more." Maya jerked away but Marcus caught her. "I'm sorry." He chuckled. His voice was heavy with sleep yet playful. He kissed her and she could feel his eyes on her. "You alright?" He asked.

"Yeah."

Marcus's hand found her thigh and he squeezed it.

"I feel like you got something on your mind." He replied. He gripped her thigh again and all the blood rushed to Maya's center.

Bad timing to be aroused but it felt amazing.

Maya ran a hand through her tangled curls and exhaled. "I'm giving Sterling my notice."

Marcus shifted to an upright position. The sheet slipped from his lower half; Maya swooned at the way his rich, brown skin shimmered in the moonlight, but she directed her eyes to his face.

"Baby, are you sure?" He asked.

"That firm has been my life since forever and I have given them all I can give. When I pitched my initiative, I was confident that this would prove to them that I was..." She paused, unsure of the exact word she was looking for.

Worthy.

Faithful.

She sighed. "It's just time for me to leave."

Marcus said. "But baby, what about making partner?"

"I'm five years away from actually being considered." Maya said. "And that partner talk went out the window with my initiative. Tim never wanted me to launch that project anyway." She said.

Marcus kept quiet beneath the darkness.

Maya said, "You were right, I have been a token for that man for too long."

Marcus pulled her into his arms then kissed her shoulder. "Baby, when I said that..."

Maya cut him off softly, "I know what you meant. I just didn't want to admit it."

"Are you sure you want to resign? Are you really ready to throw all that time and prestige away?" He asked.

"Yes." Her response was rapid. "They threw me away when they decided to cancel my project." Maya's voice broke, she could feel the tears looming behind her eyes.

"You know Tim made me send letters to the interns personally?"

"Babe." Marcus let his voice trail.

"Yep. He canceled my initiative then made *me* break the hearts of six Black and brown undergrads. Marcus, they didn't deserve that. And this project means everything to me. Our community needs this and I'm going to make it happen."

"And you will, baby. We will." Marcus said. "What about Robert? Are you going to talk to him first?"

In the midst of her tears, Maya smiled. Marcus' shoulders perked up and scanned her face in the moonlight. "You already told him, didn't you?" He said.

Maya replied, "I told Elena. So naturally, she told him."

"Then it is true what they say about marriages." Marcus chuckled.

"What?" She asked.

"That in a good marriage, there are no secrets."

"I only know that to be true with Elena and Robert." Maya said. She wiped her eyes and laughed. "Which makes me wonder." She turned toward Marcus then climbed on top of him.

"What's up?" He asked. His hands latched to her hips. Maya could feel his energy in the darkness.

"How did you infiltrate Sterling, Turner and Associates?"

"Infiltrate? Ooh, that's a sexy word." He laughed. "But I didn't infiltrate. I just reached out to Robert."

"Robert helped you?" Maya asked.

"He did and he's helping us fight this Wayne Carlson fallout."

"I can't believe it." Maya said.

Marcus nodded. "I came to him, humbled as hell of course. I told him everything. I told him about Kiana coming over and you walking in." He paused. "I told him that I made a horrible mistake and that I was in love with you. I begged him to help me."

"Just like that?" Maya said. "He helped you?"

Marcus laughed. "Hell no!" He said, "He had some choice words for me, which were fairly similar to the words I heard from Darnell and Olivia only with less colorful vocabulary."

Maya looked away in the dark until Marcus pressed his heated chest against hers. Maya's body tingled and she could feel the mass between his legs shift.

"Maya, I knew that I loved you the moment I saw you at the gala." Marcus said, "You took my breath away. I was so sidetracked by you, your intellect and your beauty, I damn near forgot about that deal with Carlson. And the more time I spent with you, getting to know you and learning about you, all I wanted was you. And now." Marcus' arms tightened around Maya's waist. "I'm never letting you go."

Maya could feel Marcus' smile radiating.

"Promise?" She said. Marcus kissed her gently.

"Promise." He said as they fell back onto the bed.

Twenty-Four

♥

M arcus sat across from Darnell in a large room surrounded by glass. They were in the formal meeting room of *Sterling, Turner and Associates.*

Marcus sat quietly dressed in dark green dress pants and
a burnt orange dress shirt. He had the cuffs rolled up to
his forearms. Darnell wore khaki slacks and a white button
up.

Darnell was scrolling through his phone when he set it
down and fell back in the chair. "Man, what is taking so
long?" He said.

"I don't know." Marcus said. "Robert told us to be here
at eleven." He glanced down at the gold watch on his wrist.
It was a quarter past eleven.

"Aren't lawyers supposed to be punctual or something
like that?" Darnell said. His attention went back to his
phone just as the glass door opened.

"Gentlemen." Robert Turner said as he stepped into the glass box with a large smile on his face.

Marcus eyed the thick folder under his arm.

Robert's bald head shined under the fluorescent lights and his teeth seemed to glow too. Robert wore a brown suit, accented with a pale orange shirt and a tie similar to the color of Marcus' shirt. His suit jacket had large gold buttons that Robert unfastened before he hugged Marcus then shook hands with Darnell.

Robert and Darnell were not there yet but Marcus believed that Darnell would loosen up around the lawyer more when he experienced Robert's humor and the fact that he could probably drink the both of them under the table any day of the week.

Robert took the seat at the head of the large, dark wooden table. "Fellas, today is a great day. You hear me?" He said.

Darnell looked at Marcus, he raised a bushy eyebrow, and his eyes widened. Marcus shook his head quickly; a cue to Darnell to let the man continue and Robert did.

"Today is a great day for InnovateCore because." Marcus eyed the manilla folder again that sat in front of Robert. He opened it then handed one piece of paper to Marcus and another to Darnell. "It appears that you gentlemen weren't the only ones who were taken by Mr.

Carlson's generosity. Dozens of companies have come forward to speak on the fact that they knew nothing of Mr. Carlson's doings despite losing thousands and thousands of dollars. We weren't the only ones seeking justice here."

Darnell looked at Marcus then back to Robert. He asked, "What does that mean?"

Robert's smile widened. "That means that Carlson' legal team has decided to settle all lawsuits that have been submitted targeting their client. I assume they already have enough on their plate with this money laundering fiasco."

Darnell's nose crinkled and Marcus laughed. For a man who knew numbers; he was struggling to put two and two together.

Robert saw it too. He cleared his throat and proceeded. "Gentlemen, what we have in front of you is a lump sum settlement payment from the contracts you lost due to Wayne Carlson. It's not all of the funds you lost but it is a substantial amount if I say so myself. And this." He stopped to pass out more paperwork. "These are documents concluding and confirming that InnovateCore was not aware of Mr. Carlson's illegal activity and had and has no connection with money laundering."

It was Marcus' turn to smile; Darnell scanned the document then yelped. "Shit. I mean, damn. I mean." Darnell shook his head. "This is unreal."

"Oh no." Robert said. "It's real."

Marcus looked down at the check. The green marble paper check was made payable to InnovateCore. He turned to Robert. His dark eyes were already on him. "Thank you." He said. "Thank you for this. For all of your help and I do mean *all*."

Robert nodded. "It was my pleasure. I could not let another Black owned business go under due to someone else's nefarious intentions. Plus, you make Maya happy and that means the world to me. You two remind me of Elena and I. Hard working, determined and stubborn as hell."

The three men laughed; their joy echoing within the glass box and seeping out onto the work floor.

Marcus' laughter trailed off. "I do love her." He said.

"I know." Robert said. "Just be good to her and take care of her during this time. I am very proud of her, and she will be missed around here. I mean I'll still see you two but *here*, her absence is going to be a hard one to handle."

Darnell's head jolted from Marcus to Robert. The humor drained from his face and looked like a giant question mark. "What happened to Maya?" He asked.

Twenty-Five

♥

Maya A. Thompson
2418 Cascade Tower Plaza Drive, Apt 788
Cascade City, IL 60129

August 21st, 2023

Sterling, Turner & Associates
45 Fremont Blvd, Suite 401
Cascade City, IL 60129
Attn: Claire Bledsoe, HR Manager

Dear Ms. Bledsoe,

I am writing to inform you of my intention to resign from my position as Special Counsel at Sterling, Turner & Associates effective immediately. My career goals have changed since I started working here and I feel that the time has come for me to pursue another opportunity that is more aligned with my aspirations to strengthen my community. My mission has always been to help others understand the legal system instead of fearing it. And this next venture allows me to achieve my dreams.

I appreciate the opportunities that Tim, Robert and the entire legal team has given me during my time here, but it is time for me to fulfill my greatest purpose ever.

Please let me know what assistance I can offer as I transition out. I hope that we can stay in touch going forward.

Sincerely,

Maya R. Thompson

Twenty-Six

M aya smiled at her copy of her letter of resignation. She had made four copies and distributed them accordingly. One went to Tim, another went to Robert, a third went to Human Resources, and the fourth was for herself. She planned to frame it and put it in her home office, on her desk, where it would serve as a reminder whenever she felt like giving up and returning back to an office.

After she confessed her plans to Marcus, Maya went to work drafting her letter, followed by applying for her LLC and purchasing a website domain for *TLCCounsel.com*.

The *Thompson Legal Community Counsel* was born. Not only would Maya offer legal counsel on a sliding scale basis, but she would also help law students study for the BAR Exam, review and edit resumes and create a scholarship fund for high school students ready to pursue a higher education in Law. Without Tim trying to ax every idea she had; Maya was free to dream and execute as big as she wanted.

And she would too.

With most of her office packed up, Maya took a final look around. She turned slowly until she completed a full 360-degree turn then sighed.

"There's still time to rescind that resignation." Nina said when she stepped into the hollow office. She looked around the room too. "Damn, this place is empty."

Maya said, "Yeah. I didn't realize I had so much stuff until I started packing up."

Nina nodded toward a small box on Maya's former desk. "Is that the last of it?" She asked.

Maya said, "Yeah. Just some knick knacks. You wanna look through them and see what you want?"

Nina's pink lips curled into a Cheshire like grin. "Hell yes." She scurried to the box and started to sift through it. Maya watched her with a bittersweet smile. She had been on the verge of crying and felt her eyes welling up again. When she blinked and adjusted her eyes, Nina had an armful of trinkets. "Thank you so much, Maya." She said.

"You might as well keep the entire box." Maya laughed.

Nina said, "I didn't wanna be greedy."

"Take it." Maya replied.

Nina dumped her loot back into the box before she picked it up. She looked past Maya and smiled. "You here to take her away from us for good?" She asked.

Maya turned, Marcus and Darnell stepped into the office. Darnell nodded to Nina who bowed her head to hide her schoolgirl blush.

Marcus approached Maya, wrapped an arm around her waist then kissed her forehead. "You all packed up?" He asked.

"I am. And what about you two? How was your meeting with Robert?"

"Rewarding." Marcus said with a soft smile that activated one dimple.

"We gotta meet Olivia downstairs for the mural unveiling. Nina, are you coming?" Maya asked.

Nina's arms shook beneath the weight of the box. "I umm. I gotta take this to my desk first then I'll meet you downstairs."

"Whoa." Darnell said. He stepped closer to Nina then grabbed the box from her. Nina's eyes beamed at him. "I'll take it. Where do you want it?"

"Let me show you." Nina purred. She walked out of the office with Darnell in tow.

"You're gonna miss this place, aren't you?" Marcus

asked. Maya turned to face him; she tilted her head to meet his eyes. "Be honest." He said.

Maya smiled, "I will miss the people."

Most of them. She thought.

9 MONTHS LATER | MAY 2024

Twenty-Seven

♥

It was almost midnight when Marcus' Land Rover pulled into the empty lot of Sapphire Plaza, a newly constructed development with a total of six suites, all recently occupied. At the southern start of the plaza was a frozen yogurt shop, followed ironically by a dentist office, then a neo-soul centric boutique that advertised psychic and birth chart readings. The fourth suite announced that a coffee shop called *Daily Grind* was coming soon and at the end, filling the last two suites was the new and soon to open home of *Thompson Legal Community Counsel*.

Marcus parked in the spot in front of the double glass doors covered with large pieces of brown, craft paper. When he cut the engine, Maya looked at him, her right brow raised.

She said, "Baby, what's going on? Why are we here?"

When he smiled at her, Maya felt the blood rush to head

and her heart thumped against her chest.

"Come on." Marcus said.

Maya climbed out and let Marcus lead her to the front entrance of TLC. He pressed a finger to his lips and grinned.

"Isn't this considered breaking in and entering?" Maya asked.

"Not if we have the keys." Marcus said. He wiggled a set of keys between his fingers. "Besides, I have something to show you."

He opened one of the doors then motioned for Maya to walk in.

Maya obliged and when she stepped in, she drew a quick, sharp breath. "Oh my God." She said.

After six months of meetings, money and headaches, Maya had created the ultimate space for herself and her future clients. Her vision was a space that was welcoming, encouraging and far from intimidating that made people feel welcomed. She sought to establish a professional space that was also cozy, especially since she knew that she would spend most of her time there. The main room had an open floor plan with a reception area, a small cyber cafe with four computers, chairs and two printers.

Within the open space, Maya carved out areas for a free library and coffee bar equipped with a brewing system for coffee and tea. Beyond that, there was a two-stall bathroom, complete with a changing station, a kitchenette, a utility closet and of course Maya's office. But before her, the professional space she expected had been transformed.

Flameless, pillar candles created a path leading to a round table adorned with red, pink and white roses. A bottle of champagne sat in a bucket of ice with two crystal flutes standing beside it. More flameless candles created a perimeter around the table and two chairs, along with bouquets of roses lining the reception desk. Maya's jaw dropped as she walked the lit path.

"Marcus." She breathed. It was all she could say as she took in the moment.

He came into her view, his eyes glowing beneath the flameless flicker from the candles. Marcus took her hands in his, leading her to the table. "I told you that the day that I saw you, Maya, I fell in love. I watched this beautiful woman speak so candidly and openly on the beauty of our community. You were poised, perfect and fine as hell." He chuckled. "I didn't think that I had it in me to love again but you came along, and you challenged everything that I thought I knew. We have endured a lot in this last year all while trying to claim seats at the table for ourselves. We dealt with so much that anyone else with a weaker state of mind and heart could have never endured and going through it all made me realize that you are the only person I want to endure the tough times with forever."

Marcus knelt down; his eyes fixed on Maya. He reached into his pocket and pulled a red velveteen box from it. He opened it slowly.

Maya gasped. Her hands cupped her mouth at the sight of an oval halo engagement ring. "Maya, will you marry me?"

Maya's eyes welled with tears until Marcus became a glowing, wavy mass. The tears burst from her eyes before she nodded her confirmation. "Yes. Yes, I will." She said.

Marcus slipped the ring onto her finger then rose to his full height. Their tearful gazes reflected into each other.

"I love you, Maya." He said.

"I love you more." Maya wrapped her arms around Marcus' neck then pulled him close to her until their lips met beneath the soft glow.

Acknowledgements

♥

W riting this book was a challenge. I almost gave up on this story, but I don't think I would have made it this far without the love and support from the people who are near and dear to my heart:

To my children: My *Star*, *Samurai*, *Mr. Gray* and *Jelly-bean*! The four of you are my forever reason to do what I do. I always want to be the best example of hard work, faith, love and dedication for you. Thank you for being my greatest elements of motivation. I love you with all my heart.

To my cousins, Ahmed and Icy, I have to thank you both personally because you two have been such a gift to me. I have no idea what I would do without you two. As long as I have you two, I will always have a little piece of Chicago with me at all times.

And to my Muses: Danielle, Juliana and Nadia, thank

you for being more than friends but sisters and inspiring me through your creative journeys.

All of you helped me bring this story to life and I am forever grateful for it!

About the Author

P. Rose's passion for writing started at an early age when she would make up fairy tales about vampires and princesses. Today, she's a contemporary author who wants to share diverse stories about love, life and things that go "bump" in the night.

When she's not brainstorming or writing her next book, P. Rose can be found dabbling in food photography, reading comic books, drinking iced coffee and obsessing over Optimus Prime while spending time with her beautiful kids.

For behind-the-scenes updates, exclusive short stories and more, subscribe to whoisprose.substack.com

Made in the USA
Middletown, DE
21 November 2025

22112622R00210